Blind Walls

Also by Bishop & Fuller

Galahad's Fool

Realists

Co-creation: Fifty Years in the Making

Mythic Plays: from Inanna to Frankenstein

Rash Acts: 35 Snapshots for the Stage

Frankenstein (DVD)

The Tempest (DVD)

King Lear (DVD)

Descent of the Goddess Inanna (DVD)

Available at www.damnedfool.com

Conrad Bishop & Elizabeth Fuller

Blind Walls

— a novel —

WordWorkers Press

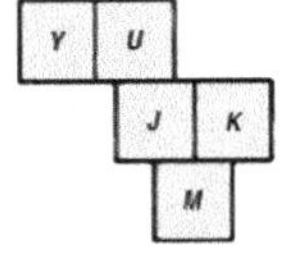

Blind Walls

© 2019 Conrad Bishop & Elizabeth Fuller

Printed in the United States of America.

For information:
eye@independenteye.org

For purchases:
www.damnedfool.com

ISBN: 978-0-9997287-2-7
LCCN: 2019900747

Book design by F. Ackerman

One

As always, I stood by the *Here* sign under a fig tree sprinkled scantily with small ripe figs. Behind me, as always, I felt the looming massive labyrinth of Weatherlee House.

Being a short man, I habitually assumed a military stance, stretching myself upward at least a quarter of an inch. My clipped hair, which I'm told is mostly gray, added gravitas to my otherwise bland face, or so I imagined. My tour guide's uniform—crisp navy blazer, burgundy rep tie—bulged only modestly at the midriff. A brass name plate, over the buttoned pocket where my heart might be, labeled me *Raymond Smollet*. Today I didn't wear my hat. The hat was optional. My round wire-rimmed black glasses were the only discordant feature in my demeanor. The fact is that I am blind.

The figs and my necktie hue I knew only by report. The wire-rims made my nose itch. I had tried wrap-arounds, but my supervisor Mr. Bottoms said they looked creepy. In fact, Management surely discerned that I looked even creepier with wire-rims, hence they preferred the wire-rims. I could intuit patrons peering in sideways at my fixed milky orbs, a perfect match for those haunted-house billboards that sucked them in. People would pay top dollar to tremble their way through alien worlds where the only true risk was blurring a snapshot.

Today was the final day of my life and now the final hour. Final, at least, for life as I had lived it. I stood cockily under my fig tree on the brink of my retirement—a Friday that marked the completion of thirty years as a tour guide of Weatherlee Ghost House. The forthcoming jaunt would be my final tour of the day. My pocket beeper would burble at four p.m., and I could trust my instinct to have my ducklings back at the gate precisely when the ancient garden bell clanged its perpetual five o'clock clang. Friday afternoons were generally scant, and I would allow the patrons a few minutes' grace after warning that if they needed the bathroom they should "pee now or forever hold your pees"—one of my little wisecracks. It sometimes roused a titter and in some souls an urge to pee.

Final day, final hour. I had a devilish urge to mark it somehow, the way we played jokes the last night of the high school play. I might neglect to remind my group of their bladders and then mock their whimperings. I might pretend to get lost. Or after a lifetime of spouting the market-tested Legend of Weatherlee House, I might tell them the plain unvarnished truth. That yearning lay deep in my bowels, though I would never risk it: better to fall into the rut of my rhythmic spiel and let the clock run out.

Time to begin. Eight tourists, I could tell from the shuffles and snorts. From a few sighs of exasperation, I already envisioned a mom in a floppy hat, with her surly daughter chewing a wad of gum as if to torture out its confession. You've made it through four tours today, I told myself: best to play it for yawns, phone it in and then creep home to my little rooms, feed Gertie (my ancient cat) and get an early start on drinking myself to death.

Retirement yawned up to suck me down—just one last feeble yawp of my thirty-year stint as Mouthpiece of the Dead.

I'm quite aware that I'm telling this story to myself, as I'm the only one who can be forced to listen. I'm also aware that I'm the least compelling character in my life, though like most men I live by the illusion that I'm the only true human, the star of the show, all others being merely my supporting cast or my stage crew. Blindness aids this delusion.

Skilled memoirists start with a mid-life crisis, then backtrack to getting born. But I prefer to begin with my childhood, since from there the story has nowhere to go but up. I was the only tangible consequence of Mr. and Mrs. Barnett "Barney" Smollet, who termed themselves middle-class by virtue of their wall-to-wall carpet. We moved from Ohio to Arizona to allow my father to die amid cactus. When he complied, my mother brought us to Santa Cruz, California, to be near her sister, whom she despised. Simpler to hate each other at close range and save the long-distance charges.

My earliest recollection is of a violent crying jag. I was curled on a bare floor while a babysitter tried to calm me by flipping the pages of a catalog. She pointed to the picture of a football. "That's a football," she said. I kept on crying but stopped by the time I'd finished high school.

In my adolescence I envied boys who could blame their hand-wrought guilt on religion, so I went one Sunday with Billy to his church. Billy might have been my first lover if I'd had the least notion of what it entailed and if I could have jumped the line of females enraptured by his gold-flecked irises. The preacher was a skinny old man with a shock of hedgehog hair. His topic was *The Seven Last Words of Christ.* (Now it would be *The Seven Last Tweets.*) That visitation of spirit did nothing to sidle me closer to Billy's thighs, but it did offer me vital insight to my future career. I learned that you could spout pure drivel if you spouted it loud and clear.

I was also attracted to girls—anything anthropoid would do—and in high school I achieved a few feels before trotting off to the collegiate hunting preserves. But girls terrified me. I would become an intimate sister inside their minds and feel their nakedness long before I ever saw a girl naked. Males were safely armored. I feared them, but we could maintain a mutual anonymity. I could make love without actually being there.

In those days I still had my sight and could see my pathetic longings with great acuity. College I managed to survive with only a single lackluster suicide attempt, trying to overdose on aspirin. I had no great ambition. I double-majored in theatre and heartbreak, faring better in the latter.

After graduation I was hired in the local school district's business office, typing, filing and managing deliveries to the schools. I was meticulous in my work and was well liked, or at any rate people said hello. The job was a snug cocoon from which the worm might emerge one day with translucent wings. But this prospect was shattered by my arrest. On a pre-Lib Saturday night the police raided Harold's Lounge, and I was one of two dozen gentlemen nabbed for disorderly conduct, a.k.a. being queer. I told my mother I hadn't known the nature of the establishment, but my employer was not to be fooled. Innocent children might be polluted by a pervert typing purchase orders. I was given the opportunity to resign—*to pursue other interests*, my letter said—and two weeks' severance pay, generous by prevailing standards. So ended my career in public education. The case was dismissed.

At that time I lived with my mother in a small two-bedroom cottage on what was then the outskirts of Santa Cruz. As a child I had wallpaper depicting cowboys and Indians. In my teens it was repapered with hallucinatory spaghetti of intersecting vines. In my twenties I stripped the walls and repainted them dark green in a thick impasto, like a stubbly beard over a skin disease. When my mother died I saw no reason to move, and so I have occupied the same bedroom up to the present day. Same desk, same bed, a corner armchair on the verge of collapse—the only concession to my approaching antiquity. Recently I brightened my room with chartreuse curtains, which of course I can't see but can envision the dubious effect. The rest of the house, except for meals in the musty kitchen, is long forgotten.

I was past thirty, immature for my age, and had bounced through a straggle of jobs that required little more than staying propped upright. Still, I held hopes of a career that would make all those high school jocks who'd scorned me swallow their bubblegum in envy, bubble and all. From time to time I had acted in amateur plays—which offered a few liaisons, including Kenneth, the neurotic pharmacist who brought me to Harold's—and so it happened that Roxanne, one of my theatre friends, called to tell me they were hiring at the "Ghost House." She worked box office there.

At that time I was not at all blind—no more so, at least, than the average man. I was hired for the garden crew, and at first those little floating specks in my eyes appeared to be dancing gnats. But at night they swam in the murk like tiny fish, and soon they bred swarms. Luckily I was soon promoted, and at some dim tick of the clock I led my first group of tourists into the twisted intestines of Weatherlee House.

From there on, nothing of any consequence occurred for the next thirty years.

By the time I was stone cold sightless I had spent several years telling the same story five times daily, five days a week. The weekend staff were younger, more lovable, more vicious—so vision was no real advantage. I had hopes, as my diagnosis progressed from "Let's hope" to "Tough shit," that the cliches of blindness—the echolocation of bats, the olfaction of bloodhounds—might emerge, but I only heard the creaking of floor joists, smelled mildew and cheap perfume. Still, before utter darkness fell, my frail theatrical background brought me a degree of popularity. I had learned to feel my way through the maze, offer shuddersome cheeriness to my groups, and I had learned to see.

Not literally, to be sure. I would never be able to spot the soup stains on my shirt. But I came to trust my mental delineations. I could see—or at least imagine—each little clutch of gawkers whom it was my duty to astonish and amaze before shedding them like dandruff. Spurred by their scuffs and grunts, I could conjure up my past life's catalog of hairdos, noses, buttocks and hats into stereotypes that would follow me up the stairs and down the halls and into the heart of the sorry dead beast.

Stereotypes are small-minded but as convenient as plastic bags. In my head I beheld most of the women in wide hats, flowered blouses, polyester slacks, carrying small water canteens from which they took butterfly sips. The men would be in safari jackets, Hawaiian shirts, Bermuda shorts, or those flat cartoon burglars' caps that executives wear to confirm they're on vacation. Few made any distinct impression, though I recall a lady who said she had slept with her dead husband—slept beside him a final night—and next day they buried him. That image still came to me at times, alone in my swaybacked bed.

I never asked names and they never offered, so I named them secretly, each one, each tour, each decade. Like the TV in bars or airport lounges they couldn't be turned off. Each day after work I envisioned them all, no matter how much I drank. I strove earnestly to please them—my flock, my squad, my brood—while hating them as only a passive man can hate.

Soon, within the demise of sunlight, my world took shape. Freed of vision, I could create my own picture shows. My imagination ran rampant in its pajamas, scurrying down the passages. I could see the woodwork, the turrets, the exquisite dadoes, the iridescent glow of the Tiffany windows. I could even see movement in the empty rooms as you might see a cat flashing across the highway: ripples of serving maids, carpenters framing the stairs we climbed, nailing each tread in place as we stepped upward on it. Eventually I saw the little lady herself: Sophia Weatherlee. On this final tour.

"Okay? All here? Anyone not here, speak now!" I got a few chuckles, or it might have been stifled coughs. "Fair warning, I tell jokes the way some people belch. Nervous habit." Dead group, I could tell, wondering what they were in for. I never aimed for guffaws at my wisecracks. They simply moved my pilgrims to think *He's quite a character*, and that helped with the tips.

"The structure you will enter was built by Mrs. Sophia Weatherlee over a span of nearly four decades. Born in 1839, she married the heir to the Weatherlee Repeating Arms Company in 1862. Their only child, a daughter, died of a rare wasting disease, and she lost her husband a few years later. Seeking counsel from a Boston spiritualist, she was advised that in order to stay alive she must live with the sound of hammers. Why hammers? We can only guess." I paused a moment to let them guess.

"Keep in mind that Weatherlee rifles were the weapon of choice in the Civil War, the Spanish-American War, the First World War and the winning of the West. They killed hundreds of thousands, millions perhaps—all bad guys, we assume. Mrs. Weatherlee fancied, perhaps, that she had to frighten away their angry spirits with the clatter of construction. Or to confuse them with convoluted arteries. Or to offer them free lodging. We know not what. Did they tap at her window? Did she hear?" Another pause. No more shuffling: they were hooked. In thirty years you develop a knack.

"And so she migrated to California, bought a small farm near Santa Cruz and began construction of Weatherlee House, where we now stand in awe. Anyone not in awe?" No laugh, but I'd made my point, a veiled threat to the unbeliever. "Her carpenter crews worked seven days a week, twenty-four hours a day, for thirty-eight years, until her death in 1922. Despite the advice of her spiritualist, she did in fact die. She must have been quite surprised." I laughed. My little hoot gave the joke an extra poke, so I got a few chuckles. The last time I'd ever hoot it.

"I should mention: no smoking, no photographs, no chewing gum. And please stay together. People do get lost." With a slightly ghoulish intonation: "This is not recommended." I stressed that if anyone needed to leave the tour they should ask for safe escort. "The rules are there for reasons that may not be apparent," I said with a trace of perversity. It was the story they paid for, not the architectural pastiche. A labyrinth with no horned beast at its core would be a waste of plywood.

I entered through the plain green door that must have once been a servants' entrance. The group followed, and I heard the lady in the floppy hat pick a fig. I stopped in a small bare room with empty shelving along one wall and waited for my gaggle to gather.

"Pause here, please. Here you see a door which is five feet six inches in height. Not remarkable, considering that Mrs. Weatherlee was only four feet eleven. Of course people were much smaller then. All of us were, I suppose." I chuckled. "However, what may surprise you is this." I tapped my knuckles on it, then opened the door to a solid brick wall. "This must not have been a place where Mrs. Weatherlee cared to go."

They followed me. I always felt a twinge of astonishment that they did. Strange that nobody questioned my blindness. Perhaps they were sightless themselves. Perhaps they were accustomed to being led by the blind. Or perhaps I wasn't blind at all: the blackness that held me was reality.

"Careful on these steps. You'll notice the four-inch risers, a concession to Mrs. Weatherlee's arthritis." My covey climbed the midget stairs, and we came into the small rotunda with archways to corridors gallivanting in three directions. The mansion's original furnishings were long gone, so Management had sprinkled the rooms with mismatched antiques. Here would be a rocking chair with ottoman and on the curvature behind it a narrow stained-glass window—the brilliance of priceless Tiffany. A pleasant nook where a quaint old lady might sit and read, philosophize and die.

When my tourists had coagulated I continued my spiel. "So in summary: Weatherlee House contains one hundred sixty rooms in four stories plus basement. Forty bedrooms, two ballrooms, forty-seven fireplaces, fifty-two skylights, ten thousand window panes, two thousand doors, seventeen chimneys, six kitchens, three elevators and, significantly, thirteen bathrooms. Once rising to seven stories, with an estimated three hundred twenty rooms, it sustained severe damage in the 1906 earthquake. Its floating foundation saved it from total destruction. I would advise that we all maintain floating foundations. I'm joking, of course."

I heard a creak from the rocking chair, turned and saw her.

Sophia Weatherlee reached out and stroked the colors in the air. Her hands showed age—half-bent fingers, liver spots, a roadwork of blue veins, skin the texture of chicken skin. But the hands didn't match the face. Even without the heavy powder that caked it, her face might have been thirty years younger—round, smooth, delicate features with only a hint of cheekbones. The hair was abundant but dutifully fixed in a bun, tinted pale blonde with an underglaze of gray. The eyes, though, were sisters to the hands. Deep, ancient, knowing eyes that had looked on death. That looked on it every day.

"Mrs. Weatherlee's inheritance made her one of the wealthiest women in . . ." I continued speaking but didn't hear a word I said. I was seeing what I had never seen before.

Two

She rocked gently in her rocking chair, head resting against a small silken pillow painted with trees and rivulets by some mystic Oriental. She held a clear glass bowl containing seven agate marbles. She stirred the marbles with her finger.

I had seen wisps of her before. Never a solid image, only a translucent sea fog. My glimpses may have been an urge to hold onto sight, to keep a flicker in that little movie screen we call reality. I would conjure up a clouded face that only I could see. A few times she came into my dreams. When my seekers badgered me about ghosts, I wanted to tell them to press their thumbs to their orbs, gouge, dig hard and then they might see. Of course I restrained myself.

Patrons came to Weatherlee House in hopes to witness the crime of its conception, the worldwide slaughter of innocence. Certainly one ax murder would be more shocking than a knowledge of millions dead, but there was no atrocity to view, no flash of ghosts fleeing the gruesome scene—only the gradual crime of the building itself, the framing of thousands of doors, the carpenters extending a hive cell by cell for the queen. But I would have expected the tremulous warbles of a theramin, not the heavy tread of workmen.

Sophia Weatherlee sat sharply etched in the morning sun. Behind her the Tiffany window blazed, a festoon of rigid foliage with a luminous scrolled Shakespearean quote in the colorful glass: *Wide unclasp the tables of their thoughts*. Whose thoughts? I had no thoughts except those that I stifled under endless babble. *Wide unclasp the tables*? If I were truly to unclasp—

Her hands moved. I heard a knock. Did my tourists hear? Time stretched like a rubber band, then snapped in my face.

"Marty? Is that Marty?"

"Morning, Miss Weatherlee."

"Come in, please. You're late."

"Took me a while to find you."

A tall chunky man appeared at the opposite door. He wore coveralls, a blue carpenter's apron and a utility belt with dangling tools. He held a brown billed cap in his hands, cradled like a sleepy pet.

A pause for her to focus. "Our sunrise was lovely this morning."

"Yes it was."

"You saw it?"

"No ma'am."

"You're very trusting. How are your little ones?"

"They're not so little now." The man seemed familiar with the litany. Her soft cutting voice had an interrogative twist, not quite accusatory but as if some hidden guilt in the world might be found before lunch and flicked away like a vagrant ant. Sophia Weatherlee fumbled for an object on her side table. "Oh dear, I've lost— Here." She held up a ring stiff with keys. "Here. What are these keys?"

"Ma'am?"

"We have unidentified keys. I have never seen these keys."

He took it from her insistent reach. "These here?" Obviously *these here*, but he didn't know what else to say. Her lips flattened, her eyes widened and went slightly crossed—a sign she was about to give an order. One of the carpenters, Clyde, did a goofy imitation, though Marty as foreman warned him against it.

"I do not want keys that have no locks nor locks that have no keys. How do you rationalize these keys?"

"I couldn't say."

"Of course you can't. How would you know? They were in amongst my jewelry: strings of pearls, bracelets, things I can't conceive myself wearing, can you? How little we know ourselves." She paused for a reply that was lost in fog. "But there they were, as if from another reality, as they say in cheap novels—*Dracula, The Book of Mormon,* that sort of thing." She regarded him expectantly. Marty saw she was waiting for a chuckle, but he didn't see what was funny. He was accustomed to these occasions, sensed when to speak and when to let the seismic tremor pass. "I want these keys tagged. See to it, please." Her fingers pressed the heavy carved arm of the rocking chair.

"Right." He slipped the key ring into a canvas apron pocket and waited for the woman's next eructation. Marty—I heard his name as Marty—endured Mrs. Weatherlee's quirks as part of the job. Her wages were generous, and the working conditions—rest breaks, overtime, sick leave—couldn't be matched. For his money the upper classes could use more of her eccentricities. Her finger in the glass bowl stirred the marbles.

Had someone spiked the staff lounge coffee? Was I having a stroke? Were ghosts popping out of the woodwork to give me a last hurrah? The shock of these babbling apparitions might have struck me senseless to the floor, but no such luck. I might have expected this: I was sinking into retirement. Death has a touch of dignity, but retirement is a hunched faceless wretch sneaking out the side door, holding a piece of angel food cake on a paper plate. A fumbling erasure.

I tried to pick up my train of thought, but the words fell lifeless from my tongue. "The cost of the construction, in today's dollars, would have been more than . . ." To mimic being awake was a vital professional skill, and I jabbered on by rote. I wanted only to rattle my script and stop on the way home to pick up my dinner of pizza and Johnny Walker. I gulped down a tiny ooze of stomach acid, stood there and watched the movie.

"Go to the window, please, Marty. If it's good weather you could work on the roof." Her lids were closed. The Tiffany window—the alcove's only window—was directly behind her, but nothing could be seen through its myriad panels.

"The roof's done," Marty said.

"What about the weather?"

"It's fine."

"I lose track. Inevitably it changes."

"We've got the lumber for the porch."

"So much tumult."

"Just hammers."

"If there were no hammers or nails, might things simply . . . come together?" Her voice had an upward lilt. Marty decided that it wasn't a question.

They listened to the distant hammers and the cries of a wrathful crow, then the foreman ventured, "I brought in the new man, ma'am. As I said, we need another hand. So he's all set if you want to give the go-ahead. He's right out there on the stairs."

Eyes closed, she stirred the marbles. "There was the question of the pipe. What about the pipe?"

"Well that's a problem. We've had trouble getting the galvanized. They've only got the black in that dimension."

"Why can't we use black?"

"That is an option."

"It's under the ground?"

"It's under the ground but it's not as durable. That's why you wanted the galvanized."

She opened her lids. Her mouth went softer, almost a smile. "If it rusts in thirty years, no matter, so will I. Let's proceed."

"Fine."

"Fine. And the weather is fine. Fine and dandy, as they say."

The foreman's fingers brushed the tools on his belt. His habits had been shaped under the scrutiny of tight-assed contractors, and despite the old lady's offhand ways he was anxious to get to work.

"Did you want to see the young man, ma'am?"

Her lips went tight again. Marty knew his timing was off. Never push things, he told himself. After a moment she spoke. "Marty, that breezeway must be secured before the rains come. There was a vagrant found in there, was there not?"

"I know, Miss Weatherlee. He was escorted out."

"You know, yes, I'm aware that you know. And he had a name."

"Smoky."

"That's horrible. You know I rely on you, Marty. I won't have it."

"No ma'am."

Her voice rose from a murmur to a shriek. "I am not responsible for these people!"

After months on the job, Marty was used to her blurts. "She's like a pot of oatmeal that thinks it's lava," Clyde had joked. Clyde was a funny kid. Marty couldn't imagine him in the Army, shooting people, but Clyde would probably crack a joke about it. He rubbed his nose—large and bony with a crook. She seemed to find that gesture vaguely threatening and would usually change the subject.

"Well, so." Her gaze fell to the slow stir of her marbles.

He ventured further. "Miss Weatherlee, I said we'd lost the two boys that went off—"

"Where?"

"They joined the Army."

"Peter and Clyde. Of course they would. They're so young."

"So I said I need help. So this young man I think is—"

"So where is he? Bring him in!"

My tour guide jabber failed. For a moment I guessed that the staff had concocted a little show to delight my final hour. I was in the midst of a play whose title I'd missed, and despite my tries at acting, plays rarely appealed to me: I preferred my own misery to that of others.

These figures trod freely across my stone-dead retinas. I sensed their thoughts. I heard them speak—babble from shadows etched into the walls, but shadows with crisp articulation. Some people suppose they have dreams that seep in from another world. My would-be girlfriend Shirley dreamt of being an ancient Egyptian girl whose mother scolded her in hieroglyphics. What world of bony noses and vagrant keys was seeping in?

A young man came down the hallway. Medium height, curly dark hair, red plaid shirt. He came to Marty's side, nodded hello to the personage seated across the room. Awkward silence, then he shifted his weight and hooked his thumbs in his back pockets, thought better of it, stood there, hands dangling, aware of being graded.

The old lady scrutinized him. Pug nose, eyes wide-set, suggesting competence if not high intelligence, and blue jeans freshly laundered and pressed. "Is this the young man?" she said at last, then answered herself. "Well of course it is. Who else would it be?" The young man started to grin, then checked himself.

"This is Chuck," Marty replied.

"Come here." She pointed at the floor to the side of her chair. Chuck came to the indicated spot. He stood nervously as her finger stirred the marbles in the bowl. "What is your name?"

"Chuck."

"Chuck Ratowitz," Marty offered.

Chuck Ratowitz had gotten a call from his Uncle Frank, whose son knew the foreman's sister-in-law, about a possible job. He had taken the bus to the edge of town, walked three quarters of a mile to a farmhouse, eight or ten rooms but with new foundations laid for future additions. The foreman asked some questions, told him to wait. A long wait. Now he stood before a lady in a rocking chair, a stained-glass window throwing light on the side of her face. Old, but he couldn't tell how old. She had a glass bowl in her lap.

Her gaze narrowed. "Is he Jewish?"

"No. No ma'am, I'm—"

"That's no concern of mine," she said tartly. "We're not arranging a marriage. Is he trustworthy?"

"He's got good references. High school graduate, journeyman, four years on the job," Marty reported. Chuck shifted his weight.

"He's extremely young."

"I can't help that," Chuck mumbled.

She looked back to him, mildly surprised. "And quite strong-willed, apparently." She gave a brief smile, as if offering an apology to a child. "Do you have a family, Mister Chuck Ratowitz?"

He nodded, took a deep breath, as if commencing an oral book report. "Girlfriend. And my sister, she's in Texas, she's a lot older. My dad's dead, he died my junior year, construction accident. But it was mostly my Uncle Frank, my mom's brother, that really taught me everything, from when I was a kid . . ." He hesitated, unsure if he'd touched all bases, then added, "My mom's a bookkeeper in Arizona."

"They keep books in Arizona? Fancy that." The woman glanced toward Marty, then to Chuck. "Are you strong? Do you play sports?"

"Oh sure, I'm strong, sure. Yeh, no, I liked sports, but in high school I never had time to play cause I was working. But I did play on the church softball team, my mom went to the Presbyterian church, but there you didn't have to practice. I played second base." He wasn't sure he'd answered the question.

"And they play softball in church. What a vivid image." She stirred her marbles. "You have not said why you are seeking employment."

Was it a question? He shifted his weight. "Well, we need the money. I been out of work a couple of months, I—"

"*We?*"

"My girlfriend—"

"Of course you do. I am aware that people need money, that's why they work for me. Do you think they are so passionately devoted?"

The young man glanced at Marty, who made a gesture: stay calm.

The woman stared at the Persian rug directly in front of her rocking chair. Her voice became quiet, clinical, like a doctor cataloguing symptoms. "Why do you hide your hands?"

"No, I'm—" He brought his hands to his sides.

"Are you afraid of me?"

"No ma'am."

"Why are you rocking? Do you need to urinate?"

"N— No ma'am, not at all—"

He tensed for the next assault, but she calmly picked up a pair of delicate reading glasses folded on the side table, put them on and held up the bowl of glass marbles.

"Pick one of those, if you please." He hesitated, then stepped forward and picked a marble out of the bowl. Strange way to demonstrate his carpentry skills, he thought, but she's the boss.

"Now put it in your mouth."

Chuck hesitated, looked at Marty, who nodded. He put the marble in his mouth.

"Thank you. Now spit it out. Just out of your mouth directly down into the bowl."

The distant rasp of a handsaw cut through the silence. He stooped and let the marble drop from his lips. She studied the bowl. He waited for an explanation or a failing grade, like back in high school, struggling with his book report on *Moby-Dick*. He hated book reports, but that book got to him. The captain was nuts and everybody knew it, but they just went right along taking orders. They deserved what they got. He did like the parts about whales.

Sophia Weatherlee turned to Marty, apparently forgetting the marbles. "Will that pipe be delivered tomorrow?"

"Yes ma'am."

"That's all, thank you. And a report on those keys."

"Right."

"Well, he's fine, he'll do." She smiled toward Chuck, then waggled her fingers in a gesture of dismissal. "You'll get used to me."

Marty gestured to Chuck to follow him and started out, then turned back to the woman. "So is that it?"

"How is your leg today?" she asked. Chuck had noticed Marty's limp.

"Shot off."

Sophia laughed quietly, then waved to Chuck as if to a child. "We joke about this."

Three

On the cusp of change—your past life looming like a slag heap of soiled undies—there comes a reassessment. I had always sought to avoid such challenges, and now as this odd spectacle faded from my sightlessness, I persuaded myself it was merely hallucination, daydream, the leftover scraps of a screenplay I'd once tried to write or seismic quivers up the support beams. Otherwise I would have to admit to premature dementia. I was, well, frankly, befuddled.

Or might I be a medium giving voice to the walls, channeling a corpse's madness?

Nothing so exotic. My nightmares had never been wispy, warbly affairs: I would feel the beard stubble, smell the sour milk, hear mangy dogs whining, taste the grit. I would see an old scar hidden by the eyebrow and feel its patch of numbness. So I wasn't surprised at the clod-footed solidity of the dream, even as it descended into nonsense: a guy walks into a farmhouse where they've just started work, but inside it's a stately mansion and he's given a marble to suck. Grown men are named Ratowitz. These blind walls were throwing me a freakish retirement party.

"If you listen," I said to my tourists in muffled desperation, "you might hear the hammers." I waved my hand toward the silence, gave them time to strain their earlobes. Could they hear?

"Excuse me?" It was a high-pitched male voice, German, Austrian perhaps. I pictured a pudgy fellow, mid-thirties, sporting a blond pompadour and the profile of a chicken. His name might be Herr Gerg or something throaty. As my sight fizzled out I had developed the habit of naming my nomads, striving to put a face to each, the way as a child I'd poked features into Mr. Potatohead.

Herr Gerg asked the cost of Weatherlee House. I answered by rote. "Construction expenditure was five million dollars. In the present day that would be well over seventy-five million, apart from the Tiffany windows, which are priceless. And you're dying to know something else, yes you are, try and stop me!" I gave a squeak of a laugh. "It is built of the highest-grade redwood, renowned for the beauty of its grain. But Mrs. Weatherlee did not like the appearance of redwood. It took 25,000 gallons of paint to suit it to her taste." I could feel their eyes glaze over. They were straining to see ghosts.

I groped my way up the narrow servants' stairs to the second floor, slowing my pace for my less nimble followers. The hat lady puffed, and I heard a soft growl from her daughter. Call the mom Mrs. Padgett of Cedar Rapids, Iowa, and the girl would be Samantha—Sammie to her friends—frantic to escape her boredom. Now my groupies were taking form, creature by creature, the better for me to despise them.

Halfway up the stairs, another slippage. My dreams had always transmogrified through architectonic anomalies—a classroom morphing into Penn Station, tropical jungle into women's lingerie at Sears, a church basement enclosing the killing fields. I had stumbled down hospital corridors into oncoming traffic, so I shouldn't have been surprised at the appearance of a room that didn't remotely fit what I had traversed for thirty years. I froze on the risers. My tourists may have continued directly through me up the stairs.

A small drab kitchen, a sour dirt yellow. A table, two chairs, cluttered counter, cracked linoleum floor, a ceiling fixture lined with dead flies, an electric stove— There were no electric stoves in

Weatherlee House. It might have been a decrepit trailer among the used-car lots on the outskirts of town or a drab little granny unit behind the two-car garage, but it surely resembled nothing on my thirty-year route. Then I recognized a face.

Chuck Ratowitz sat at the tan Formica table reading the paper. He sipped his coffee and scanned the business pages. Corporate mergers, Dow Jones, carnivorous CEOs—an alien world, but to him it must have glittered like a rip saw's teeth. He'd been holding his breath all day with news to make known, but she didn't get off work till six.

He heard the back door. She came into the kitchen, dumped a ruptured grocery sack on the table, gave a heavy sigh. Blonde hair in a ponytail, pale pink uniform, white collar and cuffs, tired blue eyes. She leaned over and kissed him by habit. He rose, embraced her, and then they were kissing as if they meant it.

He pulled away. "That's pretty good."

"How about this?" She kissed him deeply.

"That's good too."

"I've been thinking about that all day."

He nuzzled her neck, nibbled playfully at an earring hoop. "I know why those guys come into the diner," he whispered. "The food's for shit. They like what they see behind the counter."

She bit his chin. He laughed. "That's not funny," she snapped.

"Sorry. Sorry, Dee."

"I feel crappy."

"You feel pretty good to me."

He hugged her but she pulled away. She got enough of that male-adolescent teasing at work. She knew he meant well, but a keen suck of depression drained out all the sexiness she'd felt a moment before. A five-pound bag of potatoes had split the sack down the side, and she began to unpack what was left. "You know what I caught myself doing today? Talking to myself. Totally nuts, like my mom." She checked the egg carton to see if any had broken. "Nobody's tipping. This guy in a suit, shiny brown suit, tells me a joke, goes off, no tip. Big fifty-cent joke. I'll call up the landlord, tell him a joke." Dried beans, tomato sauce, a package of Krispy Kremes, plastic garbage bags. Chuck moved close behind, not quite touching her. "Didn't you say you were gonna check on a job today? We got the rent coming up."

"I did. Let's get married." He stroked the back of her neck. She ignored it.

"Let me get supper on. Spaghetti okay?" Right now the idea of cooking was a swamp too deep to wade. She'd once had dreams of a family, whipping up sumptuous meals for husband and kids—*Little House on the Prairie, Little Women*—but facing the task every day for the next fifty years—

"Dee? Hey? I got a surprise." More of Chuck's jokes. When his humor didn't score with her he couldn't stop. Like little boys on the playground teasing the girls, he just couldn't stop.

"You won the Lottery. I'm glad."

"I said I'd check on the job."

"Chuck, I'm not in the mood for jokes. I'm tired and I feel really mean. Just let me get supper on."

"So I got it."

"You got what?"

"I got the job."

She had taken the spaghetti package out of the cabinet over the stove and grabbed a pot to start the water boiling. Midway to the sink she stopped and stared at him. Another joke?

"They're adding onto this house," he went on, "more than just a couple rooms, I guess. Some rich lady, kind of a real nut but the foreman's okay. He's married to some woman, her sister's a friend of my cousin's, and I did some work for my cousin on their porch, so that's where I got the tip. Old farmhouse, but it's in pretty good shape and they're adding on—"

"What does it pay?"

"Six hundred a week."

Another seismic quiver. *Six hundred a week* had vastly different values from year to year to year. Here, it sounded like a lot. Was I in the 1880s now or the 1970s or some cracked linoleum limbo outside Time? Would the young man drive to work or ride a horse? If construction began in 1886, whence came electric stoves, Krispy Kremes, plastic bags? Where were we on the official timeline? Clocks and calendars were playing peek-a-boo.

The flimflams of Time. For years I had joked with tourists that I started working here during the final years of Mrs. Weatherlee's life. "Don't I look well preserved?" No one ever laughed, and after a while I stopped trying to chuckle my way past the ontological hush. Now, for all I could tell, it might be true. The old woman might be young, the carpenter facing retirement, or myself a toddler crying myself silly in a lost fluorescent limbo.

I told myself more vehemently that it was all in my head.

"Six hundred? Come on."

"No shit."

"Six *hundred?*"

"I ain't seen that in a while. Like never."

"For how long?"

"I don't know. It's a big job. Quite a while. Foreman says she's rich. Marty the foreman, Marty Wenger, my cousin's friend is Wenger, Edith or Edie— I don't know, but they're laying these whole foundations, it's a big job."

"Oh honey!"

A pattering on the floor: the last spaghetti sticks slid out of the package in Dee's hand. "Oh!" She started to stoop for retrieval, then tossed the plastic aside and rushed to embrace him. The pasta crackled underfoot. "Oh God, Chuck, oh, why didn't you tell me? Here I am being a bitch, I'm sorry— Oh Chuck, even if it doesn't last, it's— Just for you to be doing something that makes you feel good—" She squeezed him as hard as she could. All the gall of the day turned to joy. They fell again into the kiss that might last for minutes or years— those kisses faked in the movies but seen so rarely in life, maybe only in memories that never happened. At least never on guided tours.

"Let's celebrate," he said. "Put on your blue dress. We'll go out and eat someplace nice, then a movie?"

"What time you gotta be up? When do you start?"

"Tomorrow. Seven. Be up by quarter to six. No, five-thirty, I gotta check my tools."

"I don't want to get you too sleepy before we come back here." Another hug.

"Put on your blue dress." He swatted her on the butt, and then they moved gently into a calm embrace, each reflected in the other's face. An exquisite intimacy made manifest by six hundred a week.

"Hey," Chuck mumbled, "I was thinking, we oughta think about— We could buy some rings?"

"Rings. What kinda rings?" Her eyes danced, though her lips held a twist of doubt.

"Gold rings."

"Just like that?"

"Yeh. Just like that."

"Okay."

"Okay? Just like that? Okay?"

"Okay."

Though I had never known it, I had imagined there might be times between two lovers, if they were very lucky, either too young to know better or too old to hide it, when their passion became laughter—clowns making love, a silliness in their joy. Now I saw it, in this hazy year when *six hundred a week* was meaningful. They hugged, laughed, tickled and wound up with Chuck lying backward over the kitchen table, Dee pinning him down.

"This is a pretty intense lady to be married to," he gasped between laughing jags.

"Careful I don't get you pregnant."

"If you think you can do the job."

"How many kids are you up for?"

"Six. Even number. Fit'em in a six-pak."

She coughed from too much laughter. It hardly mattered what was said: just talking was funny now. They were both too dizzy for words.

"Careful," she said, "I don't want no stretched-out husband here."

He twisted around, managed to prop himself upright on an elbow, still snagged in the snaggles of laughter. "Hey, come on, I'm hungry, let's go eat. Put on your blue dress."

"So you can take it off?"

He rose, grabbed her roughly with a growl, and then everything went soft between them. They touched each other like some sweet precious thing found in the surf.

"Chuck?"

"Hm?"

"Could we get a waffle iron?"

Four

A waffle iron meant home to Dee. The times when her mom made waffles for breakfast were the only times she ever felt part of a family. Sometimes maple syrup on top, sometimes strawberries. "Want another? Dee, Sally, anybody?"

Her father was career Army, and when she was little they were all over the country. He took early retirement, and two days before her twelfth birthday he deserted the family. She would hear her mother crying at night and hated her for it. It was hard to love someone you had to feel sorry for.

When they heard the news that he died, Dee remembered those times around the table. Families: you couldn't expect love. If people got that, they wouldn't have to make movies about it. Just be thankful if you got an extra waffle. She cried more about the waffles than about her dad.

My phantasms were a relief from the tedium of sanity and its terrors. I chased my panicky thoughts the way three-year-old Raymond had chased his grandma's squawking chickens. Were my voyagers ahead or behind? Might I get fired just fifty minutes short of my pension?

Dee wouldn't let me go. Her boyfriend didn't intrigue me so much. I assumed I knew his type: one of those high school kids who'd yell out, "I smell a faggot!" when they spotted little Raymond Smollet sitting alone in the cafeteria. No malice intended, just fun. Guys like that, their faces were a blank, their thoughts were in simple subjects and predicates. But Dee drew me in.

I was still lost in the depth of their kiss. I felt my own first kiss. Janis—what was her name? Her lips were thin, dry, clamped. Brief peck, quick glimpse of a world, and then she looked at me an instant and never looked again. Janis. Right now, though, I wasn't quite ready for my life to flash before my shuttered peepers.

No need to fear for sanity. It was long gone.

Dee Giddings—soon to be Ratowitz—sat at the kitchen table with a cup of instant coffee, leafing through a yearbook. She wore a man's blue workshirt over a pale green pullover with a scoop neck, a bra strap cutting into her shoulder. She tugged absently at the strap. Strange, imagining such foreign details.

As she turned the pages of high school, her face flickered with changes. A slight hopeful smile, then a cloud of quiet desperation, a flash of childish panic, a glint of sunlight on her cheek. Chuck had been up early as usual, and after fixing breakfast she went back to bed for a while to gaze at the ceiling. Finally she got up, put on Chuck's old shirt and rummaged in the closet. She hadn't opened her senior yearbook since graduation, not even to read her classmates' *Good luck!* scribbles inside the covers, and now she was paging through it. *The Blue and Gold*, and guess what, the cover was blue and gold.

A whole day to herself, and this is what she did with it. The diner was closed for Good Friday—her boss was religious—so she had the whole day to herself. Chuck was working, of course. If he could get off next Friday afternoon they'd go down to the county office and get married. She hadn't told her mom. Her sister had just got divorced and was pretty sore on the subject of marriage, so Dee would keep her mouth shut with the happy news.

First page, the front of the school, kids coming down the steps, with the header *We're Stepping Foreword.* That's not the way you spell it, but she'd never noticed. Maybe somebody had thought it sounded more educated. And a photo of the football scoreboard: Home 17, Visitors 6. It was the only game they'd won that year. Chem lab, sewing class, library. Yearbooks had a smell, a whiff of ink and locker sweat.

Sipping her tasteless coffee she glanced around the kitchen. Everything had been denser, more intense in high school—the whole world shrunk down into Abraham Lincoln High. *Memories Play an Important Part in Our Lives*, the header said. Cheerleaders: *Yea team! Fight!* And the Homecoming Queen, Judy something, and the ladies of the court, Sandy, Peggy, Chloe, Jolene something, something, something. And there she was herself, pinning up Easter bunnies on the bulletin board.

Drama Club: she wanted to be in a play but her mom would have killed her, so she never tried out. John Duckworth, he was nice, always smiled at her. Faculty photos: Mr. Henkel, Miss Rickard, Mrs. Eiler, Mr. Deethardt, Mrs. Weems, Mr. Killian—and in her mind she saw Chuck Ratowitz coming out of shop class, old Mr. Killian's class, like a god or a movie star. She noticed his walk, no hurry, but a confidence, a quiet determination, as if he were going somewhere and why not come along? Oh did she want that up close!

And then, in the fall of her senior year, there he was, across the aisle in history class. Mrs. Coad, an old hawk-nosed lady with a big fluff of gray hair, had a sarcastic humor in talking about the kings and the queens and the wars, and most of the kids didn't react to her jokes. Dee had a hard time not laughing too loud, but Chuck Ratowitz was laughing too. And then they saw each other laughing.

History was just before lunch break, and they started to walk down the hall together. He wasn't pushy, but he wasn't shy. One day in the cafeteria, right in the middle of her Velveeta sandwich, their eyes found each other. He reached over and touched her hand.

"Hi there."

"Hi."

No point in asking her mother if she could go out on dates. Despite Daddy's Army career, they were Seventh Day Adventists— never underrate your parents' illogic. And after he deserted, Mom dried up like a prune. She bore down on Sally, Dee's older sister, haranguing her if she came home ten minutes late from school. At eighteen, Sally left home and it was Dee's turn. She was a defiant smarty-mouth, but encounters with her mother always left her in slobbery tears. Going to a movie, with or without a boy, was just half a step from Hell.

When Mrs. Giddings got a job as church secretary it was easier for Dee to spend time with Chuck: Mom couldn't know what went on between the end of school and five o'clock. End of January, they waited for her to go out to her Wednesday night Bible study, and Chuck came into Dee's room. They celebrated that day as their anniversary.

"You okay with this, Dee?"

"What do you think, dummy?"

Two months later Chuck's brother Stan was killed in the war. Chuck had idolized his brother, and he was devastated. All Dee could do was hold him. When he got through it, they knew that love would get them through anything—they just needed to hold onto that.

A couple of her teachers believed she should go to college, and they even talked with her mother, who was astonished to learn that her daughter had a brain. But they didn't have the money, and the only thing she could think was to study to be a nurse. Did she want to spend her life carting bedpans? More tempting to have kids with Chuck, and she didn't have to study for that. She knew how.

They graduated, and Chuck pushed to get married as soon as he got a steady job. She steered away from the subject. Maybe her dad's desertion made her shy of marriage, or maybe she just liked keeping her love life secretive, doing the forbidden, being one of those women that people wrote books about.

After Chuck's brother died his mother didn't have much feeling for her remaining son, and he realized it. She told him that as soon as he graduated she was moving in with her cousin's family in

Phoenix. He could live in their house till she sold it and then he was on his own. So he had the house a few months and Dee drifted back and forth. Her mom took in what was going on but stopped with the sermons after a final screaming fit. She'd called Dee a slut and a liar and an ingrate and a devil, "just like your father," but Dee just stood there glowering at her. No tears, not any more. *Not any more, Mom.* Dee Giddings would not be a victim.

The first time she slept overnight with Chuck she was appalled that he snored. And he was appalled when she told him. He asked her to imitate how he sounded, and as soon as she started in he yelled, "Stop it!" He told her to shove at him whenever he did it, so she did and sometimes that made him stop. When it didn't, she put a pillow over her head or just snuggled around him and pretended he was a barrel organ. He laughed when she told him that.

The house got sold that fall and they rented the tiny cottage. Mrs. Giddings launched a few final salvos and Dee suffered the sting. She faced it coldly but those years still clung like a cigarette smell. "You're cursed by your own mother," Dee whispered to Chuck, "and you know she means it literally."

"Hey, hon, forget it."

"I know. Right."

She turned the page. Volleyball.

Her yearbook wouldn't let me go. My own had the same slick pages, the same fake leather binding, the same promise of freedom, the same door opening to the blank brick wall. In those lost days of sightedness I would flip through its pages, a hand at my groin, to find the boy I lusted for who was off with the girl I loved. If my tourists wanted ghosts I should rip open my breast and let them surge out braying.

I knew these people.

Volleyball. Dee hated volleyball. Another headline in sentimental script: *Forward, remembering.* Got it right this time. Forward without remembering worked better for her. She was happiest with their living together in the here-and-now. She wasn't the greatest cook and Chuck wasn't a born dishwasher, but she swiped a cookbook from her mom, started from page one, and after a while the stuff tasted good. She found a waitress job, and Chuck got short-term hires on projects but nothing steady. His uncle said there was a lot more construction in San Francisco, but they liked their little cottage. Her mother had been sick, and even though they weren't on speaking terms Dee felt she should stay nearby.

Finally Chuck got hired on a big development, a whole subdivision that promised at least a year of steady work. After two days on the job he was fired. Dee was on early shift so she got home first, and when he came in he slammed the door as if to blow it off the hinges. He couldn't mutter more than two expletives at a go. All she could understand was that he'd got fired, he wanted to kill somebody, and she could see he was trying not to cry. At last he found words. They had a dozen code violations—utility-grade studs on bearing walls, sloppy notching, faulty blocking between the joists—anything to build it quicker and cheaper. He wouldn't do it, so they fired him. She told him she was proud, but every month they faced the first of the month.

Then this new job popped up. Not only the dollars but the quality of the materials—the wood, the tiles, the finishings—sent him to seventh heaven. Dee joked that he'd never leave her for another woman, but she couldn't compete with a piece of fine walnut. Chuck laughed. When she heard herself say it, though, it didn't sound like a joke.

Why am I scouring this wasteland? She closed the yearbook, rose and put her coffee cup in the sink. Quarter till eleven, time to get started doing something with the day. Doing what? She ought to get a library card. She used to read a lot in high school, but now it didn't seem right—too private, too childish. She sat down again with the yearbook, opened it at random and found herself staring at her own senior photo. Same smile as all the others, as if a pair of plastic lips were stuck on every face to brand them with brainless glee. She shut it. On the back of the yearbook in raised cursive script, gold on blue, was the same phrase again: *Forward, remembering.* Some kid had *remembering* on the brain.

Then it came to her why she was riffling through the stupid *Blue and Gold.* She was terrified. Marriage: next week if Chuck could get off work. They were pretending it was only a scrap of paper, but her gut knew otherwise. There was something of death about it. She would no longer be young. She would be in a world where half the marriages crashed and the rest were hell on a thirty-year mortgage. She would be in that dream driving up a steep hill that got steeper, steeper, until at last the car tipped and began the plunge over backward. She'd seen Grandma the day before she died. Grandma's eyes.

No, no reason to fear. She had no burning ambition beyond loving Chuck, having kids, quitting her waitress job, making a life. Maybe her dad's desertion had shaken her and she still was rocked by the tremors, but she trusted Chuck and he trusted himself. He wasn't afraid. She loved him. He saw her.

If I had had a sister, it might have been Dee. I would have seen her smiles and frowns without her knowing it. I would have been jealous of any doofus who touched her. I would have drunk in her joys and terrors more deeply than my own. I would have yearned to tell her, *You can speak to me, I know you, we're kin.* But possibly I wouldn't have. I stay outside people, even outside myself.

When I raised my focus from the yearbook, she wasn't there, nor the kitchen. It was only hallucination, fantasy, some late-night movie I'd forgotten, an escape from the quotidian into another quotidian. Once I had tried to write a novel, but after a dozen pages I stopped, appalled at what I might make happen. Better to tell a market-tested tale over and over until I could no longer hear the telling, no longer fear the consequence. Better steer clear of whatevers.

Immediately I was surrounded by daisies: the frantic giddy decor of the Daisy Room. I was the tour guide again, and my tourists, huffing from the climb up the stairs, awaited my pregnant words.

Five

"We're now standing in the Daisy Room, as you may guess from the wallpaper rife with daisies. Mrs. Weatherlee's favorite flower was the daisy." I was relieved to discern no phantoms in the Daisy Room. Perhaps they were repelled by daisies, as vampires were by—what was it, broccoli? I might have worked that joke into my spiel if I hadn't been on my last official legs. No, forget the phantoms, Raymond: just do your job. Strange that I could ignore the most outlandish singularities if I simply had a job to do.

A steely female voice cut through the murk. "How is it known that her favorite flower was the daisy?" I visualized a tall severe woman, a history professor perhaps, call her something tart—Dr. Quint—with a faint mustache and perfect teeth. Strange, I had never had that question before, and it goaded me to tell the truth.

I didn't. "Extensive research." That appeared to satisfy. I went on to acknowledge that the Daisy Room furnishings, as in most of the house, were not original; that Sophia's movables had been auctioned off *post mortem*; that it took a full eight days to transport twenty tons of furniture to the auction house. Those figures were the result of the same extensive research.

"This, however, was not Mrs. Weatherlee's bedroom. This room was occupied by Isabella Pardee, her niece. Historical record shows that she came west a few years later than her aunt, served as Mrs. Weatherlee's secretary and sole companion. Eventually she moved to a house in San Francisco. No telling how Izzy Pardee regarded daisies. Let's forge on."

It was the only subversive speech I allowed myself. Meaningless but I treasured it. Sometimes I named it as Isabella's favorite flower, which conjured up a daisy-like Izzy waltzing blithely through the monkey house. Sometimes I charged it to Sophia, implying a tyrannical urge to tattoo daisies over every inch of her hapless niece. If Management had ever discovered my deviation I would have pleaded a slip of my aging muddled tongue, but they never did.

"So, continuing on to Mrs. Weatherlee's bedroom. Let's see if she's had a pleasant sleep." I chuckled, then led them up the passage to a staircase that descended seven steps to a landing where it ascended eleven steps. "This wing of the second story is three feet higher than that. So, up to go down, down to go up. Healthy exercise for ghosts."

As always, my domino row of jokes fell flat. Yet as I said, the jokes had their function. *Is that joke really lame or is he hiding something?* They evoked a faint terror, the efflux of an aging dog giving out a few sad yips. No fangs lurching up from the cellar, only that soft workaday despair that crusts over a late afternoon.

Continuing my rote babble, I entered Mrs. Weatherlee's bedroom, and my brood crowded through the doorway. "The room where she passed away . . . eighty-two years of age . . . sumptuous furniture . . ." On and on by rote as two figures came into my sightless gaze in the early morning light of late afternoon.

Sophia Weatherlee was propped in a handsome Victorian half tester bed, its high posts supporting the canopy, with mahogany panels of ornately-carved vine leaves and a low curved footboard with tastefully modest finials. Her breakfast of tea and biscuits was on a lap table before her. Her niece Izzy sat in a side chair at some distance, with a steno pad and fountain pen in hand. She was framed by a sunny window alcove, maroon valance and curtains.

Isabella Pardee was a trim woman in her mid-thirties. Her pale green dress made a brightly vegetal contrast to the dark drapery, its simplicity more suited to a working girl than to a Late Victorian heiress-to-be. She had her aunt's direct intelligent gray-green eyes, a smooth round face and thick auburn hair pulled into a bun. A slightly hooked nose suggested a woman who might mount the barricades for female suffrage, civil rights or Peace Now on any day over the next hundred years. Her only delicacy was a raw silk scarf loosely draped around her neck, imprinted with yellow daisies. Perhaps she did in fact like daisies, or else I was wishing them on her.

Her aunt was dictating a letter to a lawyer regarding a bequest for tuberculosis—curing it, presumably. "Dear Frank," she began, "I am entirely in accord with your suggestions of trustees for William's memorial. Designating a board of trustees to the memory of my husband is a rather ghoulish notion, is it not? It made me smile and then weep a bit. Still, a hospital is a hospital and requires a healthy budget for pills and purgatives, to coin a rude phrase."

"Rude phrase?" Isabella asked.

"Rude phrase, yes. Continuing: I have not yet reviewed your bylaw proposals, though I'm sure I trust your judgment. As you know, my trust in your advice is absolute, and my only reason for insisting on full oversight is that if anything were to go amiss I should have only myself to blame."

"I never thought of it that way," Isabella murmured.

"Well, aren't I special?" Sophia smiled. "I do my best, Izzy, to make up for my shortcomings, in both my height and my heart."

"More tea?" Izzy asked. "I'll ring."

"Sufficient."

"Continuing?"

"Just a *Yours gratefully*, and that will do."

"Right away." The young woman started to rise.

"Izzy, wait a wink, if you please."

She sat. "Yes?"

"What do they say about me?" Izzy absorbed the question. "You go into town," continued Sophia, "and you say you work for Sophia

Weatherlee, or that you are related to Sophia Weatherlee, or you say nothing but you just have that look about you, since in these tiny towns people are obsessed by strangers or the strangeness they project onto strangers. And so then what do they say?"

"I'm sorry, Auntie, you ask me that about once a week in fact, and I still don't understand the question."

"Of course they wouldn't say it to you, would they? That's absurd. They would say it once you left the shop, with your lovely hair fixed in a bun, very handsome, of course. And so how would you hear them say it? I talk in riddles, I know."

She took a biscuit from the tray and daubed it with a tiny spoonful of marmalade, then made a cryptic gesture with the biscuit and set it back on the tray.

"Of course they have to speculate. The human quest for meaning: rooting to find some tiny speck of rationality in my doings. We still name the constellations, even though their stars have no relationship whatever, except to our solipsistic brains. I love the word *solipsistic*, it describes me so well, and we're all so enraptured by our own grotesque reflections. And so they must construct some ghoulish meaning to my bizarre endeavors, lest all their foundations crumble. And so must I, I suppose."

I was surprised at the old woman's humor—far better than mine. Ghosts are known for their moans and clatters but not for their jokes. She should be the tour guide, I thought, and I the haunted heiress.

For a moment I was lost in Sophia Weatherlee's face. Its smoothness belied her age. She was old, no question, yet the carpenters spoke as if the building had just begun, and she would have been in her forties then. Simple answer, of course: it was all in my mind. These ghosts, these rooms, these hammers and yearbooks and biscuits were quilted from scraps of the only world I had known, tatters of little Raymond's blue shirt that his doggie chewed up—call it the Schnauzer of Time. Chronology was as jumbled as this peepshow we groped our way through. So much down-to-go-up, up-to-go-down.

The brightness felt softer, as if the sun were squinting its one mad eye. My voice droned on, rumbling along the ruts. I heard a sniff from the reedy nostrils of Dr. Quint. Herr Gerg asked a question about the window—the same narrow Tiffany window visible in the earlier room. It looked to be following us like a stray cat we'd made the mistake of feeding. Multicolored cut glass in concentric spider-web patterns, blazing with sunlight, and the quote on simulated scrollwork down its length: *Wide unclasp the tables of their thoughts.* Jerked back to reality I replied, "Its meaning? We can only speculate."

He persisted. "Whose thoughts? Ghosts?"

"My granddad called 'em ha'nts." Another voice, and a face flared up in my cranium: a short wiry black man with a Band-Aid across the bridge of his nose. His expression was harmless but the Band-Aid glared. It might have been the man I spied as a toddler. My mother told me that the first time I saw a black man I cried, and I was retroactively ashamed for being a bigot at the age of three. His name might be Ike.

Again I tasted a burning acid reflux. Words pressed against my esophageal sphincter and would not be swallowed. This was my last day, my last tour, and my pension was guaranteed unless I incurred a criminal liability. Why not stop with the haunted-house prattle and just release a full-out liberating vomit of truth?

I restrained myself.

"Izzy, do you believe in ghosts?"

"No. In a word."

"Then where does it go? Whatever's left of us?"

"Into the ground."

"Must be quite chilly," Sophia said. "Good thing we're dead then." Isabella said nothing. "And then after thirty years we begin to seep, do you think?"

"I should think we're dried out by then, Auntie. We needn't worry, truly." The silence hung there a short time. "Should I get this into the morning post?" she asked, holding up the letter.

Sophia ignored the question. "This is what they say when you leave their shop. Purely for your information—"

"I know, yes, I know—"

The old woman's lips sharpened. "That I was married and had a child. That my child died, as did my husband. Tuberculosis. Yes?"

"So you have said." Izzy had heard it all.

"That I was advised there was a curse from the sins of my father, my father's rifles, artillery, firebombs and his many appliances which produced several millions of dead. Soldiers, Indians, Mexicans, Filipinos, brown, white, yellow, red, all the colors of the rainbow brought into a single bloody communion by improvements in accuracy and penetration—"

"Auntie—"

"The consequence being vast hordes of displaced spirits, specters, spooks who have no home, who cry for a home, and so I am giving them a home, you see, all these many rooms to house the dead and the forthcoming dead. Is that what they say? That's what the newspapers say. Don't you read the newspapers?" Her jaw clamped tight and a tremor shook her. The morning sun blazed. Both women's eyes were hidden in shadow.

Isabella was accustomed to these flights. "Are you finished?" she asked quietly.

Sophia absently crumbled her biscuit on the tray. "Yes, I suppose I am." She picked up a crumb and put it in her mouth. "You certainly have my sister's temperament, but you're a wee bit more tractable. Or less obnoxious at any rate. Poor Sis, I miss her abuse."

"Auntie, you have asked me to tell you frankly when you sound compulsively antagonistic."

"And so I am. It must be the tea. Green tea is a failed experiment, I fear." The young woman smiled and Sophia reflected it. "Yes, thank you for taking me at my word."

"Any more letters, Auntie?"

"Well, let's see: perhaps an invitation to all my friends to visit me. An enormous dinner party. A gala. A Saturnalia."

"Which friends?"

Sophia looked up with a smile from the crumbled biscuit. "I can't think of a single one." She dabbed her tray with a napkin. "Yes, please try to get it into the morning post." The young woman rose to go, then came to the bedside, reached out for her aunt's hand. They shared two half-smiles that made up a smile between them. "You shouldn't pull your hair back quite so severely," said the aunt. "Leave it softer to catch the sun."

"I like it this way, Auntie."

"Yes indeed, you inherited my sister's willfulness. Someone had to: it came in great gobs. We'd have needed a warehouse to store it." She giggled, then glanced at her niece. "Ask Millicent to take my tray, if you please. No, I dismissed Millicent. Who is my newest victim, I forget?"

"Grace."

"Ring for Grace then." Isabella pressed a button beside the bed. "It is such a blessing to have one sole person on the premises I can't abuse. Though I certainly try."

Yes you do, said Izzy's look. She left the room quickly.

Grace, the new maid, came to clear the breakfast things. A slender light-footed girl, her movements were in keeping with her name. She kept her focus defocused, as well-bred servants should do, having been told that Mrs. Weatherlee disliked being visible. As she picked up the tray her employer spoke. "You are Grace, is that it?"

"Yes ma'am."

"Well, I hope you will find your work pleasant here. They have you in the third floor quarters, yes?"

"Yes ma'am, they do. It's very roomy, nice."

With a quiet tartness: "I can be quite human, you see."

Startled, the young maid glanced into the old woman's deep eyes, then, unsettled, to the window.

Sophia watched her. "*Wide unclasp the tables of their thoughts.* I'm puzzled why I chose that. Shakespeare was a genius, to be sure, but he doesn't always offer the best advice."

Hesitantly the girl found words. "It's beautiful, ma'am."

"That will be all. Thank you."

Sophia Weatherlee raised her frail hand, spread her fingers and waggled them in the sun. Grace gave a nod and departed.

"She's black." Ike's voice, amazed.

I went numb. I shrugged, made a sound that might have meant *Very true* or *Who knows?* or *Yams are tasty*. I scanned the other faces but they were only smudges. Snatching up a thread from my school-group lecture: "Yes, Mrs. Weatherlee did hire African-Americans, Mexican-Americans and Asian-Americans among the nearly sixty members of her household, which included the building, gardening and agricultural crews. Yes."

Mrs. Padgett spoke up. "Were there African-Americans then? I imagined they were all Negroes."

"Mom!" Sammie the daughter. They came into sharp focus. Mrs. Padgett, a buxom middle-aged woman with a wavy flowered hat and wide bottom. Sammie, fourteen, probably considering suicide. She might succeed better than I had.

"Well, everybody's human," said husband Bud, in shorts and sandals, safari hat and tan fishing jacket with a small flag pin on the lapel. He smiled a lot and probably sold insurance.

Nothing from Ike.

"So let's move along." I led my little flock of fledglings away, I the mother hen clucking down the hallway. But I was deeply unsettled. Shaken, stupefied. *She's black.* The tourist had seen her.

Six

She's black. My ghosts had been spotted. I clasped my hands behind me so none could see them quivering. I felt exposed, as if someone had flung open the toilet-stall and caught me mid-fantasy. Ten minutes into my final hour I was stark naked.

We stood in a narrow passageway with wide bay windows and a skylight ceiling. "You're now in the Conservatory," I said. "Mrs. Weatherlee's house plants, all the decorative foliage, would come here for a drink and a sun tan." I pointed to the floor. "You'll notice the unusual flooring, removable panels, where the plants would be placed to be watered. The zinc subflooring is tilted so that the water could run down troughs and refresh the garden beds. *Sustainability*, we call it today. She was well ahead of her time, was Mrs. Weatherlee."

Bridging two wings of the house, the Conservatory offered a dazzling interlude between dark and darker, the sunlight scouring out all presumptuous *ha'nts*. I had a few moments to bathe in brightness before approaching the Ballroom. "Mrs. Weatherlee loved flowers, as is evident even in the woodwork. While Victorians covered vast landscapes with industrial blight, they surrounded themselves with lavish arabesques of ivy carved in walnut and wallpapers in blossom. They worshipped the nature that they so avidly destroyed." These little sallies of social comment enhanced my aura of creepiness.

I nodded to signal moving on, then stopped. My flock had gathered along the south wall, staring out the bay windows. It appeared to be early summer before the springtime green had faded to tawny lions' breath. Men's voices drifted upward. Two figures sat below— ghosts fully lit in the noonday sun. I noticed that we stood in a wing that had not yet been built.

Chuck Ratowitz and the foreman sat on the cinderblock foundations of a partly-finished veranda, lunch boxes at their sides. Marty peered into his sandwich. "Peanut butter," he muttered. "That means my wife's pissed off about something and I'm supposed to guess what." He chewed it as if munching gravel. "Piece of advice. You and your lady friend, what's her name, Dee-dee?"

"Dee."

"If it gets serious with her, establish territory. Never let'er know how much you're making. You cash the check, handle the dough, always be the banker. Cause the time comes, couple years, you wanna play around, you know, see what else is out there, you got a little freedom. You can tell her they cut back on your hours and just keep a little back. I don't say that's the right thing, I mean it's kinda pathetic in fact, but otherwise they got you by the balls. You go to the movies and see the movie star getting his, and don't you wish."

"Well, I don't think—"

"Take it from me, I've been there. I've fought the fight and chomped the sandwich. They won't respect you unless it feels like, hey, any time you can walk. It holds a marriage together. Otherwise you get fuckin' peanut butter. Course tastes differ. Some guys like peanut butter."

"I hope you don't mind if I don't take your advice."

"I didn't figure you would." He gave a curt laugh.

Chuck finished his liverwurst sandwich and poured a second cup of black coffee from his thermos. *Play around a little.* It stirred a ripple of rage. "Three deep breaths," Uncle Frank once told him, "will save you lots of grief." He took a deep breath.

But *play around* struck a sore spot. He'd had a couple of high school crushes before he met Dee. Charlene was the class slut, but after a few dates she moved on to the basketball team. In his junior year he met Gail—short, roundish, full of fun—and when his dad died, her presence offered a quietness, as if life would wait patiently until his pain was done. Over that summer they started having sex. They never talked much about the future but it seemed real.

Then he met Dee. She was beautiful, she was smart, but there was something unpredictable about her, something edgy, and he wanted that. Gail had seen him walking with Dee and she knew what was coming. In her room, when her parents were gone, he finally got up nerve to tell her straight out. He had rehearsed what he was going to say, but the words came all in a jumble. "Maybe we could all be friends," he said, not knowing what the hell he meant by that. She broke down, flood of tears, raw red eyes, twisted mouth, ugly piggish sounds rising up from the gut—he couldn't stand to see her. He ogled the clowns and circus riders on the wallpaper, the stuffed animals perched on her pillow. Finally he just walked out. For the rest of the year, whenever he saw her at school, her face was a chalkboard, erased.

One thing stuck: he would never ever be unfaithful to Dee. He had hurt someone badly and would never do it again. Late fall they first made love. Two months later his brother was killed and Dee was an anchor, though he ached at the memory of the same hugs from Gail. From then on he felt married.

"Well, Dee's working too. We're both making the money, so—"

"Good for you." Marty poured a cup from his thermos and took a sip. Chuck looked at the cup and Marty noticed the look. "As far as you're concerned it's coffee."

"Right."

"Miss Weatherlee is very tolerant of what she doesn't know."

Chuck blew on his coffee to cool it. "She's a character."

"Character. That's one way to put it. She's okay. Anybody with bucks is either a nut or a sonofabitch. I got no problem with nuts."

"Is she kinda . . . funny?"

"Funny? Yeh, she'd get a few laughs on a comedy show, I guess. But we got a job and if you don't want it other people do. Free country, you got the right to starve to death, it's in the Constitution."

"I guess."

"You damn sure better believe it."

A silence set in. This conversation with his foreman made the young carpenter feel . . . guilt? inappropriate intimacy? Clearly the older man had a need to talk, but Chuck was embarrassed to have a conversation he couldn't share with Dee.

"So, Miss Weatherlee . . ." Chuck began. "Is it Miss or Missus?"

Marty took a sip. "She was married back East, I dunno." Chuck waited to hear more. "She's supposed to've had a husband who was where the money came from, and he died. Guns and bombs, good future in that. That's all I know. That's all I want to know. Call her whatever. Guess I wouldn't call her Sweetie Pie."

It was all he had to say, but he rambled on. People have that compulsion to talk, Chuck thought, like scratching an itch that's never quite where you scratch. "Look at this." Marty took a folded paper from under his lunch box and opened it out about eighteen inches wide. Its fine cream surface was covered with pencil scrawls, ink blots, intersecting rectangles, arrows and tiny indecipherable blocks of print. "Now here, this is the finest quality art paper. This'll set you back a bundle. She grabs these sheets from her niece, who tries to do art stuff, watercolors, so on. Scribbles all over it and then every morning hands me something like this."

"What for?"

"What for? This is our blueprints. This is the architect plans."

"Architect?"

"Well, she had an architect for a while, big reputation, ego like a watermelon. She canned him. Now it's her. This is the plans for today." He waved the paper. "Tomorrow more scribbles."

"You mean she—"

"She's the genius. There's another guy, Overton, Project Manager, sort of a contractor for the foundations, plumbing, electrics, pretty much of an asshole. But I never see him. She just says what to do and

I pass it along to the night shift guys, Carlo, Gene, sub-foremen. Fact is she's pretty good. Hard to believe. She studies these books, comes up with stuff, it knocks me for a loop. I'm here more than a year, we got twenty rooms. Who knows, maybe it won't stop. Do they stop building skyscrapers?"

"This is what you're building from?"

"This is it. This is the Gospel. Fact, it works out pretty well. Except you ask her a question you get this whole life history. Then you get the third degree."

Chuck was silent. That's not the way it's done. You submit your plans, get your permits, build what's approved, then you get inspected. This wasn't some other century: this was now. "How does she get away with that?"

"Money. Any other questions you got, same answer."

They drank their coffee. Chuck scanned the gardens. An array of sunflowers along the walkway led to a post-mounted bronze bell eight inches in diameter with a rope hanging from its rocker. A squat young plane tree sheltered it, and a statue of Cupid stared from a respectful distance. A wrinkled Japanese gardener—Mr. Kurosawa, Chuck recalled Marty saying—made his way toward it from a supply shed. Peculiar sight: the old man wore bib overalls bleached nearly white, a blue workshirt and a fur-lined trooper hat with dog ears dangling, ready for a Minnesota blizzard. He rang the bell five times a day on the canonical hours, Marty said, though no other Catholic traces were evident on the property. Mr. Kurosawa pulled the rope, and the plaintive bell of Weatherlee House rang out thin and clear. In his other hand he held a sickle. He smiled at the men and waved it.

"Tengo que irme!" My brood turned to gawk. Edged faces, but their sockets were smudged, unfinished. To my beclouded sight, the exclamation came from a Mexican lady, rotund, florid, past forty. She might be clasping a rose-embroidered shoulder bag and a small stuffed bear. Perhaps reassured by the bear, her panic dissolved. "Es okay, no lo hace."

"Es okay? Es okay!" A young man's thin voice, mocking. I found his face at the back of the group. A skinny kid in his thirties with little spasms of beard splotching his jaw. "Darrell Oswald," he said. "Easy to memorize." His eyes were a murderer's eyes.

They all had faces now. I counted them: the Iowans, the Mexican señora, the black man with a nose, the Austrian chicken face, the toothy lady prof, the scrawny assassin. I had gathered the cast for a major disaster movie.

We were still looking out the Conservatory window. I struggled to come up with more statistics and chuckles. Sometimes when drunk I would spew out bits of my spiel to Gertie, who never made the least twitch—good practice in running off at the mouth to no effect. Another minute passed. We had years to go.

Below, Marty brushed the paper, scanned the scrawls, took a pencil from his utility belt, made a note. "One thing. Just don't ever tell the old bat that something's wrong or it can't be done. She doesn't like the word no." He picked up his thermos. End of lunch break. "What about your girlfriend, Dee-dee? She easy to get along with?"

"Dee. Yeh, good. We got married last week."

Marty gaped at him. "When?"

"When I took off early Friday. You said that was okay."

"You got married?"

"Yeh."

"You said you had stuff to do Friday."

"Well, I did."

Marty absorbed it. "Well, I did that once. I made more noise about it though."

"I guess I don't talk much."

"Just go down to the county office or something?"

"Yeh."

Chuck had wanted a ceremony though they didn't have the cash or friends to invite, so he didn't push it. They went down to the county office, said the words and that was it. He wanted to tell the foreman that Dee had been reluctant, but that was too private a thing to say to this cynical guy. She was scared of trusting that final step and her agreement was impulsive. "We don't need a piece of paper right now," she'd said. "Let's just be together." And he'd agreed, okay, sure, what's a piece of paper? But pieces of paper held a heavy charge—your report card, your diploma, your paycheck, the building plans. Maybe she just felt she wasn't quite ready, or maybe she knew herself better than he knew her.

He realized they didn't have much in common except that they'd both lost their dads. She'd been good in school while he'd just scraped by. She used to read all the time, but he'd never be caught with a book unless to smack a bug. She said how lucky he was that his mom didn't interfere, and he thought how lucky she was that her mom cared at all. But their bond was deep. Hearing about other guys' marriages unsettled him. A roofer, Benny, said they had a big TV in their bedroom, and Chuck thought, damn, when we're in bed we've got better things to do than that. She was happy about it, he thought. He just wanted to make her happy.

Marty screwed the lid onto his thermos. "Yeh, me and my old lady, we made a big deal of it. Preacher, church, wedding gown, all her mom's friends. Course, most guys now, if it doesn't work out they move on, but I wasn't raised that way. My folks were farmers. You had problems you stayed together for the sake of the pigs." He had cracked that joke many times and waited for a laugh that didn't come. This kid was no conversationalist.

"No, I take it seriously, yeh," Chuck said. Stupid thing to say.

"Yeh, Ginny and me, our assumption was if we were gonna make each other miserable it'd be for life. And we do. *Till death do us part.* I believe in that. Gives you something to look forward to."

They sat for a time contemplating the skeletonic veranda. Marty took the last bite of his peanut butter sandwich, grimaced, picked up his lunch box. "Well, congratulations." He rose. "Back to work."

They moved on. As did my tourists. There were so many rooms to be seen.

Seven

My litter proceeded into the East Wing, the pudgy blond Austrian leading with his pointy nose, but I was rooted like a leftover philodendron. Never before had my puppies ventured unaided into the bowels. Never had they seen a glimmer of ghosts. Never had my dead eyes been so focused. Was this part of my retirement package?

No rush to catch up. As if shuffling to the toilet at midnight they had already slowed their pace. I held an odd affection for them, the way I'd loved the guppies my mother bought me for my birthday, all of whom were soon floating in food scum on the surface. My throng were sucked into the gloom. They became my brethren, and I hated them with the fetid hatred reserved for siblings.

The light changed. It was morning again, perhaps late April, rainy. A row of butterfly bushes, newly planted five minutes ago, were nearly waist level, and the unfinished veranda was now an elegant gingerbread mongrel: tile roofing with filigree latticework skirting the rails, classical white columns with acanthus capitals, and stonework steps. I entered a new season of hallucination.

Chuck sat on the steps. Lunch break again. His face was overcast and he was eating a tuna sandwich, his favorite. The work was on the north side now, but he came back here to eat lunch where he could be solitary. With his free hand he ran his fingers along the crease of his collar. He wore a clean shirt every day. He prided himself on that and was thankful to Dee.

He would sit here at lunchtime avoiding the rest of the crew. Marty appeared to grasp that he didn't want company and left him alone. The foreman taught him a lot, he was great to work for, but Chuck couldn't see him as a friend. Himself, he was friendly always, but he had no time for friends.

He was a father now. One flash and he was a father. Dee had come home one day, said, "Sit down, I've got something to tell you." He didn't sit down, he just grabbed her and hugged her and spun her around, and when he set her down she was in her seventh month. By the time she started dinner, baby Joey was teething. That's how it felt. Life was so sudden.

His mind jumped back to the job. A new guy hadn't set a king stud straight, had measured the top plate wrong, and the whole window header was leaning. No excuse, the jerk was in a hurry. Nice that Marty trusted Chuck to fix the screw-up, but it left a sour taste.

The pregnancy. That was a job done right and Dee knew how to do it. He joked that he was no longer part of the construction crew, now he was just the watchman. It was hard to believe those months had actually happened. He tried to remember the first time he felt the baby kick—the quickening they called it—but he couldn't. What came to him, oddly, was the time they'd decided on the name. Joseph. Joey. That was the moment he knew it was real.

In Dee's seventh month they had repainted the kitchen a bright lime green and put in new cabinetwork. She had gotten off work early, and when she was home alone she gravitated to the kitchen. Sitting at their sturdy old table skimming a book of baby names, she heard Chuck come in the back door. "Hi, hon," he called.

She put down the book and rose. He set his lunch box on the counter, came into her embrace. They held each other briefly, then he pinched her nose, turned to open the fridge, took out a beer, popped it, slouched down at the table. "You look kinda beat," she said.

"Long day."

"What about Joseph?"

"Joseph who?"

"The baby. Name for the baby."

"Oh. Hey, wait'll I sit here a minute." He gave a weak laugh. "I'm not set up for major decisions, okay?"

"Sorry."

"No, that's . . ." He gave a sigh, getting his bearings. Deep-sea divers had to come to the surface slowly, he recalled hearing, and it was a strange passage, always, from the world of hammers to the world of this woman. "Hey, maybe it'll be sextuplets, the way we were going at it." She always liked it when he tried to be funny, he thought, even if he wasn't.

She smiled. "Yeh, there's a point where birth control just doesn't stand a chance. Pork chops?" He nodded.

"Or if it's a girl, what about Esther? Esther, Heather, no, I guess that sounds like an old lady with geraniums." Chuck took a swig. He didn't really want to talk but she clearly needed to. "I go kinda crazy going through girls' names cause I start to think about changing my own."

"What's wrong with Dee?"

"Well, people ask you, *What's that short for?* It's short for Dee. My mom liked me short, I guess, so I'd always be her baby."

He had suggested they do the test for girl or boy but she didn't want it. She was afraid, she'd said, that with a girl she'd wind up acting like her mother. It had been his job to tell Mrs. Giddings that Dee was pregnant and fend off the woman's hysterical demands to "be of help." Dee didn't want her anywhere near.

"Well, it's probably gonna be a boy," he said. "I mean it better be if its name's gonna be Joey." She smiled at him, though she didn't react as if it was funny. Would she be mad if he called the kid Joey instead of Joseph? "No. Yeh. Joseph, that's nice. That's cool. Joey. Joey Ratowitz. Tough little guy."

"Well, give it some thought, for heaven's sake!" More tart than she'd intended. "Sorry, I'm kinda nutty right now. Hard day?"

He didn't know how to answer. Would he speak of the web the old lady spun when she'd called him in that day, talking to him as if he were her foreman or her pastor—stuff about drainage and reincarnation? Or the fog that rolled in from Marty's sullen looks? The foreman hated her talking to his men, but that wasn't Chuck's fault. It had happened twice, and when Marty asked him what she'd said, it was like trying to do book reports in school: the guy who wrote the book had the words, not him. And Dee's question, *Hard day?* He was glad that she wanted to know him, share his darks and his dreams, but he needed words for that and his skill was driving nails.

His ironworker dad had been that way. He was the guy up on the skeleton of the bridge, cranes swinging in girders that could crush him like a peanut shell. Always reliable, always faithful, always providing, never speaking. "Like trying to mind-read a coconut," his mom told a neighbor lady. Chuck had bristled when he heard that casual mockery of his dad, but he could feel the woman's desperate thirst. Now the same.

"No big deal."

She didn't seem satisfied with that. She'd probably had a hard day herself. She was into her sixth month, or seventh, he couldn't keep track. They could afford for her to quit and she'd have to quit soon, but she was stubborn that way. It was hard to talk things out when he never could find the words. She got up and started supper.

"Well, it's okay," he tried again, "it's good. The lady, she gets weirder all the time. Foreman, Marty, says she pays her maids and kitchen help by the day so she's able to can 'em when she wants. But Marty's okay, he don't put up with stuff as far as the crew goes." It wasn't what he wanted to say but it was words at least.

Dee picked up the book of names. "Hon, you don't have to do it, you know. There's other jobs." His gall rose like a bubble, a blurt in boiling oatmeal. She was trying to be kind but she had no clue. There weren't other jobs that paid this well. None. *Just shut up with that.*

And it was the job he'd dreamt of. With other foremen he'd been told, "You're not building furniture," meaning don't build a house with the tolerances you'd need for cabinet-making, it's a waste of time. True, but for lots of guys that was an excuse for sloppy work. Go more than a quarter-inch out of plumb on an eight-foot wall, your work is sloppy. The first day Marty told him, "Chuck, think of this job like building furniture. Take your time. The lady's got shitloads of time." Chuck could have hugged him right there. And he knew he was a hotshot, but a hotshot who still had lots to learn. The contractor, manager, whatever he was, came out from town once in a while to coordinate things. Not very well. More than once they'd had to take out structure they'd just put in because he'd miscalculated the notching. Chuck learned a lot from that guy's screw-ups. He still couldn't understand how they did without the countless permits and inspections required for every job he'd ever been on. "Money talks," Marty had said, but it was spooky.

"The lady calls me Mister Chuck." He laughed. Once in a while his dad had tried to joke, but nobody could ever tell if it was a joke. "*Mister Chuck.* I had to laugh." He hadn't.

"Well, I guess my labor's gonna be easy," Dee said. "Hard part is naming the baby and we've got that done. If Joey agrees to be a boy." She put the book on the shelf with the cookbooks, turned and smiled. Their eyes met and they laughed together.

I stood looking down from the Conservatory at this young guy innocently eating his sandwich while I made up his story. I was braiding old yard-sale rags into some fable no more tangible than the fairytale I had spouted endlessly for thirty years.

But if I were fabricating these people—their faces, hearts, yearbooks—whence came the raw materials? I couldn't hammer a nail. Once I'd tried to build Gertie a litter box, but even a frowsy dishwater cat doesn't want nails protruding where she licks her butt. I had seen men eating sandwiches, but I never watched carpenters doing the work they do—fitting, joining, fastening, whatever—and here these terminologies were flowing out of my head. I had knowledge of drinking a beer but not how to frame a window. Nor had I ever lived with a woman or named a child Joseph.

Once, at my grandma's, I read a *Reader's Digest* story about the original Siamese twins. Circulatory system, liver, nerves connected. It must be the way a mother feels or a lover. That scared me away from Billy, from Shirley, from others—part of yourself outside yourself that has a will of its own. I learned to uproot it before it blossomed, to flee from what I didn't want to see.

Even in my days of sightedness I rarely went to the movies or read much fiction. That was like riding a crowded bus and smelling body odors, or being trapped in someone else's itchy skin. It might wrench me out of my damp nest of self-pity that was so much like home. Even now I rely on beginning my day with a gentle whimper for breakfast and another as a nightcap. A young lady is paid to come in each month to read my mail, process my bills, those things you need eyesight to do. Her name is Colleen. I've never asked her who she is.

Chuck was there with Dee through a twenty-six-hour labor, bearing the steel-jaw grab of her hand each time the tide rolled in. He had expected her pain but he hadn't expected seeing the sheer brute work of giving birth—the hardest labor he'd ever seen anyone do. Like the Bible story where Jacob wrestles the angel all night: sinew and strain and the terrible not knowing.

It went on. Chuck held her hand, stroked her forehead, wanting to absorb the pain, take it into himself.

"Want some water?"

"I'm fine."

"How you doing?"

"I'm just gonna get up and go home."

They smiled together, but Chuck saw her doubt. She didn't think she could do it. He wanted to tell her, hey, billions of women have done it, but he realized he didn't know diddly-crap—dumb as a bag of hammers, his uncle would say. Every minute or so he glanced up at the clock. The doctor hadn't been back since six o'clock.

"Should I call the nurse?"

"Some water."

The doctor walked in at nine, asked Chuck to step outside, and after a few minutes came out and said they had to do a Caesarian. Chuck came in, put his hand on her brow, kissed her forehead, tried to find words. Their eyes didn't meet, exactly. He went to the waiting room to sweat it out.

At last a nurse came in. "She's fine, it's a boy." She directed Chuck down the corridor to a viewing window for newborns. On the other side of the glass a nurse pointed to the third pod in the second row. There it was: Joey. It looked exactly like a baby. Chuck felt something he'd never felt before. It ought to feel good, but he couldn't tell, it was just weird, like the first taste of beer or the first ejaculation—it took getting used to. Then Joey twitched.

Just a twitch, but none of the other babies twitched. Why did Joey twitch? Chuck flushed. Something was horribly wrong. Should he yell for help? The nurse had paid it no mind, so he said nothing. They must be tending the babies. They must know better. If he asked about it they'd take the baby and start doing tests and make the nightmare real. Just a twitch, he told himself.

Most of that day he could recollect only in fragments. When he came into her room she was lying with her face toward the door. "Hi. How you doing?" he asked. No reply. "It's Joey. Joseph. He looks great." She said nothing. "I mean, right, it's a boy." She smiled faintly. Later they brought the baby in, and Chuck stared at this little animal on Dee's chest, at her breast, finding the milk. The milk was already there. She startled, then smiled.

Still, he continued to brood. What makes a baby twitch? Do their nerves just fire willy-nilly? Can dreams be stirred from their brief glimpse of light? Are they already dodging traffic? Was that the spasm of his brother at the shock of death? He put those thoughts behind him as best he could, but for several days his hands held a tremor. A part of him was outside himself. He would never be safe. He felt delight—and cold horror—at what he'd begun.

The first months were what they'd expected: no sleep, nerves raveled, a tiny alien dropped down the chimney. Chuck was a father now, so he sensed that he'd better grow up fast. He found himself wishing that life was the way it had been, just the two of them, just their love. Then, washing the dishes as Dee sat nursing Joey, he would glance over from the sink and be shaken by a crazy surge of joy.

Despite first impressions I developed an odd attraction to Chuck. Not so much that he was a beautiful young man but that—despite his marriage, his family, his crew mates—he was alone. I wasn't the only one. Others so different from myself were out there rambling down the passage to nowhere. Both of us accepted our life sentence without possibility of parole. My words were graffiti scrawled on the walls he erected. He made a baby, I fed a cat. We did what we had to do.

I looked again: he was gone. Below, there were only the ornamental shrubs and the spectral gardener approaching with his shears. I groped for a touch to guide me to my tourists. They were as alien to me as my savage schoolmates, but they were mine. Their search let me touch mystery, let me curl into the dark lush corner of a world gone frigid in fluorescence.

They hadn't gone far. They had turned into a hallway that ended at a toilet stool. They stood gazing at it, baffled. As I approached they turned to me for comfort, but I could offer them nothing more than the waterless throne. I had forgotten my lines. My mind was grease. I could only do what I had to do.

I had fantasized it before. From the start, my script changed very little. Management allowed deviations to give it a personal flavor but demanded fundamentalist adherence to the gospel of Weatherlee House as written up in travel guides and splashed on billboards. At times I was seized with a suicidal impulse to tell the truth as I understood it, to admit how shaky were the facts of my spiel. On each occasion I stifled the urge. Now eight pairs of eyes riveted me, plaintive, merciless. Nature abhors a vacuum, they say, so at last, without intending to, I spoke the simple truth.

"In actual fact," I said with dead calm, "the legend of Sophia Weatherlee's guilt-ridden obsession—the spiritualist, the homeless ghosts—is pure speculation based on fanciful newspaper accounts.

She was a very wealthy recluse who owned multiple properties, even a houseboat in the Bay, and moved among them. Far from seeking eternal life, she executed a will including instructions for her burial in New Haven and a bequest for her husband's memorial. The so-called legend grew from one hack quoting another until it became a billboard slogan with ghosts flitting in and out." I scanned their imagined faces. No response.

"The architectural anomalies—stairs leading to nowhere, a door to a drop-off—are likely the results of earthquake damage. The number thirteen occurs frequently—thirteen bathrooms, thirteen-candle chandeliers, thirteen coat hooks, stairs with thirteen steps—and then others with ten or fourteen or eight. Tell me she had thirteen fingers, I'll give it some credence."

My voice rose to a ringing whine. "Another quote from Shakespeare: *Do you smell a fault?* It makes an appealing story, granted, without which Weatherlee House would have been quickly replaced by a subdivision or shopping mall. Instead, within five years of the old woman's death, it became a tourist attraction. The rumors became my scripted babble and we have been exploiting your fantasies ever since."

I went mute, awaiting the explosion. A breathless eternity. Then the Austrian spoke. "So are there ghosts?"

They had heard nothing at all. The best of both worlds: I had purged myself of falsehood to no effect whatever. Truth is best if unheard. I shrugged in response.

"Could be."

Eight

We stood at the south entry to the Ballroom. My ducklings were grouped in the archway, gawking like devotees of an execution. I wedged my way through to a place of command, then turned to follow their gaze.

Sophia Weatherlee sat in a far corner of the enormous room, silhouetted against the migratory spiderweb window. *Wide unclasp—* It might be Shakespeare, might be from a fortune cookie, a tombstone, or instructions for a cell phone. Now she was perched in a Savonarola chair, a cheerless squatting device evoking the legendary severity of the Florentine monk. Weird thoughts swarmed in my brain like blowflies, and me without a swatter.

"Thursday we went to the beach. My hair was so beautiful. Catherine was quite jealous." The woman's mumble was wafer-thin, intended only to tell herself, *I'm here.* She peered across the ballroom, perhaps at me or at the ghosts she'd invited. As before, her hair was gathered in a tight gray bun, but a strand had come loose and hung across her cheek. She brushed at it. "Squirrels on the roof, skittering, hideous . . ."

I addressed my flock. "We're standing now in the most costly room in the house, the Ballroom. Notice the inlaid flooring, the paneling, mahogany, teak, walnut, eleven varieties of rare and expensive wood. The Tiffany glass, of course, and the gaslights, the chandeliers, the imported fireplace tile would have cost a small fortune. Strange to say, it was never used. Mrs. Weatherlee was no dancer. A ballroom without a ball."

No one was listening to me. I was only a skitter of squirrels.

"Marty?"

Marty stood framed in the opposite entryway. "Ma'am?"

"The light is so dim here. We need a skylight."

"Skylight?"

"Skylight? Of course not, we have two stories above us. There are limits even to my absurdity." She plucked at a spot on the chair arm. "But have you noticed? There is lint everywhere."

"Lint?"

"Somehow we have an echo." She smiled, picking up the leather-bound book in her lap. "I have been trying to read Proust. Have you read Proust?"

"No ma'am, I'm not much of a reader."

"Why should you be? And if you were, why read this little French twerp? He's nattering endlessly on every nuance of his useless life. I should be sympathetic, given my own eccentricities, but for that matter I have difficulty forcing my mind to descend into reading. Books are the ultimate terror." In a flash she was animated, almost gleeful. "The ultimate terror. Corpses embalmed in leather, shelf upon shelf. What sane woman would spend her life visiting mausoleums?" She placed the book on the tea table to her left. "I'm joking, of course." She picked at the arm of the chair.

Marty was accustomed to her morning ruminations. "You've got new plans, Miss Weatherlee? I think you said? We're done with the veranda. Waiting for deliveries on the elevator shaft."

She gave a querulous wave. "Well, it's not working out. I seem to be building these corners. Corners by the dozens."

Elucidation was not forthcoming. "Well," he ventured, "a room's got corners. You build a room you build four corners."

"As a small child I was terrified of corners," she said, again with quiet glee. "The things that accumulate there . . ." She took a folded sheet of watercolor paper from beneath the book and held it out to him. He crossed the floor as if treading on fragile skin, took it from her and studied the new plans, then took a pencil from his pouch and made a mark.

"And my baby's bedroom, eclipsed, like gazing into the maw of a ravenous orchid." She brushed at the strand of hair. "Because it came clear to me that my father— Not my father, my father-in-law, lovely man, he was like a father to me, but all the fathers, whoever— It became clear that they were guilty of so much. All the young boys. The wars that made us our fortune, they built us this lovely ballroom." Marty scanned it. "How easy was it, do you think, for a young woman to reconcile that? To justify her own comforts, her privilege, her futility? How easy, Marty?"

"How easy was it?"

"Very. No trouble at all." She smiled. She likely enjoyed this sort of banter. "But no, my father-in-law was strongly opposed to war, spoke on the subject, spoke out against it despite his reliance on it. He might not have done so, I suppose, if men had actually been listening." She turned her face to the daylight.

Marty knew when to speak or keep his mouth shut. "And then also we finished the breezeway," he said. "Flooring, Chuck's doing that. He's a good worker. And we finished sanding the stairs—"

"Did you see the sunrise this morning?"

"In fact I did."

"Remarkable. What were you doing up?"

"Ruth and I were having a discussion."

"Fighting about your boys? They're good boys." Marty was silent. "But then how would I know? I'm always doing that, constructing fictions. From the finest exotic materials." She made a vague gesture toward the walls, brushed at the strand of hair.

Marty stepped closer, pointing at the paper. "Now I'm trying to figure, Miss Weatherlee, you've got these notes. Does this mean this wall goes out? That can't be done. That's a weight-bearing wall."

"We can discuss it. Meantime you can make the necessary preparations."

"It can't be done, Miss Weatherlee. We already talked about that." *Never say no*, he had said. He was violating his own rule.

She spoke in a measured tone. "Otherwise we would be unable to enlarge that room without losing the interior window into the stairwell, what do you call it, the transom, and it feels much too—"

"It might be done but it's very—"

"And I'm fond of the window. I'm accustomed to the window. I have lived in these rooms."

"Then what if we just—"

"I have lived in these rooms!"

For an instant her face contorted. Rage, Marty wondered, or just arthritis? Then her features settled back to neutral and she brushed her brow. Marty rolled up the sheet of paper.

"Would you call your new man in here, please? Chuck, what's that silly name, Ratowitz? Would you call in your Mister Chuck Ratowitz, please?"

"Chuck?" Marty hesitated.

"Please call Mister Chuck."

Marty crossed the floor to the entryway, disappeared into the foyer. "Chuck! Would you come in here a minute?" He hesitated, then reappeared.

They waited in diagonal corners. Sophia had no apparent urge to fill the silence. These premises were hers, including the silences, hers to fill or not to fill as she chose. She might have noticed Marty's hands clenching and unclenching, but she made no sign of it. At last she spoke. "We can discuss this another time, since I fully understand that there are complications which you are wise to bring to my attention. However, we cannot enlarge a room and keep the walls where they are. There are limits to illusion."

Chuck appeared in the doorway beside Marty. "Sorry, I was—"

"You laid the black pipe?"

"What? Oh. Yeh. While ago." It was only the third time he had been summoned by Mrs. Weatherlee other than when she had hired him. The safest course was to question nothing. Still, strange to talk about plumbing across a parquet floor with a strange hunched woman forty feet away. He still felt the marble in his mouth.

"Thirty, thirty-five years, you say, and then what happens to that pipe?"

"It starts to deteriorate, ma'am."

"Marty, are you in agreement? Is that correct? From your vantage as foreman?"

"Yes ma'am."

"And what happens to the water in the pipe?"

"It can seep into the ground table, ma'am."

"Seep. Do you think it will seep?"

Chuck's breath shortened. What was the upshot of his answer? Was he being blamed for seepage? Trying to follow her ramblings was harder than finding his way through the house. Just glancing into her eyes, or the way she looked at her fingers, it seemed like some other century. Sometimes it was just funny. Once she had directed Marty to ask if they could hammer more quietly. "Cry quieter, Joey," became a joke he shared with Dee. But mostly it was okay. As his uncle used to say of his grandma, the lady stayed confined to her innards.

Chuck met the old woman's insistent gaze. "It might seep," he replied.

"You have had experience with seepage? At your age?"

Was she making a joke? No matter, he was on solid ground with seepage. "Oh yeh, my brother, he had seepage, we had to dig out the basement, refinish it."

She paused. Marty unrolled the sheet of plans, glanced, rolled it up. Again she plucked at the spot on the armchair. The sun had gone behind a cloud and Mrs. Weatherlee lost her luster.

"So it is," she said. "Very well. Then you will see that a plan is made so that in thirty-five years, before those black pipes rust, when it seeps we will have a plan. We will all feel infinitely more secure if we have a plan. Even though we may all be dead by then. Will you take care of that?"

"Uh, sure, yeh . . . Yes ma'am."

"I'll have him take care of it," Marty hastened to add.

"Well then do," she said. Her eyes pierced him like needles. "Why are you both standing across the room? We're not playing tennis, are we? Come here where I can see you. I'm not all that sinister." A quiet laugh. "Or perhaps I am." She paused and they approached her. "You know, I once dreamed this house was in flames. But very slowly. The very slow flames of oxidation. Rusting that would take decades but flaring high in the night." Marty fingered the pocket watch in his utility belt but didn't risk checking it.

She addressed Chuck. "Have you taken out walls?"

"Walls? Sure. Walls, yeh, I took out walls. But you have to know what you're doing there. It can be tricky. You gotta work out if it's—"

"You are so very young."

Chuck froze. He was in his first day on the school safety patrol, fourth grade. The teacher handed him his white patrol-boy belt, said, "Here you go," and walked away without telling him which corner to stand on or how to put on the belt or what to do if some kid got hit by a truck. *Just keep thinking six hundred a week.*

Marty interrupted. "Miss Weatherlee—"

"Come around, Marty, and pick this up, please." She indicated a large cardboard box. "You had suggested that an additional one of these items would be useful to the crews, and so I am providing it as promised." Marty picked up the heavy box. "Please look inside." He balanced the box on his knee, opened the lid.

"Fine piece of equipment, ma'am."

She gestured for him to take it out of the box. He set the box on the floor, lifted out a compound miter saw that still bore its tags.

"Would you hand it to your subordinate, if you please." Marty did so. Chuck hefted it. "Well, Mister Chuck," she said, "do you know how to use this?"

"Oh sure— yeh, I— ma'am? That's a Porter-Cable 12-inch right there. That's a nice piece of equipment."

"We are agreed on that point. Would you like to have it?"

"Well, yeh, that'd—"

"Why?"

"Why? Well, you know the corners you can cut on that, you can pivot that around, you can tilt it, that'll give you angles like butter."

"Butter. Imagine that." She reached for her teacup, realized the maid had removed it, and wiped the doily where the saucer had been. Her face was shrouded. "Well, you see, the problem is this," she continued. "This is to be for general use of the crews. However—" She brushed at the fugitive strand. "However, it should actually *belong* to someone. Property is to be owned. It is in the nature of things to be owned, lest my sister cry down from Heaven to charge me with multiple counts of socialism. So whatever shall we do?"

Sophia waved her hand toward the miter saw as if it were a child's toy. "Now I would like for you two gentlemen to work out between you which of you is the owner of this object. It's entirely your decision." They glanced at each other. Marty had a notion what was happening, Chuck was clueless. "And I will be eager to know how you decide. I'd like a report on that, please, Marty. And the wall. We need a plan for the wall."

"Yes ma'am." He twisted the roll of paper. Chuck hesitated, then carefully placed the heavy instrument back into its box, lifted it and offered it to Marty. Marty ignored it, gestured for him to go and limped after him.

The men were gone. Sophia's brow squeezed tight and her lips flattened. A high girlish voice formed the words: "I am acquainted with walls."

Porter-Cable saws? Were there such devices in Sophia Weatherlee's time? My fantasies were being seen by others, and I blushed at my ghosts' anachronisms. Dr. Quint's steely voice cut through my fog. "Could you offer us the historical context?"

History always irked me. Either it was all past, thus futile, or else it repeated itself—a notion too depressing to bear. In school it was a few compacted tick-tocks of madness and waste; an oceanic symphony of holocaust; a pathetic juggler whose lone talent was a mindless dingbat cycling of blades and balls. Where were we now in relation to the timeline? Could even a stone-blind tour guide misplace a world war?

My salaried function was to offer clean well-lighted nightmares, devoid of dandruff. But who really cared if my story took place before or after we slaughtered Filipinos, before or after we dropped the Bomb, before or after *Howdy Doody Time* or JFK or napalm? History, like the sewage system, worked in the background, flushing headlines, prognostications, bodies for the body counts. The years fell off the calendar and clattered on the floor.

To answer the question I launched into an amusing story about the death of my first cat Max on the night of a Presidential election. For the present that seemed to suffice.

Nine

Sophia Weatherlee stood erect in a deep green velvet dressing gown. I had never seen her standing. She was as short as I had always said she was.

A bare chamber, dim except for a naked bulb in the ceiling and a glow from a tiny high window: the Sewing Room. It had never been used for sewing, though it had once been stocked with bolts of fine imported fabric. Spread on the cutting table before the woman was the familiar sheet of watercolor paper scrawled with rectangles, figures and tiny cursive. An empty tea cup and saucer rested on a high stool to her right. She stared at the paper blankly.

"Mrs. Weatherlee, the carpenter's here," the maid announced. She departed, Chuck appeared. Sophia continued to scan the scribbles.

"Well, Mister Chuck. We have business here."

"Yes ma'am?"

She picked up a pencil. "Your wife is well, I trust, and your child?"

"Yes ma'am, they're fine." He guessed he was expected to say something more. "The little one's quite a handful."

"I lost mine, you know."

"Ma'am?"

"Sara Lynn. Two years, eleven months, twelve days, very near her birthday. A wasting disease. The official diagnosis was marasmus, a kind of malnutrition commonly found in darkest Africa but rarely in the private estates of New Haven. Embarrassing, you may surmise, apart from other emotions that attend upon the occasion." She made a pencil mark on the paper before her.

"Sorry."

"As was I." She was gazing into another world. "Sara Lynn. She was so well-behaved, never complained. *The hand of death squeezed out the juices and left the rind*, as I recall from some poet. Morbid but true. I still smell the rotten stench that rose up out of the lungs. In literature little dying girls lie there in angelic repose. You never read of them exuding a stink." Sophia's hand clutched air. "She had a little rag doll, a Raggedy Ann, that somehow got lost the day before she died. She cried only for the doll. Your little boy will not play with dolls, I expect."

"No ma'am, I don't suppose."

"Just as well."

She looked older. I tried to penetrate the lady's blurred eyes, to peek into her naked heart. All entrances were shut. In the other ghosts I could see feelings that fluttered through them like shadowplay, and they drew me into their sticky fly-trap innards. Only Sophia Weatherlee was closed to me. I could hear each word of her surgical articulation, but to the motions of her soul I was blind, blind, blind.

What came to me was an image of a woman in labor. So foreign to me, yet I was overwhelmed with the face of a woman giving birth, screaming out her mindless confession, but the torturer was implacable. Then the labor was done, forgotten, and the work of mothering began.

For this fabled heiress that task was aborted. What might have sprung from it? A dancing girl child, luminous as ruby, gentle as moonlight, sweet as rain. Instead, she nursed this architectural fetus, this elephantine infant, this toddler heavy with bloat, prinked out in Victorian lace.

It was too much to be seen by a sightless male. The image was there for an instant, then smeared by some greasy distracted thumb.

"Well, we have business." She reached for her tea cup, but it was empty. "Mister Chuck, would you please ring for the maid. Grace, is it, the colored girl? That button there." He pressed a button at the side of the door. "An ingenious system. Though it takes them a bit of time to find their way. We might install pneumatic tubes. Shoot the poor dears through tubes." She studied her papers as Chuck stood waiting.

"I find it difficult to talk business without tea," she said. "Awkward to wait, I know, but since it has always been the privilege of power to have others wait for you, then it must be the duty of those in power to exercise that privilege. Not entirely Christian, granted, but as my father-in-law would say, even Christ had to wait His turn. Of course he was joking. He was staunchly Episcopal. What do you think?"

Chuck hadn't understood a word. He nodded.

She smiled. "You are so agreeable." Grace appeared, tea was ordered and she left. Sophia made a delicate wave of her hand: more waiting. Chuck shifted his weight. From his few encounters with the lady he'd learned that waiting was part of the job.

The tea appeared. Sophia took a sip, then turned as the maid was leaving. "Do Negroes drink tea?" she asked.

Grace stopped at the doorway. Chuck caught a squint that might have been confusion, anger or fear. Then her eyes fell to the empty tray she held. "Some do, I think, ma'am. People are different."

"I ask the most idiotic questions. They just come frothing out. Thank you, Grace." The girl disappeared.

From beneath the paper Sofia took an official-looking document. "So. Very well. We have new developments." She smoothed the pages. "This has been drawn up. I prefer doing things more informally, but my lawyer Mr. Landreau, who is a dear friend and upon whom I rely— What was I saying?" She glanced at the paper, reached for her glasses on the table and inspected the typing closely. Chuck knew in a flash that he was being fired.

A voice chirped through the silence: Mrs. Padgett, the Iowa lady in her wilting hat. "How is it that we know so much about her? Did she leave memoirs?"

My phantoms dissolved. This jerk between realities was irritating my digestive tract. "From various sources," I said, but the silence was broken and they wouldn't let me off the hook.

"It is my understanding," said Herr Gerg in his creamy Austrian slur, "that there were no spiritualists in Boston. Did not the Puritans burn them at the stake?"

"That's part of the mystery." It was my stock reply to any hopeless question. I heard a squeaky smirk from the whiskery Mr. Oswald, but I simply wanted the words to stop. I was nauseated by the pond scum, apple rot, the tissue wad of words.

"Were there murders here?" The first words from surly daughter Sammie.

"Not as such."

Now the questions fluttered like frantic bats. "Did she have a pet?" "Why hammers?" "Will it seep?" Thirty-eight years of questions, but at root they were asking *Why?* Why the madness of Giza, Stonehenge, the World Trade Towers, the fossilized strata of Weatherlee House? She built it to piss off the neighbors? To protest the oppression of women? To lay waste to forests? She built it out of a boredom as profound as high school civics class? We could only surmise.

A more modest answer, perhaps. She did not build at the direction of spirits or from guilt at the killing that gleaned a vast fortune in bones. Out of terror, no. She built it simply as a tourist attraction. And built it very well.

"You are being promoted," Sophia told Chuck. "You will be foreman of the day shift. With an increase of salary, of course." She looked up from the lawyer's draft, appearing a bit surprised at discovering those facts, and gave the paper a wave.

He swallowed his surprise. "What about Marty?"

She ignored the interruption. Chuck would begin tomorrow as foreman, reporting to the south kitchen entry where someone would lead him to wherever she happened to be at the time. "One never knows," she said, "nor do I."

"But I mean—"

"Let's be less formal, shall we? I'll simply call you Chuck, not Mister Chuck. And you may call me Mrs. Weatherlee. *Ma'am* sounds like those old Negro mammies on plantations, and I recall we freed the slaves some time ago, did we not?"

He stifled a *Yes ma'am* and stood there.

After a moment she answered the lingering question. She and Marty had disagreed about a partition requiring removal, and he concluded that in good conscience he could not carry out her directive. He was a good worker, she acknowledged, so she had generously offered to continue his salary at the same level. He accepted the decision like a gentleman.

"I won't ask if you're capable because of course you are. You're qualified by virtue of your salary increase."

"So . . . I'm gonna be foreman, is what you're saying?"

A stupid question and she paid it no mind. She reassured him that her Project Manager would continue to coordinate the construction—plumbing, wiring, foundations—and offer help for unfamiliar challenges. Things were becoming complex, so hereafter blueprints would be provided. "Although," she said with exasperation, "I have had my differences with Mr. Overton. He seems to feel that a woman's capacity for architecture ends at the second layer of a chocolate layer cake. And even that is a challenge."

"The only thing is—" Chuck hesitated, then plunged ahead. "I don't know I'd be as good a foreman as Marty, I mean he hired me, he's got a lot more experience—"

"Did you see the sunrise this morning?"

"Sunrise? No."

"You must in the future. It begins the day." She tapped her fingers impatiently. "And so is this agreed?"

Chuck shrugged. "I guess . . ."

"Please don't guess and shrug. A simple yes will do."

"Sure. Yes." He recalled that she didn't like to be told no. "But it's gonna be kinda funny for Marty being under me."

"No one is making that decision for him."

Chuck knew that wasn't entirely true. Marty had doctors' bills for one of his kids and another in some kind of trouble. He was behind on his mortgage. He was no longer shooting the breeze with Chuck, but the other guys said that money was his favorite topic.

"But won't the union have something to say about that? I mean don't they have to . . ." He had spent the last of his words.

"That is the purpose of lawyers." She smiled, took a sip of her tea and handed him the three-page document. "These are the terms and conditions. Please don't mind the legal terminology. Mr. Landreau is quite a nice man personally. He goes to concerts and the theatre. Myself, I can't put up with the theatre. I don't enjoy being entertained by the sufferings of others."

Was she waiting for an answer? The young man stood silent, then the words seeped out. "Well, so, sure. Thanks. I really— Thank you. I really appreciate . . ." And again he stood silent, embarrassed at his gush of feeling.

"Then we have settled our business." She glanced down at her scribbled plans. Chuck, unsure whether the interview was at an end, started to fold the document in his hand, then hesitated. The school librarian had lectured him about turning down page corners in a book. And he ought to read it, which he hadn't, but that might look as if he didn't trust her.

He wasn't stupid. He realized the old lady—she kept appearing older—had used the miter saw to threaten Marty. He was aware that no bundle of hotshot skills would make a good foreman, and he was at least five years away from being the guy he'd want to be supervising himself. He had been on the job for what seemed like about ten minutes, replacing a smart foreman with fifteen years' experience. What he didn't know— He didn't even know how much he didn't know. Dee would tell him how proud she was, and he'd try to hide what would be plastered all over his face: that he was scared shitless.

He felt a tremor in his hands. It was worse than being fired. But he'd said yes. Fear? Pride? The pull of the tide?

"I have a further question." She sipped her tea. The oddity of this tiny woman in a rich dressing gown sipping tea while standing by a bare cutting table gave weight to her words, though her voice was only a bird-like whisper. "Tell me your purpose in life."

Chuck was unprepared for the pop quiz. "Purpose . . . Well, mostly just take care of my wife Dee and Joey. My son Joey. As long as—"

"I'm not asking about your responsibilities or the proper way to hammer a nail. I'm asking the purpose of it all!" The newly-hatched foreman stood befuddled. Sophia softened. "Of course we form bonds that create the illusion that there is some virtuous need behind our waking up each day. And we engender the little dears who spin their own illusions. A delicate pattern like a minuet, and woe to those who fall out of step. As do I, spouting this drivel, I know."

Chuck's jaw tensed. She continued with sudden vigor. "The Church tells us that the whole purpose of man is to glorify God. But have we glorified God or shamed Him miserably? Has He even within memory shown His face? Has He become a recluse like myself?" She brushed an imagined crumb from the cutting table. "Do you know that a recluse is a spider? A poisonous brown thing whose bite produces necrotic lesions, though I produce only more rooms, more troughs and sewers, more horrors. Is it all a wasting disease? A candle devouring itself? Hollowness, echoes, stench?"

Sophia pressed her hands against the table edge, drew an audible breath. Chuck exhaled. She scraped her flat-soled slipper across the stool's shadow and gave a slight laugh. "As a small girl, you know, I would stomp on people's shadows. Trying to hold them in place or perhaps to rip them free from the ankles. And once I saw a terrible monkey, white ruff around its neck, the sneer of an Old Testament prophet, and I— What was I—"

Chuck watched her foot scuffing at the floor as she erased a line on her drawings.

"So perhaps we were created for the divine purpose of building a vast stygian funhouse in praise of God's insanity. Otherwise I see no earthly purpose. Only to build more catacombs, caverns, deep holes in the sky." She sipped her tea, and for a moment she held the cup poised in the air. Chuck expected her to let it fall and shatter, but she set her tea cup primly on the saucer. "Or perhaps to play Chopin. My mother said how well I played Chopin, but when I married I gave it up. I have my Bechstein grand, of course, but I'd rather knit."

Chuck was lost. What fairy tale was it, where they followed a trail of bread crumbs until a bird ate it up?

She looked at him. "I do this to stay alive, they say. But I have no idea why it should be so important that I stay alive. Can you think of a reason?"

"Well, no, yeh, I mean, yes ma'am—"

"Then what is it?"

"Well, we all do. All gotta stay alive. Long as we can."

"You are so young."

She lowered her eyes to the work plans and folded the paper methodically. Chuck wasn't sure that his answer was satisfactory, but he sensed that she'd finished her interrogation. "So, yeh, so— Thank you, ma'am, and for the saw, when you— The miter saw? Marty said go ahead take it. But I never had a chance to say that I— I mean we're using it out there, so I appreciate it."

"That's all," she said abruptly, shooing him. He left, relieved to see daylight ahead. Tomorrow he was foreman. By the time he got back to the worksite his fists were clenched to stop the shaking.

Purpose in life?

I stood frozen in the acrid glare of the question. In fact I slept with that question nightly, an old decayed bride I might hug in the dark but never get intimate with. I would stare across the table, sip my morning coffee, smile, shrug, avoiding its interrogative eyes. I had no answer to live by, only a set of fortune-cookie slogans to set me in motion each day.

Each day for thirty years I awoke in my two-bedroom cottage with one room bare, ate my cornflakes, made my way to the bus stop, rode the two miles to Weatherlee House. I touched the grooves of my name plate to make sure I was still Raymond Smollet, danced my tap-dance, sang my song, went home, sat petting Gertie and sipping Scotch, listening to Beethoven string quartets or the drone of a CD murder mystery. Normally I dozed off before I'd drunk enough to do much damage. But now I would have whole days to fill. With what? Check the weather report every five minutes? Write my one-sentence memoir? Plan my own murders instead of checking them out from the library? Anything but the meat-hook snag of that question mark.

A half hour left till the five o'clock bell. I discerned a faint glow above the cutting table, then the blurred outline of a blazing window, the words forming again: *Wide unclasp the tables of their thoughts.* The window had followed her like a faithful doggie. Sophia's lips moved in a silent mumble as she straightened her papers. She stared at the Tiffany window's imperative.

The splotchy-faced Mr. Oswald picked up the empty tea cup from the cutting table. He handed it to Dr. Quint, who examined it closely, then passed it to Mrs. Padgett, who whimpered at its delicate beauty and returned it to the table. Despite regulations, I did not interfere.

Sophia Weatherlee stood fixated on the window. Suddenly she covered her face, and her throat gave out a burst of strangled squeaks like a tortured rodent.

"Who are all these people?"

She fled with tiny frantic scuffles down an endless passage into the dark. I waved us on, toward the staircase that led to a ceiling.

Ten

The curse of blindness: no way to shut my eyes. I needed a moment to collect myself. I hesitated, grasped the doorframe and picked up a dropped fragment of my spiel.

"The domicile would be classified as Queen Anne Victorian, although clearly it reflects the tastes of its creator. It featured state-of-the-art heating, plumbing, lighting—gaslight and later electric. Plus elevator systems and kitchen conveniences including a sink feature invented and patented by Sophia Weatherlee herself. Eccentric, certainly, but a highly gifted woman."

As I droned on, sight seeped into my sockets. The tea cup sat on its saucer. Sophia Weatherlee remained standing beside the stool, fixed like a fly in amber. She had not fled but my rovers had. Panic: might they scrawl the walls or scar the teakwood paneling? No, I could trust their innate cowardice. And the discontinuity of my delusions held no surprise. My past always had a way of canceling itself.

The old woman gave no hint of seeing me. I tend to fade into the walls. I brushed my lapels to make sure I wasn't stark naked, but I was only a servant trained to invisibility. Her fingers fumbled a small reticule at her waist; their spindly motions held me rigid. For the first time I could see bits of memory stirring, tiny dust devils across a vacant acreage. I saw—

—Her brother Stevie playing with his soldiers. The figures were cast of lead, hand-painted, some in postures of attack, others standing guard as if their mere presence might ward off the savage hordes. Several had missing heads or arms, from the days when Stevie lined them up and threw gravel to slay the Huns or Redcoats or Reds. He was lining them up again, barking merciless orders to the standing and the fallen.

—Her doll house, an opulent three-story gingerbread affair with servant rooms in the garret and furniture that exactly matched the scale of the bride and bridegroom cadged from Auntie Letitia's wedding cake. Nothing existed outside it: no neighbors, no wars, not even farmers to feed the happy couple their daily angel food. Only that sweet fairyland—until the bridegroom began to cough.

—Her Nativity crèche, delicate porcelain from Italy, figures like jade albinos, white with a greenish tinge. The humble stable was edged with gold leaf, and a delicate wrought-iron shaft spiraled up to a silvered reflector for a votive candle: God's little girl could kindle the Star of Bethlehem. An arm from the star held a mobile of tiny circling angels. Below, the Wise Men, two shepherds, animals— sheep, donkey, ox, camel—and the Holy Family with the Christ Child nestled all snug in His wee little bed. Safe, all, from the rage that Herod would wreak the day after *Silent Night, Holy Night* on other infants less tender and mild. She had loved the little figurines until the Christmas when her cousin Suzanne had picked up Baby Jesus and dropped Him. It only chipped the toe, but thereafter she could never pray to a chipped Messiah.

And I knew my odd kinship with this wealthy derelict female. We had each constructed our hollow echo chambers, shelters against a world of brutal playgrounds, of rampant cousins, dying parents, tubercular bridegrooms, wilted babies with tiny fat men's bellies. We built our shelters against whispered secrets, shame in the dark, spiders under the toilet seat, and built them well, mine within hers like the Jack-in-the-box with a tiny Jack popping out the head of the greater Jack. Like her I could smother my soul the way we put down an old wheezing dog.

Purpose in life? How foreign that sounded. Of course I had pondered what to do with my years and even how to end them, but a purpose? That was like having some exotic pet that had to be kept in a climate-controlled terrarium and fed rare bugs, and even then the creature might just lie there cold, torpid, reptilian. My various cats from time to time had the right idea: *take what's offered, don't go shopping, embrace detachment.* Very wise, those cats. Of course they'd always been neutered.

My veiled squint noted what she saw but not what she felt. Though perhaps I couldn't feel it because there was nothing to feel—no pulse, no blood, only an arid prairie thirsting for rain. Sophia stared into the void that clamped us together. But her Star of Bethlehem summoned no Wise Men, no donkeys, not even Herod's butchers—only a stubby blind tour guide on the brink of retirement.

"Who?" she called in a whisper.

If I opened my lips it would come in a flood. *My name is Raymond Smollet, I work as tour guide for Weatherlee Ghost House wherein I conduct five tours a day, and I had a man once who said his wife died at Mount Rushmore but that's all he said, and a woman asked where the horses drank and I said outside but I didn't really know—*

"Who?" more insistent.

I held my silence dangling by its fingertips. She gaped, pleading, into the pit she had dug in the daylight. A black fist held us. I was a ghost haunting a ghost.

"William?" Her voice was pale yellow.

I kept silent. A thousand times I'd regretted my choice of words but never keeping silent. No, well, maybe the last time with Lynnie when I grasped she was asking *Yes?* Or the boy I loved briefly who recounted his dreams in aching detail but who never invited me in. Or Mother dying. I should have had words but they failed.

Panic welled up. She would see me. I turned to flee and slammed into the doorframe. Behind me a whisper: "William?" Dignity shredded, I fled from the asphalt with playground laughter burning my ears, cheeks wet with shame. Mother would check the rip in the "nice-looking slacks" she insisted I wear to school and shake her head sadly. Then I remembered, no, I'm sixty-five and Mother's dead and I'm twenty-nine minutes short of retirement. Soon I'll come home to Gertie and my rooms and begin the long slow descent.

Meantime I needed to corral my throng. I'd be responsible for damages. I groped for a support and hobbled off-balance into the tangled morass. Limping like the demoted foreman, I might pass for another casualty of war. Gertie might take pity, meowing her love, the crafty little bitch, haggling for a tin of tuna and a scratch on that sweet spot right above her tail.

I found them again in the Conservatory milling aimlessly. Their brief spurt of rebellion had dribbled away, and their instinct directed them back to the same location, perhaps to be watered like geraniums, begonias or bromeliads. As I straggled in they turned to me with bovine eyes.

"We must ask that nothing be touched," I said with fretful authority. "As mentioned, these are not the original furnishings, but nevertheless they are valuable antiques and therefore . . ." I faltered, lost in my own sour mouth.

None were listening. They had congregated along the windows looking out on the veranda. The black man methodically ran his fingers through his hair. It was shiny with pomade, harking back to the days when movie Negroes sang mellow ballads to the scrubbed and polished lovers in a night club where no one ever paid the tab. He pressed his oily fingers onto the window glass leaving perfect prints. Nothing malicious: just artistic inspiration.

The ex-foreman Marty sat hunched on the top step eating his lunch, focused on the old Japanese gardener in the distance eternally trimming a rose hedge. He tossed a half-eaten sandwich back into his lunch pail and poured another cupful from his thermos. Chuck appeared around the corner to his left. Marty gave no sign of seeing him. Chuck approached.

"Mind if I sit down?"

Marty made a vague gesture. Chuck sat on a lower step six feet away. He opened his lunch pail, poured coffee from his thermos, began to munch his sandwich, following the gardener's work. "He works pretty hard for an old guy." His voice was bright but strained.

"That's his job," Marty said, peering up at the clouds. Chuck concentrated on his sandwich. Peanut butter and tomato. A long minute, then Marty relented and broke the silence. "Lose your ticket?"

"What?"

"You act like you won the Lottery but lost your ticket."

Chuck was silent. He wasn't sure what was meant. He never played the Lottery, didn't believe in it. There was something sleazy about winning something you hadn't earned. When he told Dee about the promotion she was so happy she was hopping up and down like a little kid, but then he told her how he felt about it. She couldn't understand. With all the jobs she'd had, the boss was stupid, the employees despised him, and you never got what you deserved. But Chuck had skills, so he deserved it. No, he said, he'd just been handed it on a platter and guys could get hurt if he made a mistake. But she kept saying, "You can do it, honey," and he knew he had to.

He had a hard time sleeping. Dreams dragged on for hours, then he'd wake and it was only midnight. He'd be writing down figures, calculating board feet for the hardwoods, and the teacher would loom over his shoulder and mark it wrong. He'd be building a bird house in shop class, planing the base, checking with the try-square, hitting knots, planing, planing till all the wood was gone.

In the first weeks Marty had helped him a lot. The older man was sure as hell resentful at having been kicked in the balls, but he made the best of it. Now, the silence between the two had the smell of dead meat. Chuck had to make the first move.

"Marty, I really— I just really appreciate the work you've been doing, helping me out. I mean I know I—"

"Well I try to make the foreman happy. You know me." He emptied his cup with a swig, poured another.

Chuck let it settle, made another try. "So I was gonna say, Dee wanted me to ask if you'd like to come over for dinner sometime." The instant he said it he heard how stupid it sounded.

"No, but tell her thanks."

Chuck heard himself nattering on, warding off the silence. "She's doing pretty good now. Glad to quit her job although Joey's a real handful. Toddling around like he's training for the Olympics. He figured out that the toilet paper unrolls, so he unrolled the whole roll all over the place." He laughed. "No, Marty, but I just wanted you to know—"

"No sweat. I still got a paycheck. Not as big as yours, but I got it."

"—just that I appreciate your feedback, you know, I—"

"Feedback?" Marty's voice was low and flat, disconnected from feeling. "I told you if you did what you're talking about doing, the damn ceiling is gonna fall in and the rooms on top of it. I don't know if that qualifies as feedback."

Three weeks after Chuck's promotion, Mrs. Weatherlee had brought up the question of the wall. "Where in your forthcoming schedule do you see the removal of the structure we have discussed?" They hadn't discussed it but she spoke as if she could swear in a court of law. It was a weight-bearing wall, she understood, but Mr. Overton had assured her that it could be done with the proper cantilever to support the structure, and Mr. Overton could advise on it, though she foresaw that she could not put her full trust in Mr. Overton since Mr. Overton did not put his full trust in her. "Trust exists only in a climate of mutual respect," she said, "so you must use your own judgment."

Overton was no help. He smiled his doggy smile as he rambled on about brace walls, flush beams, tension from the outward force of the rafters, but did his best to avoid giving advice for which he might be held accountable. Chuck knew they would need a temporary stud wall and angled supports to shore up the structure while installing the I-beam header. It would need a new foundation for the beam's support posts. Overton would supervise that, but Chuck was left with everything up to the final removal of the ratchet straps. Overton finished with a lecture on dropped headers, then said, "But use your own judgment. And consider the torque."

Consider the torque. Chuck was ass-deep in the swamp of his own ignorance. Dreams, more dreams: calculating the lumber for a room already built, maneuvering a backhoe around a sinkhole, counting nails spilled from a bucket nail by nail, waking up forgetting the count of the nails. He should talk to Uncle Frank. "Any time you need me," his uncle had said. But Chuck hadn't said a word about his promotion. He couldn't face the shame of confessing it.

Uncle Frank had been like a second father to him. Chuck's dad was focused on work, work, work and barely spoke to his sons, but Frank had no kids, so Chuck was his kid. Once when he was four his uncle took him to where he was working on a house. Only a single stud wall was up. That's not a house, he thought, it's just a bunch of boards. The next time they went, the walls were up, the men were installing the drywall, and the little boy could see a house taking shape. "That's what a carpenter does," Uncle Frank said, "he builds things." Next time some old biddy asked Chuck what he was going to be, he said, "A carpenter." He never stopped saying that.

As soon as he was big enough to hammer a nail and bash his thumb doing it, his uncle taught him. At school they'd say to draw a flower and his mom would tape it up on the fridge for a week, but Frank never gave the boy a job just to make him feel good. It was always work that had to be done. When he was seven or eight he was on the worksite a few hours about every week. Which led to apprenticing on weekends and summer—not actually apprenticing, he was too young for that, but by the time he was out of high school he had journeyman skills. It took some hassle but they shortened his formal apprenticeship.

His mother hated the whole idea. Brother Stan, six years older, was a whiz kid in school. Chuck idolized him even though Mom held him up as an example. "He's going to work with his head, not his hands," she'd say, as if that was so much better. Stan went to college, joined the Army, got his commission. He could have gone into supply and logistics, intelligence, engineering, anything that meant sitting at a desk instead of leading out grunts to be blown apart. Three days after deployment, during Chuck's senior year, he was killed. Friendly fire. Mom never mentioned Stan again.

When Chuck was canned from the first big job, he yelled at the foreman, "If you'd wanted a third-rate shit-ass carpenter you should of hired one!" It got back to Uncle Frank, who chewed him out, really ripped him. "You're gonna get a reputation," he warned. "Give people lip and you'll be blackballed from here to Denver. Don't ever *ever* let me hear you use that kind of language to a foreman." And then he said, "Come here, dummy." He gave him a big hug. "That's for being a first-rate carpenter who don't take no shit from assholes." That made it all worth it.

Now he was ashamed to face Uncle Frank, pretending to be a foreman.

"C'mon, Marty, do I have a choice?" Chuck's anger flared. "How many jobs are out there? Do I see you jumping at some other great job?"

"I'm telling you that is a weight-bearing wall and you don't just do it out of a Boy Scout manual—"

"Overton's signed off on it, he says that if—"

"Overton couldn't build a doghouse. He knows maybe how to play with Tinkertoys. She picked him up at some yard sale. Look, I told you once I'll—"

"You told me more than once—"

"Then I'll tell you again. You don't know what you're doing and you're gonna get somebody hurt. Maybe you do it, give yourself a big pat on the back, then a month from now some guys are standing under there and it all comes down."

"Or else we do the job and it's fine and we all get our paychecks."

"The only carpenter that could do that job is Jesus Christ."

He had heard that joke from Marty before and he was in no mood for humor. Talking to him was a bad idea to start with. Chuck pictured his dad complaining about a nicey-nice foreman on his bridge crew: the men wouldn't respect him. They were used to being bossed around and finding ways to slack off or swipe materials or pad their hours. Now here was this over-the-hill loser chugging his coffee-and-bourbon right under the foreman's nose—Chuck could smell it—and spitting jokes in his face. He was the foreman and had no obligation to be this man's friend. He wanted to finish lunch and get back to work, but peanut butter didn't chew fast. He watched the old gardener clipping the hedge.

"How'd you get this job?" Marty asked quietly.

"You hired me." Chuck took an apple from his lunchbox, bit into it. Granny Smith. His favorite.

"How come?"

"Cause you needed a good carpenter." He felt Marty's eyes on him. Okay, give him his due. "And my cousin's a friend of your sister-in-law and she said you needed a good carpenter." Did that satisfy him? "Okay, I mean, right, that's the way you get jobs. Somebody knows somebody and it gives 'em an edge. Nothing weird about that."

Marty frowned at him, began to chomp a raw carrot noisily. "My take on you," chomping, "is," picking a chunk from his teeth, "you're the nicest, most honest, lovable kinda guy in the world. That's my take on you." He slammed his lunchbox shut and flipped the clasps.

"You don't make that sound too good."

"Don't I?"

Neither wanted to prolong the pain, but their antlers were locked in a brotherhood of impotence. They staggered back and forth, struggling to unhook.

"Well hey . . ." Chuck ventured, though whatever he said, Marty would slam it back the way his brother slammed the ping-pong ball. "So any idea how long it's gonna last?"

"Last? What?"

"Job?"

Marty's lips twisted into something like a grin. "What, you get married, put a kid in the oven, buy a big TV, and now you start thinking if you're gonna have a job?" Chuck was aware he was being mocked, way out of bounds, but Marty couldn't help it. He glanced out at Mr. Kurosawa in his dog-ear cap clipping the hedges. The gardener looked friendly but he never spoke. Sometimes he'd raise his shears and go clip-clip as a way of saying hello. Chuck wondered if Mr. Kurosawa dreamed of roses. That would be a better dream. Work on the wall was scheduled to start next week.

Marty drained his cup, poured another. He would have liked to scrape the Ratowitz kid raw with his words, but there was no point insulting numbskulls. His words were retreads and would gain no traction. "Well, it's gonna be a while. Who knows? Maybe it won't stop. Do they stop building shopping malls?" He sipped slowly. As long as the foreman was sitting there on his ass he'd take advantage of it. "Hey, did she give you the what's-your-purpose-in-life ramble? She came at me with that, I told her, *Well, Miss Weatherlee, I'm saving my wages to buy a new one. New purpose in life. What I'm driving now, all the valves are shot. Blue smoke coming out its ass.*" He gave a dry laugh. "No, I didn't say that. I wanted to." From indoors came a muffled cry. "She does that," he said.

"Okay, Marty, she's nuts, we know that, okay, but maybe you don't need this job so bad so you can afford to—"

Asshole! Marty wanted to scream it out, but he held his anger tight, just above a whisper. "No, right, I don't need it. I got a mortgage, two kids, one's living in the basement, one's in rehab, and a wife who's so pissed she won't even look at me—"

"That's not my fault—"

"No. No, that's right. That's absolutely true. That is not your fault." Between them the silence spawned the first shimmers of a quake. "So you go home to your little cutie. What's her name?" he asked. "Dee-Dee?"

A mumble. "Dee."

"High school sweethearts?"

"So what?"

"So what? That means you think you know everything about her and you don't know nothing. That's what that means."

The words cut deep—a sliver dug out with a needle. Chuck was poised to grab Marty's thermos, give it a sniff and fire the man on the spot—no excuses, no mercy—but he was frozen. If he raised his voice he knew it would crack. The quiver in his spine was rage, panic, both. Marty pretended not to see it.

How could he be stung by words so far off the mark? He was closer than ever to Dee, and she was more passionate. On their anniversary she got her mom to take Joey for the night. She made lamb shanks for dinner and they spent the evening together. They hadn't realized how much they needed that, how much they loved just looking in each other's eyes.

Or maybe she sensed his neediness, some smell about him whenever his mind played over the phrase *Consider the torque.* He was coming home tensed up, either complaining about the job or just sitting silent at the table. Still, she'd laugh when he described the old lady talking about her pet cat who died forty years ago, then asking if he accepted Darwin. Mentioning books he'd never heard of—he was no reader—or long-dead politicians. Dressing the way they did in the old days, out of another world. He did an imitation of the way she'd squint and flatten her lips. It made him look like a frog. Dee laughed. He loved to make her laugh.

But questions marked her face. At the table she would stare into space and then flash him a smile when she felt him watching. She would stand at the sink and continue wiping the Formica counter with the sponge until Joey toddled up and tugged on her pant leg. Joey would be throwing a fit and she'd grab his arms to hold him still, but as if she were holding herself with tight fists.

His refuge was the child. Dee loved seeing him hold Joey and make funny faces or pretend to give the child orders like one of his men. "Hey Joey, that door's hanging crooked. Reset the hinge, would ya?" Sometimes he'd echo back the sounds the toddler made, mimicking his burbles and wawas and snorts, and Joey loved hearing his daddy speak his language. Sometimes—

Chuck rose to his feet. "Marty, damn it, I'm trying to— What's your point? What are we talking about?"

"You tell me. I was just sitting here."

"You resent the fact that I'm foreman, right?"

"Oh, you noticed that?" Marty took a sip from his cup, saw Chuck staring at it. Ceremoniously he dipped his forefinger, sniffed it, pretended to suck it dry, then gave Chuck a clown's wide smile. Chuck turned away. Marty's face darkened. "You telling me there's nobody on this job knows it better than you? She took one look at you, tell me that, she took one look at you, she thought, *This guy's incredible, I can feel it, all that energy, the way he sucks a marble!* Tell me that."

Chuck sat again, screwed the lid onto his thermos, twisted it sharply to numb down the rage. Marty drained his cup, shook the last drops onto the steps. "You know why I hired you? Not because you knew somebody's cousin. That's about the dirtiest thing anybody ever said to me. No, I checked up. I know why you lost your last job. Cause you wouldn't follow half-assed orders. You wouldn't use low-grade lumber. You wouldn't build a piece of shit, so you got fired. That's why I hired you, little boy."

"My uncle taught me." No reason to say that, but Uncle Frank was seeing him with that funny walleyed glare from steely blue-gray eyes, and he had to say it.

"Here's what's gonna happen." Now Marty's voice was on a tight leash, low and flat. "You're gonna put that in and maybe it's gonna be just dandy and it'll last till the Day of Judgment. But Overton don't know shit about it and you don't know shit about it and two shits don't make a devil's food cake." Chuck might have laughed at the joke if it wasn't being smeared on him.

Marty's voice flattened. "And eventually, if you don't have a qualified structural engineer on it, you got a fifty-fifty chance that section's gonna collapse, all right? I was not willing in good conscience to put my men at risk. Hey, that's your decision, but if somebody's hurt on that job you're gonna live with that the rest of your fucking life."

Schoolyard fight, fourth grade. Artie pounded him but Chuck kept coming back for more, his face battered and wet. Now he bit down hard. He held his voice in the same flat tone as Marty's, as if they were brothers. "I'm aware of the risks, Marty, but somebody's going to do this job, and as long as I'm on the scene I'm gonna try to the best of my ability—"

"You sound like the President."

"Right, whatever! Fuck it! Okay!" Chuck rose. "You coming in on Monday? You gonna show up and work?" Stupid thing to say but he had to say something.

"When I show up I work. I show up if I got a job. Do I got a job?"

"Of course you got a job." Why say that? He should fire the man.

"Well if there's a house here I'll be working on Monday. Otherwise, no sweat."

The stags' antlers were locked, but they took a pause in their mindless stagger to disengage. Chuck's mouth was dry. Marty grinned. "Hey, what kind of name is Ratowitz? Puerto Rican?"

Chuck turned to go, then stopped. Mr. Kurosawa stood twenty feet away, gazing in their direction. The old man was wearing a blue baseball cap, not the regular dog-ears. "Oh, hi. How's it going?" The gardener gave no sign of hearing, then he smiled, made a couple of playful clips in the air with his clippers and continued down the path. Chuck looked back toward Marty, but Marty was gone.

He would never take out the wall if he thought it couldn't be done, he told himself. He'd quit before he'd do that. He wasn't that kind of guy. He wouldn't any more put his workmen in danger than he'd let Joey fall. He was certain it wouldn't collapse.

Twelve

It collapsed.

The renovation had gone according to plan, and they proceeded on schedule without complications. To avoid hassles, Chuck put Marty on the north wing crew and hired extra help. Three weeks after they finished the structural work, as the teakwood paneling was being installed, it went. The ceiling came down and three rooms above it.

Two men were pulled out of the rubble. One, a Filipino, was dead, and another had a broken spine. Several others escaped with scratches, one with a smashed finger: Reggie, who announced with a trembling grin, "That whole room shook like a sonofabitch."

It happened on the night shift. Chuck got a call at home, went out, was gone the whole night, though there was nothing much to do: the site would be roped off for investigation. He went home for coffee, came back and stood around. Same the next day.

He could feel nothing. He knew it was going to happen. When you heard the ominous chord in the horror movie you were sure the fiend was lurking behind the door the girl was ready to open. The front-row kids were screaming, "Don't open the door!" but all you could do was watch it. He ought to feel guilt, shame, or at least the fear of losing his job, but he was numb.

And he knew what Dee would say before she said it. *It's not your fault, you did your best, you did what you were told to do.* But she didn't say it, not at first. She just held him, let him bleed, and he was grateful for that. A few days later he woke up with the acid thought that he was more shaken by his bad judgment than with guys getting hurt and killed. Chuck felt sorry for Chuck.

Inspectors and lawyers scurried like roaches over the site, and he answered the same questions a dozen times. Every day he considered telling his men that he was in over his head, that he hadn't asked for the job, that he'd try to learn from his nightmares. Of course he couldn't do that. His crew started work on a wing far distant from the collapse. He dodged Marty's stare.

Two weeks, then Mrs. Weatherlee summoned him. She informed him that he bore no liability. That the weight of the beams had exerted an outward torsion on the supports. That Mr. Overton had been replaced. That the victims' families were fully compensated. "Which is to say that the matter is closed. You have my full confidence. Tomorrow we can resume the work." She spoke with flat, barely parted lips. "That will be all."

Chuck sat on the veranda and watched Mr. Kurosawa pruning.

"Are we having fun yet?" I joked. A cheery snort from the Iowa dad, a whimper from his daughter. "In the thirty-eight-year span of the project only six workmen were killed. A remarkable safety record." I don't know why I said that. Just to hear my own voice, perhaps. It might have been true.

Often in the past my mind wandered and I forgot where I was in my spiel, but now it seemed as if the house itself were forgetting and I was the bit of trivia that it forgot. Scrawled patterns of sunlight along the walls thickened the darkness, and my voice echoed in some deep ventricle of a necrotic heart. I made out the scrofulous Mr. Oswald, his dead eyes and spurts of whisker, tapping his forehead against a door jamb. About him lurked my clutch of disciples waiting to be led to glory. Ah, that was my job, I reminded myself. Or so I pretended.

The tour was now a chronicle spun by the resident ghosts. They appeared as their story required, and the rooms, the verandas, the gardens sprang up around them. Of course they were all in my skull— their histories, their yearbooks, their innermost thoughts—and I marveled at the drabness of my fantasies. No staggering zombies, no gaping wounds: only grit from the daily grind. An old movie I'd seen before my sight was erased—*When Worlds Collide*—had always haunted me. Now I perceived that when worlds collide they could simply intersect, each in the other's slipstream, smooth as silk.

We stood inspecting a kitchen, spacious and well designed. It was yellow, as before, but a freshly-mortgaged yellow, not a landlord yellow. I recognized the table, the tan Ratowitz table, with an open account ledger and a wad of receipts beside it. My tourists pressed into the doorway blocking my view, but I saw directly through them.

Dee came into the kitchen, sat at the table, began to sort the receipts. It had taken her forever to put Joey down for the night, and his crankiness had seeped into her. She glanced at a receipt. Young as she was, she needed reading glasses, but she would hold off as long as she could. From the living room came a muffled burst of laughter. Chuck was watching some stupid sit-com.

"What are you watching, hon?" No reply. She raised her voice. "What are you watching?" Then she clamped her fist to her mouth. She might wake Joey.

"Just stuff."

Dee continued sorting the stack, trying to breathe away her irritation. Not with Joey: with Chuck. Joey had wanted Daddy to tell him a story but Daddy was watching TV—not even watching it, just pointing his face in that direction. "I'm out of stories," Chuck said to her. "What do I do, read him *The Three Bears* or tell him how I killed a guy?" She understood, but understanding didn't make it any better.

When Dee wasn't older than nine or ten, her mom had said in a rasping voice deep from the gut, "You're incapable of love. Incapable!" Maybe that was true. Maybe she was. No, Dee told herself, love wasn't just a gooey grunting thing. It had days when it had to be faked. It filled a night with passion, and then next morning you woke up dead tired with the kid yowling that he'd pooped in bed. Love was holding on. You just held on, slogging through the slush till the good weather came and the blossoms burst out. And they did. They always did.

It had been two hellish months. They were sure that he'd be fired or worse. Then the old lady told him it had all been settled out of court and Chuck was not to blame. The families of the victims—one dead, one paralyzed, one minus a finger—got more money than Dee would ever see in her life. And the work went on. Chuck would wake up shell-shocked, eat breakfast and leave without a word. He was on the job longer in the day, and when he was home the job was heavy on him. She would make a nice meal, he'd eat it, barely tasting it. Sometimes he pulled back from her touch. What else could she do but touch?

Several times she had tried to talk about what happened. "Hon, it wasn't your fault. Those men, sure, they were hurt, I'd be sorry too, but they didn't have to be under there. The guys on the crew said they were slacking off, and she took care of those families pretty good, they'll never have to worry. Hon—"

"Shut up!" First time he'd ever raised his voice to her. "Just shut up!" She went ahead, made breakfast and Chuck ate it. As long as people ate breakfast they'd survive. When he came home that night he apologized in a dead flat voice. She put her hand on the back of his neck and he let her do it. Then Joey came toddling in and Chuck picked him up and hugged him.

So now it was better, sort of. Chuck still had a job, and Joey needed a dad who didn't just sit around and brood. But something was changed in his face. He would put on a big smile for Joey, then his eyes would glaze and the glee would wither away. *All things pass*, her mother had quoted from the Bible. Sure they do, Dee thought, but like elephants in the circus parade they leave stuff.

Another burst of TV guffaw. She pushed back her chair, rose and went to the doorway. "What's on?"

"This comedian, what's his name?" He was gazing past the screen.

Dee took a step into the room, her hand on the door jamb as if securing a line of retreat. "I think I'm getting the hang of double entry," she said brightly.

"That's good," he said.

She had taken a bookkeeping course at the junior college thinking it might help her keep track of their finances. Two days after she'd finished the course she noticed a card on the market bulletin board: *Bookkeeper wanted part-time. Work at home.* Something to do to use what was left of her brain.

Steiber's Used Cars was a flimsy enterprise in the butt end of Santa Cruz, a quarter-acre lot with as many junkers as could be crammed under three droopy lines of red and yellow pennants. Each car had a phrase soaped on the windshield: *One owner only. Priced to sell. Really clean. Look ma, new tires.* Rollie Steiber was a round jolly little man whose broad desperate smile marked him as about two weeks away from suicide. She told Chuck that the poor guy might do better running a lemonade stand. But she took the job. His books were in pretty much the same sad state as his cars, but she could come in once a week, collect stuff and do the work at home when Joey took his nap. She was pleased to have the spare change, and her weekly trips gave her some nutty-boss stories to share when Chuck recounted the old lady's maunderings.

"Hon, I know you're not too happy about me working," she said, standing in the doorway, "but it's not like the waitress crap. The less he sells the less work I have to do, so it's the same wages, and meantime I can actually learn to do what I'm doing."

"Wish I could say the same."

Again she was stumbling into the minefield. By now she knew better than to offer sympathy. "Well, I know we don't really need the money but it's good experience—"

"Good experience for what?"

They were heading toward a fight, but that was better than watching him sit there like a stump. "Good experience in case anything happened, in case you had an accident, say, or—"

"No problem. We don't have accidents. I'm the foreman."

The dog shit was everywhere, no place to step. "Well, it gives me something to do. I'm here all day cooped up with Joey and—"

"Okay, okay, okay!" He turned to face her. "I'm sorry you're living this lousy fucking life! I'm doing my best!" He slammed his fist on the padded arm of the chair then buried his face in his hands. Like a soap opera. Silly almost.

Dee stood frozen. She wanted to rush to him, sob with him, but if she touched him he might explode. What to do when your mate's pain overflows like a backed-up toilet? When he can't stand to be loved? Do you turn back to the tangle of Rollie Steiber's accounts? Do you pound his shoulders? Do you stand frozen, waiting for an earthquake to shake him loose?

Very slowly she approached him. Her hand found that place on the back of his head. Her touch was right. She heard a breath that sucked all the air from the room, then the letting go. She loved this man and he knew it. He brought his face around. His soul was open to her. Slowly she nodded, and he nodded with her.

The little boy cried out, awakened by the shouting. Dee turned away and went to tend him. Chuck leaned back in the chair and breathed, and breathed again.

My tourists—*We few, we happy few, we band of brothers*—stood in silence. They were watching the comedian on the TV. The goofy boyfriend had dropped his girlfriend's birthday cake and the dachshund was slurping it up. The guy gave the girl a sad-doggy look and she twisted her mouth in grim irony. The laugh track howled. The screen drew all eyes except mine.

Dee returned. Chuck met her. They went into the bedroom. They stretched naked across my dead retinas. They made love, oblivious to the muffled whoopee from the living room. I saw them as one glad flesh and I stifled a cry of pain too deep to feel.

Sitcom, soap opera, miniseries? I was tuned to some lost channel inside me. Who were these people, that I should be concerned? Were there not countless others who had worked in this rambling catacomb, doing their jobs, going home, raising their families, dying without all the fuss? Would I not be better entertained by a dachshund slurping the frosting? In the distance the TV belched its belch, chortled its chortle, but I heard the lovers' murmurings in the twilit space after love. A moan, a giggle, a touch.

"How you doing, babe?" I heard her say.

"I'm good. I'm pretty good. Right now I'm pretty good."

"We're okay. Aren't we?"

"I think we are."

The words meandered, but they were walking the path together. *We're here. We know the pain. We're in love.* Their tenderness was terrifying. I could hardly bear it.

"I touched her!" the floppy hat lady crowed. I wheeled to confront my rabble. Touched who? Dee wasn't there, she was naked in bed. She was still making love.

I had to assert authority. They were observers, not participants. No interference with history. History was trademarked, glassed over, climate-controlled, untouched by human hands. Big bucks were tied up in history. If you broke it you bought it. I don't know what I said or if I even said it, but they must have heard every word of my strangled rage.

"Sorry. Okay."

"No problem."

"Verzeihen—"

"You the boss."

I was relieved. At least they pretended I was still in charge. I reached out and recognized a panel where the plaster had crumbled away. We were in the long hallway of the east wing, and the yellow kitchen's visions were the fallout of low blood sugar—I'd had only a salad for lunch. The tour would get back on course.

"Okay, straight on down this way, stairs on your right." The group stirred. "Next stop," I paused, then in a sepulchral voice, "the Seance Room." My Bela Lugosi tone often got a laugh. This time, no.

Thirteen

It wasn't the Seance Room. There were times when the architecture hiccuped and we all lurched forth in a peristaltic spasm. Now the chambers had shuffled themselves, and we stood in a room unfamiliar to my groping. A dining room, but not the official Dining Room. Two female figures were seated at either end of a walnut table, miles apart. They sat sculpted in a half-light from a crystal chandelier above the table. They appeared to be engaged in the ghostly task of finishing dessert.

Sophia took a tiny forkful of blueberry cheesecake and held it poised to her lips. "Tell me, Izzy," she said, smiling at the young woman. "Too sweet, wouldn't you say? Be honest."

Isabella took a forkful. "Tastes fine to me. Very good."

"By normal standards obviously. But that is the curse of wealth. It must not simply be *fine*, it must be exquisite beyond imagination, a cheesecake epiphany. We're fulfilled by that expensively pungent smell of moral rot." Her niece frowned. "I'm joking, as always."

"I would hardly call it a curse. It's very good cheesecake."

"Nor I. There are so many other curses to choose from. They dwarf the cheesecake in their atrocity. Very tasty atrocity, I grant you."

Isabella shook her head. "You're way beyond me, Auntie."

"By many decades. But you'll catch up." She took another forkful. "I must apologize to the pastry. It wants to be conceived of as fine. As do we all." They nibbled in silence, Sophia taking tiny fretful forkfuls. "Coffee or tea?"

"Tea, please."

Sophia raised a finger. Out of the shade a maid appeared. "Grace, is it?" Sophia asked.

"Yes ma'am." The girl stood with lowered focus.

"Chamomile for my niece, and for myself . . . well, surprise me."

"Yes ma'am." She started to go.

"And Grace—" The maid stopped. "How is your mother? You told me she was ill when I last inquired. I hope she's better."

"She's much better, thank you, ma'am."

"I'm glad to hear it. That's all." She gestured and the maid departed. "She's new but she seems to be working out. You notice she keeps her eyes averted even when speaking directly. That's vital in a servant. She has the instinct. And I feel sorry for her. She grew up with her mother. No father. That's common among those people, I believe, and of course it's not her fault so I need to be open-minded. But that's another curse of wealth: we must have servants."

"You're digging up lots of curses today, Auntie."

"Not to mention the obscene curse of my self-pity. Though for that I may be forgiven, since I plainly acknowledge it. Does that make me a Papist, do you suppose?" Sophia forced a smile that started to warp, then fixed her attention on the dessert. A long silence ensued. Grace brought the tea and slipped away. The old woman regarded her niece. "But in fact my intent is to charm you with my bubbling good humor, addict you to cheesecake, make this delicate abode so irresistible— But I never manage, do I? You're still intending to leave."

"When I can. When it's not disruptive."

"Disruptive?" The old woman laughed. "I sit here daily longing for disruption. Panting for it. But not at the cost of your deserting me."

"I'm not—"

"Well of course you are. You'd be a fool not to." She placed her dessert fork on the saucer with military abruptness and shoved the saucer away. "My servants, my foreman, my tradesmen, whomever I can bully, they disgust me— Not you, you're too independent, you just giggle at my absurdity, but the others— I want them to flail back at my prodding, my jabberwocky questions, my genteel brutality. I would like for once in my life to confront someone who would spit back something more than *Yes ma'am* in my face. I live for that moment!" She closed her lids tightly, as if crushing what she might see, then opened them with a wistful smile. "And then of course I would fire them."

The niece sipped her tea. "You remembered chamomile. Thank you." Sophia raised her cup as if in a toast. They sat in silence.

"Well of course I accepted that at some point you would wish to move on. You've seen me as I see myself." Sophia glanced into her tea cup. "The dialogue writes itself on the walls. They always told us to sound out the words we didn't know. *I need to leave you, Auntie*—that reads very clearly."

"Auntie—"

"But I wish you wouldn't call me Auntie. That's an old rag doll with a china face and the seams popping out."

"Aunt Sophia then." Izzy chose her words carefully. "You know how beholden I was for your help in escaping New Haven and my close brush with marriage, that poor sweet man. You gave me an anchor here and I'm very grateful. But I have spoken many times of my desire to find my own path, find friends and a purpose and perhaps a husband—"

"Perish them all!"

She was used to her aunt's expostulations, like the mud pits she'd seen at Yellowstone, the burblings of gas from the depths, and she loved the old woman, she told herself, to the extent that she could love a creature whose pain spat out like hot grease.

"I'm jesting, of course."

"Of course."

It was not Sophia's generosity that held and repelled her, but the hunger within it. The gifts—of clothing, of a purebred mare, of more pocket money than she had pockets to hold—were claws that dug deep. Once she had remarked how beautiful the garden daisies were, and within a week the paper-hangers had plastered her room with daisies. Now she woke each day to swarms, battalions, legions of daisies.

"I had an idea."

"Oh dear."

"I know," Sophia smiled, "I do that. But quite seriously. We have a ballroom. I spent a fortune solely on the wood paneling of the entrance, and those seascapes, that artist—"

"Winslow Homer."

"Homer. Why I ever plunked down good money for those paintings when we could ride out any day and enjoy the ocean itself for free and hear the gulls— What was I saying?"

"Ballroom." Isabella saw the trap preparing.

"Ballroom. I have a ballroom. Why are there no people dancing? We should have a ball in our ballroom. A huge ball. That's what people do, people who have ballrooms. Wouldn't that be fun for you? Where are my notes?" Her hand scraped the table surface as if ordering her notepad to appear. "I've worked it out. I'm acquainted with several trustees of the San Francisco Symphony. We can bring them in. Surely they know waltzes and polkas and such. You would be honorary chairwoman. We can draft letters to the cultural enterprises and charities we support, requesting they invite their major donors. And we'll require them each to send a handsome young man." She offered her niece a jaunty smile.

"I can do my own prospecting, Auntie."

"*Auntie, Auntie, Auntie!* Well then let me be blunt. Your *Auntie* is alone. Even with her carpenters and servants and ghosts, she is alone. William lies in an elegant coffin on a New Haven hillside and never writes. If I went to visit he'd have nothing to say. He'd ignore me completely." Half-laugh, half-sob. "And Sara Lynn . . ."

"Well of course I'd be happy to help in any way I can." Isabella heard herself say it, cursing her entrapment but certain that the ball would never happen. Guests, if they reached the front entry, would be greeted as invading Huns.

"Our dilemma, Izzy— More tea? No? The dilemma of wealth: everyone despises it yet desires it. Except perhaps people just too stupid to live." She glanced at the dregs of her tea. "This looks like urine. I never look at my urine."

The niece was accustomed to such footnotes. Her aunt took a sharp gasp to speak, instead fingered up the last of the cheesecake. She shook her head, denying exodus to words that had no passport.

"And so?" her niece asked with frank impatience.

"And so they see me as a freak." Sophia's voice rose. "I feel like a window display, some old bent artifact to be joked about!"

Izzy heard the cramp in her aunt's blurt of metaphor. "You should be a poet."

"To spread my gloom? Yes, I should publish widely."

The young woman felt a rush of nausea, an urge to expel her aunt's ooze of words.

"I kill people, you know." Sophia stared at the crumbs of her cheesecake. "They die, that is to say, within my sphere of influence. Not my intention, of course." She waved her hand dismissing the notion, but it hovered in her eyes.

It was the first time Isabella had heard her aunt allude to the accident. She had listened to the old woman pacing the tunnels at night. Three servants had been fired for no discernible reason. Once she had heard a cry and a pounding of fists. Yet two weeks afterward, Auntie had summoned her to a bright morning walk amid the floral tumult of the gardens. No gloom until now.

"But no matter." Sophia broke the silence. "What is it Shakespeare says? *The evil that men do lives after, the good is oft interred with their bones.* Very wise, that Shakespeare fellow. Do you suppose they'll find some little crumbs of good to inter with my bones?"

"Aunt Sophia," Isabella began, "this was a lovely dinner as always, and I know you're unhappy that I'm intending to leave, but—"

"I told you, didn't I, that your great-grandfather was a hatter?"

"Yes, in fact you did." Isabella sipped her tepid tea and held to her silence. The only safety was in silence. You survived the maze by accepting its irrationality. Insistence on directions was fatal.

"And from that flowed the manufacture of shirts, shirt factories, uniforms. But I've told you all that, yes, and then armaments for all the great wars." Sophia was lost in her thicket of words. "But was it that poor man's intention to lay waste to the Earth? Certainly not. He only crafted the fact and the fact bore its fruit— Where was I?"

"We went from hats to bombs, I think."

Sophia smiled, waved her hand, sweeping away the hats and bombs. "Well, no, I can't really follow a thought to its conclusion. Only to its deathbed." She coughed, then the wall of her face crumbled like wet plaster and she wept.

Or I imagined she wept. I always mistrusted tears. My sisterly college friend Marybeth, on whom I had relied for solace in my heartbreaks, was merciless on the subject. "Tears are bullshit, Raymond," she would say. "We dribble out tears to wash away stuff we don't want to see. We always forget that it never works."

So I accepted that Sophia wept, that Izzy's comforting hand came to stroke her soft hair, that she gazed up with a frantic plea—but the vision blurred. I couldn't make out where my crew had stashed themselves, but I mumbled my set speech about the crystal chandelier with thirteen electric candles.

Still, she might have wept, if only to remember wetness.

Sophia was alone. There was no other place setting at the table. It had been cleared away or never set. Izzy might have been gone a minute or a year. The mourning black widow brushed away crumbs. The heiress' hands were a beggar's. Her retinas went black, straining as lungs strain to breathe, and her lips moved in a whisper. "*Till death do us part.* Such an earnest phrase. William . . ."

She began a sidewise nod as if keeping time to some faint marching band. "Yes, a grand ball, with couples waltzing into the night," and her mouth tightened into a cartoon grin. "All in hospital gowns." She rose from her chair, and then she was in flight, her feet making tiny frantic scuffs. Her slippers were a dark suede, navy or chocolate, embroidered with flowery vegetation in reds and golds, white collars of fleece around her ankles and delicate leather bow-knots. The sound was a skitter of squirrels.

"Out, out . . ."

She passed through a kitchen where a gaslight burned, her hand running along the rim of a new type of sink—a remarkable woman, she. She scuffed across teakwood inlay, linoleum, unpainted redwood, threadbare carpet, a metal grate. A gust of wind rattled the shutters. Her slippered feet skirted a heap of fallen plaster. She halted.

"That terrible monkey. White ruff, black pupils, hissing? *See the monkey?* they said."

She continued in tiny steps down a hallway that led to stables, snappily turned left, climbed stairs one tread at a time. Moonlight gleamed on the stairwell. She looked both directions, a choice of blackness or blackness, then moved along the passage to her right. She stopped, reached out to touch the wall, fingers brushing a rich embossed wallpaper, then touching raw plaster, and the plaster gave way to bristly slats. She clasped her hands to her chest.

"What room?" Her abrupt voice startled her.

At the end of the corridor a candle flickered. It stood in a brass holder on a round pedestal table in the center of a tiny room. She entered, seated herself in a plain wooden chair at the table. Distractedly, "Yes, the Yellow Room . . ."

I knew this room by the feel of blue against my face. It wasn't yellow, it was blue. It had been yellow when she lived, painted blue when she died, and dubbed by Management the Seance Room. I was back on familiar ground. The pilgrims were somewhere about, tucked into corners or alcoves or the shallow closet for spooks' overcoats. I could distinguish the smooth respiration of the Austrian pompadour, the Iowa dad's heavy wheeze, the sighs of his wife and child. The college prof would pop to the surface for air, gasp and sink. The Mexican lady exhaled an earnest plea to the Holy Virgin, while the black man's taped nose made a sniff. The deep steady breath was Mr. Oswald's.

"We're standing now in the Seance Room. It was here that she communed with the dead. No one was allowed in this room except herself and the spirits and thousands of tourists, of course. Just joking." *Joking, joking, joking . . .*

Sophia stared into the candleflame. Her face was chalk like those storied cliffs of Dover. It's all in my brain, I reminded myself. Twenty-five minutes more to the tour, then one vast sneeze dissolves it.

"Notice the coat hooks on the right-hand side. How many? Thirteen, of course. Was this for the spirits to hang their coats? Yet why only thirteen? They must have been the chilly ones."

Sophia raised her right hand and brought it slowly toward the flame. Her fingers approached to a proximity where a single flutter might set a moth wing afire. She held the pose, counting heartbeats, then abruptly folded her hands on the tabletop.

"Apart from the spirits," I droned on, "no person could enter this room except herself. How do we know? Notice the door has no doorknob. She carried the only key. And the door to the left? It's the door to nowhere. A door to a twelve-foot drop onto an outdoor patio. Sophia's little midnight whimsy."

She seemed to hear my words. Her gaze fixed on the door and a tremor seized her spine. She rose, slowly crossed the floor in halting steps to the door that opened on nothing. The door that opened on nothing opened. She was poised on the door sill. But we were not privileged to see a suicide plunge. She inhaled the chill of the night. The candle guttered, gasped and steadied its flame. Sophia closed the door and stumbled back to her chair.

We stood on the verge of seeing what had never been seen before: Sophia Weatherlee conjuring her spirit hordes. The walking dead, the blasted and bleeding spooks, the zombies with jaws blown away—all her twisted imaginings, necromancy made manifest in a massive billow of madness, all real. The wind gusted, lightning flashed, thunder rolled in like a frenzied walrus and the symphony blatted its blat. But there followed an anticlimax.

Sophia reached under the edge of the table, slid out a drawer, removed a deck of playing cards and began to lay out a game of solitaire: the first card face up, then six cards face down and so on. The backs of the cards were a grillwork pattern, a faint weary red.

The game was prepared. From the deck she turned up every third card in an unbroken rhythm working through the stack. Her fingers slid over the cards the way a nurse might touch a feeble child's pulse. Strange conjuration.

The silence sucked words from her lips. "I was there when my mother screamed in church. Right in the middle of church. Quite startling." She played several cards from the stock. "They say that I spy on servants. That I have special windows, they say. But why shouldn't I? Ladies should always have a hobby. You needn't answer. That's not what you're here for."

To whom was she speaking? A dark figure formed in the corner, the shape of the servant Grace. "Grace, is it? Yes, with the single mother." The girl nodded. "Yes, you may nod at intervals, Grace, just so I know you're alive." Another nod. The maid's brow twitched slightly as if it itched but she had no permission to scratch it.

The old woman continued her game. "There are times when I require nothing more than a human presence, however strange that may be. One never knows where dragons lurk." She came to the end of the game. No cards to play out from the stack, so she turned the face cards down, raked the deck together, tapped it square and dealt out another game.

"My grandfather played this game. No skill involved other than an acceptance of fate." The girl stood frozen. "An acceptance of fate: not so easy, you know. Quite difficult to win. Quite rare." The shadows of her losses played on her face. "Despite the news accounts of my spiritualism, the Rosicrucians, Madame Blavatsky, all that nonsense, no, I have no talent for seeing the unseen, hearing voices, feeling— No talent for feeling, in fact."

By candlelight the room was yellow. The cards and the aged hands were sharply etched. All else was pitch dark in late afternoon.

"And so this game, you follow the rules, simply doing the next thing, the next and the next, and it's not your fault if it comes to nothing, but no sign of merit if you win. If you stretch your neck into the noose of power, where choices lead to results, to curses— Such a game is soothing. Do I not appear to be soothed?"

Again she laid out the cards, began to turn them over by threes. The impenetrable Sophia Weatherlee was mired in game after game of solitaire, every game lost.

"These whims, they swarm in my head like wasps on rotting apples." Sophia took a catch breath, giggled. Grace flinched. "And my rooms, such a labyrinth. If I had a map I might find the Minotaur at the heart of it. And the Minotaur would stand there shifting its weight from leg to leg, saying *Yes ma'am*, smirking at me sidewise." She uncovered an ace and moved it to the foundation stack.

"But the Minotaur grows fatter and fatter. Why do I build? I surround myself with empty rooms, bulwarks of emptiness, sheltering myself in obesity. Yes, I become the fat lady in the sideshow, breaking into a wild and hideous smile, my voice never rising above a whisper. And my gardens surround the house to trap the night within."

She peered at the cards. "I need a red Jack, and it's under this despicable Queen. I recall my grandfather cheating. Cheating at solitaire, imagine, cheating yourself. We seek meaning to our existence in the most remarkable ways." She gathered the cards, shuffled them, laid out another tableau. The girl stood petrified.

"Or perhaps not a labyrinth. Perhaps a mountain of slag. I once read a horrible book about miners in France, disgusting, the book and the miners, all. They were starving, bestial, stripped to the bone. And then we jump into the mind of the round-bellied manager. How he envies them their immorality, their animal spirits, their freedom from hope! He feels himself deprived. He, the victim."

Sophia placed the ten on the Jack, the nine on the ten, the deuce of spades on the three of hearts, then came to a halt. Another game lost. She gathered the cards, tapped the deck to square it. "You see that door. Each day it comes open. Comes open to me. Some day, perhaps— Perhaps now I should scream."

The maid Grace might have turned without a word and walked out. She might have gone to her room in the servants' quarters, packed her suitcase, walked two miles to catch the late bus to Fresno. Sophia would have watched her, words stillborn on her lip. But Grace needed her wages and remained.

Sophia shivered, laid out the cards again, then went rigid, staring straight ahead. Her lips quivered, but her voice was a cheery chirp.

"What I liked about William was his laugh. He had such a good laugh. Mouth wide open, free, just a wonderful laugh."

"Put the eight on the nine," Bud Padgett whispered.

Sophia startled. "I can see perfectly well, thank you." Her eyes were fierce, her lips taut in a rictus of grief.

Fourteen

Sunlight. No cards, no candles. I veered into the old wheel ruts of the tour, but it felt too much like my stagger through high school. Watching the X in algebra class hop across the equals sign and give me the finger. Nodding from daydream into history's red glow. Glancing up from Keats' sonnet to see it was only 1:45, then straining to catch a sight of nipple down Thalia's blouse. A jigsaw puzzle where none of the pieces fit.

Sophia sat at a heavy rolltop desk in a small office alcove, writing a letter. The Shakespeare window cast its rainbow stipple on the opposite wall, but its words were a blotch. Might be *What light through yonder window* or *You cataracts and hurricanoes* or *We still have judgment here* or the same wisecrack as before. Maxims from the Bard, who just rattled on. How anyone got from room to room, from darkness to dazzle, from befuddlement to truth, was a question without an answer.

Chuck appeared in the entryway. He saw her writing at the desk and stood there, uncertain whether or not to speak. She hated being interrupted but she hated being surprised by a silent presence. Thankfully she raised a finger to indicate that she knew he was there, so he waited for her to finish. She signed the letter, folded it, laid it aside, looked up at the blurry window.

"So aggravating, you know, to be your own secretary. Izzy was very pleasant, very competent, but people feel they must live their own lives. A mistake, if you ask me." She seemed to be talking without expecting to be heard. "But why should they ask me anything? I have no answers." She half-turned her face toward Chuck. "Marty?"

"Chuck."

"Of course. Chuck. I'm always doing that. Good morning then."

"Morning, Miss Weatherlee."

"You left early Thursday."

"Right. My son was sick. Lloyd took over."

"We can't have that."

"Right."

"But of course what else could you do? I'm being absurd. You had to take care of your child. That always comes first. I'm aware of that."

"He's better now."

"I'm very glad to hear it." She scoured around as if to collect her vagrant thoughts. "How was the sunrise this morning?"

"Way too early."

She turned away to pick up the letter, put it into an envelope, seal it, then address it carefully with a fountain pen too bulky for her delicate hand. She reached into one of the tiny drawers at the top of the desk, found a stamp and affixed it. Chuck stood waiting as he was paid to do.

Turning back briskly, she flashed the whisk of a smile. "Marty, we need to explore the options here—"

"Chuck."

"I beg your pardon?"

"Chuck. I'm Chuck, Miss Weatherlee—" Her face went blank. "My name is Chuck."

"I am aware of the fact!"

He knew better than to contradict her, but that was a habit of hers that made him react by reflex. He'd always tried to restrain reactions. When he was a kid his cousin Ronnie had poked him in the ribs, and without thinking Chuck punched him in the nose. It bled and bled. Since then he'd kept a tight grip. Or tried to.

Sophia capped the pen. "We've gotten up on the wrong side of the bed. Let's start over. How is the work proceeding? What are we working on now?"

"It's fine. We're on that stairwell, should be finished next week. Oh, and the heating problem? That was funny. It was one of the ducts. A raccoon had snuck in there. We got him out."

"It's not dead?"

"No, he wasn't real cooperative, but I think he's happy to be out."

"No more death."

Chuck felt a specter pass. He had intended to tell her about Lloyd's hilarious spat with the beleaguered coon but the moment was lost.

"Tell me this," she said as if to a child who had scraped a knee. "Are you working too hard?"

Yes, that's it, yes. By now he believed that Mrs. Weatherlee had a knack for reading minds. The pressure of the work, pushing a dateless deadline, had increased, and the extra time was hard on Dee and Joey. The old lady trusted him more than she did the night foreman, so he'd get a call and have to go in for three or four hours of overtime. And he spent whole evenings at the kitchen table trying to work out construction plans. He could never say no. Maybe it was the guilt. He would still start up in the night as the first crack split the ceiling.

At times he saw Dee watching him with something like pity while hating to pity him. She would stare at his forehead, not into his eyes. He tried to joke with her about the old lady's eccentricities: ordering a porch disassembled and rebuilt three feet further to the south; asking that a doorway be sealed but that the door continue to open; railing against some President from a hundred years ago. Dee would force herself to laugh.

And force herself to tell him what a great dad he was. He was, yes, when he had time to be a dad. Joey always wanted a story and Dee would check out library books. Once she got *Jason and the Minotaur*. Chuck wondered if it was too scary for a four-year-old but he read it to him. The hero went into the labyrinth, killed the monster, escaped.

But Chuck's mind wandered to the labyrinth's construction. Had it taken years? Who was the foreman? Did the crew ever find their way out?

A new house for the family—that was a plus. They had found an affordable place a couple miles from work, two bedrooms and a big back yard. There was an old tree, and he would put up a swing for Joey when he had the time. He hadn't intended to buy a place. He really wanted to get a piece of land and on weekends he'd start to build. He could teach Joey the way Uncle Frank taught him, letting him feel useful, even just sweeping sawdust off the sawhorse. Not that he wanted Joey to be a carpenter but simply to have the satisfaction of being capable with his hands. He would lie in bed going through every step of teaching his son to drive a nail. He was great at being a father in his head.

Working too hard? Answer her. "Well, matter fact I was going to ask if I could get some Saturdays off. It's hard being away from the family. It's hard on Dee, and Joey's just about to start into kindergarten—"

She interrupted. "Your problem with the truck. Lloyd came to me about your problem with the truck."

It took him a moment. "Truck. Oh yeh, the truck. No, that's okay. He was thinking— No, it's fine. But what I was gonna say—"

"I'm concerned about the truck. People get seriously injured by trucks. I'm told by my lawyers—" She waved her hand, brushing away all fatalities. "Worried about a truck. Just think, at my age being worried about a truck!" She gave a thin laugh.

"No, the truck's fine, Miss Weatherlee—"

"Would you like a new truck? Would that make it easier?"

"Well, it's the transmission, but it's not a problem, we took care of that. What is, though, sometimes—" The woman's jaws would unlock from a bone only if thrown a bigger bone. Dee had laughed when he said that. "What is, is that it's great that I'm getting these sets of blueprints now, makes it a lot easier, safer, but—"

"Well, I should hope so."

"But sometimes where you've written over it, made notes, it's hard to see exactly where—"

Her hands gripped the edge of the desk. The ferocity of those spindly fingers startled him. Her voice was as gaunt and firm as the fingers. "I have relieved Mr. Stubblefield, as I relieved Mr. Overton. Fine architects both, but finding my plans incompatible with their standards and finding my moods difficult, for which I am profoundly sorry, Marty, I understand how—"

"Scuse me, Miss Weatherlee. I'm Chuck. You called me Marty. I'm Chuck Ratowitz."

"Well decide!"

His uncle would tap a nail gently, tap tap, then drive it straight in with a single hammer blow. She did it with words. Chuck knew in a flash that he would get the same scribbled blueprints and his crew would have a new truck. Maybe still he could get some Saturdays off.

"Is that a baby? That cry?" Sophia spoke to a presence Chuck couldn't see.

"Sorry?" He shifted his weight like a teenager under scrutiny of an old aunt amazed that he'd grown so tall. *You're older than I'd expected*, she might be thinking.

"How is your family, Chuck? I'm concerned about your family. You're working very hard, I know, and I'm appreciative, but it must have its effect on your family."

He couldn't have said it better. "Yeh, they're fine, although Dee's kinda upset about me working so much. Like we got plans maybe, then the phone rings and— And Joey, he's something, he's into everything. He's at that stage of *I want Daddy, where's Daddy?* which is great except that I'm not there as much as I'd—"

"I lost mine, you know."

Chuck was silent. Which way to turn in the snarl?

"But of course you know. I talk of it *ad nauseam*. The fairytale princess blest with a handsome young prince, a beautiful wisp of a child, wealth and all the music that wealth bestows. And then in the night the vampires come, they swarm, they suck out the marrow down to the husk. They leave the princess only the stock certificates."

Chuck stood mute. It wasn't the voice of a baby. It was someone pulling nails.

"So you know," Sophia went on, "the old bat must be crazy. How could she not be crazy? Seized by an architectural obsession to model her madness? Perhaps you should go, Chuck. Just go, just flee here, now, from this sprawling tumor before it consumes you. Madness is infectious, you know, you must know that, don't you, Chuck? Yes, Chuck. I know who you are: you're Chuck. So much older now than only a few years ago. You should go. You should just flee out the door with your family, far far away—" She shut off, eyes gone dead.

He had seen her before in that same fierce stone-faced rant, a frenzy in her wits, and could only stand breathless until it ran its course. He told himself over and over that he was being paid very generously.

At last he spoke. "I don't— I mean— You got a lotta people working for you. I mean you got sixty, seventy people, right? Nobody takes orders from a crazy person."

"They don't?" A tiny smile. "Imagine that."

Again a dead end. Chuck tried to read the words on the stained-glass window. Normally his vision was acute, but they always blurred. He ought to change the subject, but he couldn't recollect the subject.

Sophia broke the silence. "Is your wife . . . perky?"

Perky? "What? Dee? I guess." What was she talking about? "So are there blueprints?"

Her voice cut the thick air. "I don't want to putter with blueprints. I want to discuss the situation. I'm giving you this truck, full use of the truck, personal use if you like. And your perky wife can use your car for the baby, the little boy, whatever he is, and you will never have to worry. And this is the right time for you and your family to move into Weatherlee House."

The light shivered. Morning in this fantasy, but in my shreds of reality it was that much closer to 5 p.m., when the music would swell and the curtain descend.

I could understand the reaching out, the longing, the yawn of emptiness. She was letting him into her madness. Mayhap even the

Pyramids were built of a yearning in the stones. His saying *yes* to the wall's collapse had married them.

In my spiel I had spoken of a workman who spent a full thirty-eight years in service to her obsession. This was the workman. These were his years.

She let her words register. Chuck glanced to the stained-glass window. *Wide unclasp*, he made out, but the letters were changing. There was a tap-tap-tap. It might have been hammers, heartbeats, but he saw only the dust afloat in the morning glow and the woodwork's pale green semi-gloss. She had been very exacting on the color.

"It's not generosity," Sophia went on. "It's a question of need. I suspect that something is very very wrong, and I need you to be here. I hear things in the foundations. I hear them in the basement, in the floors, in the ducts, night and day I hear—"

"You're hearing the hammers, ma'am. We've got three shifts."

"You know the odd thing—" An expulsion like the quack of a duck. Chuck waited for the verdict.

"The odd thing," Sophia went on soft-voiced as if soothing a child, "it wasn't really my father's murders. My father-in-law, father, whoever he was, this enormous presence with a belly. When I was tiny I'd climb into his lap and pat him on the belly. Not out of love but just that's what you did with bellies— I've lost track. No, it would have been my father. I had no father-in-law at the age of three, absurd— But it wasn't the guilt of ill-gotten gains, those Sunday School notions, no. It was Tigger, my kitten, her name was Tigger. I didn't give Tigger her pills."

She fumbled to put on her reading glasses and her eyes became pinpoints. Her lips flattened to a single wavering line. The tap-tapping held steady.

"She was sick and they gave her pills. But I said she's mine, I'll give her the pills. And they said fine, what a good little girl you are, and I thought to myself what a good little girl I was. And then I forgot the pills."

She reached for a stack of letters, bills, receipts in an upper cubby-hole of the desk, put them in front of her without seeing them. The line of her lips moved into the parody of a smile.

"And so she died. What could I do? I put her in my closet so she would dry up and fade away, and I'd still be a good little girl. But of course she stank. A horrible, horrible stench. I hid my head under the covers."

Chuck stared at the floor. The ceiling had cracked, beginning to shudder. Soon the collapse, again and again and again.

"So what would you do? If you were nine years old? You'd cry. You'd lie. You'd stop up your nose from the stink. You'd tell them that Tigger got better and ran away, but no, that would hardly be credible. So you'd say she was killed by a rat. You'd take a salad fork and stab her multiple times so she would appear to be killed by a rat with a salad fork! Ridiculous!"

She removed her glasses, folded them in her fist, began with deliberation to breathe. "It was an education. The harsh requirements of being a good little girl. Infinitely more vivid than statistics of many millions dead."

She reached out her hand to Chuck. He stood lost in the shifting glare, then at last touched her hand as if touching a cornhusk. She seized him by two fingers.

"Marty— Chuck. Yes. Chuck. I would ask you to move your family to this house. There are working bathrooms, kitchens, plenty of light. Wouldn't that solve your problems? Wouldn't it? You need time with your family, and I am very very sorry about that, I know I make demands that are absolutely insane. And I'm calling you Marty, that's insane." Chuck fought the urge to flee. Her spindly hand gripped his fingers like the tiny jaws of a rat. "I need the energy of young people in this house. We build ballrooms where no one dances, dining rooms where no one eats, nurseries without babies, and bedrooms—"

A sharp sob. She drew back her hand as if from fire, laid it flat to the wad of papers. Her voice mimicked the gentle methodical pouring of pancake batter. "You have a wife, a beautiful child, your family needs you, and there must be energy in this house, where the light dies every day at sunset and the soldiers die in these wars that go on and on and on—" Her voice began to rise, then it cut short. She looked at him with a thin smile. "I think that's what you should do."

Chuck's mind was blank. "Where?" he asked. "Where would we be?"

"Well for heaven's sake, choose. There are rooms, rooms, rooms, and there will be many more. You can't possibly reproduce as rapidly as you build."

He had no idea what he felt. He could only think of what others felt. Dee would hit the ceiling, but if he didn't agree he might be fired on the spot. He spoke without knowing what he was going to say.

"Ma'am, I don't know how that would work— I don't think Dee— I don't think my wife would want to do that. She likes it where we are. I don't think she'd be too happy, but if—"

The window darkened. Somewhere a whisper, then the soft insistent tapping began again as if to push the clock forward. Sophia listened, head cocked to the side, then turned her face to him or to the gaggle of ghosts behind him at the portal.

"Of course not. It's absurd. It would be a disaster," she said curtly. Her voice was flat, disembodied. "Well, that was one idea. But you should select a room of your own with your toiletries and a change of clothing when you need to stay over. Not in the west wing. You need sunlight in the morning. And we will see to the truck. The truck will make a difference, I'm sure. And these are from our new man Mr. Barlow, who now is in charge of the blueprints and all the fiddle-faddle, which should make it much easier for you." She reached down to the floor and handed him a banded roll.

"I know I've kept you too long. Your men are standing idle, I suppose." She waved the notion away. "No matter, they're being paid by the hour, so they are free to survey the clouds in the sky and blossoms in the garden, which I rarely see except through glass but which flourishes, I am told."

He mumbled something about his men enjoying their work. The danger seemed past so he took the risk: "Ma'am, I was asking about maybe could I get some Saturdays off? Lloyd knows the job, and he could take over then, cause it's getting a little hard to—"

"That will not be convenient." Her eyes were closed to him.

"Yes ma'am."

My troupe parted to let him pass, then pressed closer toward the old woman at her rolltop desk. She sensed their presence, picked up a secretarial pad and began paging through it, searching for something to search for. The sun had moved into late afternoon and the window was dark. Sophia mumbled. The tourists strained to hear. Cameras and cell phones rose and took aim. Her voice burst out.

"I rely on you, Chuck." Then in a strangled cry, "Chuck! Chuck! Chuck!" She turned to look straight at me, pleading. "I don't want to be this *character*!"

Fifteen

Flash. Flash. Flash flash. A barrage of photo flashes burned her image into the air. It shimmered, white on black, and vanished. I stood stupified: no tourists, no echoes, no time. Again it crossed my mind that I might have had a stroke. Who would inform Gertie, my nearest of kin? What if my sphincter released my essence?

Then, faint as a moon through heavy clouds, a room formed itself in my mind. Low ceiling, gray-green walls, clean and spare, and the murmurs of a tour guide, very likely myself, in the tremulous air.

"These were the quarters for live-in servants, the maids and kitchen staff. In all, depending on the time of year, more than sixty people were on the property, but these were the servants on whom she relied for her personal comfort. They earned double the usual rate, a grand three dollars a day, but she paid them every day in cash so she could hire and fire them at will. She kept close tabs. As you see, this room was very spare. It was thought cruel to raise the aspirations of the servant class by providing pleasant decor."

I wondered if any of that was true. I had passed through these rooms five times a day, five days a week, for thirty years. I had never seen them.

❖

Two figures stood immobile, outlined cartoon-like against dull green. Sophia Weatherlee stood in the open doorway. The maid Grace, her negroid features lightened by morning sun, stood by a plain wooden chair at the window, a ladies' magazine in hand. The figures were almost lifelike. Their voices had a tinny ring. They still held a shimmer.

"I didn't mean to startle you," the old woman said. "I've not been in this region of our happy home, so-called, for a very long while. And I wished to test our hydraulic elevator. It's a new design, they tell me. A vertical piston shaft underground, I pull the rope, water rushes in and bobs me to the top. Like a crumbly old cork." She rubbed the back of her hand. "It sounds terrifying but better than the Otis, one hopes. I was trapped in there, you know. Or you wouldn't know, of course, you weren't here at the time, but the repairman was hours away in San Francisco. They had to crank me down. Imagine locking myself in jail between floors." She laughed vacantly. "But that's in the past. We have enough to fear in the present without dredging up the past."

"Would you like to sit down, ma'am?" Grace offered her chair. Sophia declined, took a step into the tiny room.

"Thank you, Miss Grace, no, but I did want to speak with you. It's your free day and I kept you up so late last night, myself as well, so I'll not take much of your time. You surely value the minutes that are yours, what few there are."

"That's all right, ma'am, I don't mind."

Sophia paused, distractedly fumbling a button on her bodice. "I hope you're enjoying your work." She ran her fingers along the ribbed seam of her mourning dress—a stark Late Victorian gown, black on black, touching the floor—as if to ascertain that she was still in mourning.

"Yes ma'am, I am, thank you."

"Yes, it's very satisfactory. What are you reading?"

"*Ladies' Journal.* It's an old issue my sister gave me. I like the stories, and where people travel."

"Have you traveled?"

"No ma'am."

"Nor I. Very little. Twice to Europe, Florida and the Caribbean several times, Chicago once, dreadful. And of course west, Boston to California, Hawaii, Puget Sound, that sort of thing. But I can see you have aspirations."

"Ma'am?"

"Aspirations. Hopes. Dreams. Ambitions. A desire to better yourself."

The maid heard the question, but she was uncertain of its implications. "I do fine."

The old woman took another step into the room, cautiously invading the foreign territory that belonged to her. She glanced around, then gazed out the window to the distant hills. "I'm sorry the quarters are so plain. I had intended to decorate—bright curtains, woodwork, paintings—but my sister would have been appalled. It might raise the servants' ambitions beyond what they could ever achieve. Attempting to better their lives would lead only to discontent. What do you think? Would it?"

Again the maid hesitated. Her employer was taking her into confidence like the night before—a risky place to be. The woman was waiting for an answer. "I don't think it would, ma'am. I think they'd appreciate it. I would for certain." Had she said too much?

"I didn't think so either. I judged that my sister was entirely mistaken, an ignorant bigot in fact. And of course she's long deceased. Yet I never did it." She squinted out the window. "From here one can see the building for our gasworks. Fascinating, the acetylene for the gaslights. The controls drop pellets into a water tank, and these combine to form gas which mixes with fresh air, and the operation is shut off automatically when a float rises to the top. I can't quite explain it, but I'm told that this renders explosions impossible. That's why we keep it a hundred yards away from the house." She gave a wry laugh and Grace ventured a smile.

"You know, I've never hired a Negro before. Did you know that?" No response. "Of course you wouldn't. In fact my family always supported colored people's welfare, though they never hired them for the household. Perhaps they fancied it would demean your people to hire them as servants. Of course there were many in the factories. They were less costly." She allowed the two of them a moment to breathe. "Or the old prejudice about blackness. Nonsense. For me, blackness is the norm. We begin in blackness, and we remain there. Very simple." The maid was silent. The woman looked at her curiously. "I've tried to comprehend what it feels like to be a Negro?"

Grace felt a mad urge to laugh, but she kept a tight grip. At least the old woman spoke it straight out. She gave a thin smile. "I couldn't say, Miss Weatherlee. I've always been as I am. It feels like being me."

Sophia nodded, waved her hand. "Of course it would. How does it feel to be old, white, female, encased in a hundred and seventy rooms? One hundred seventy-six now, you know? It was a ludicrous question. My family was hypocritical on so many questions, including issues of race. And I carry on the tradition. No excuse." She stepped forward, smoothed a wrinkle of the coverlet on Grace's bed. "But I've always had this curiosity, you know? To know our fellow creatures, those unlike us, alien to us, those millions, billions, so unlike we blessed souls—we few, we blessed few . . ."

She made an inexplicable gesture, as if ripping words from the air, and stood in the doorway facing the puzzled maid. Her words came from a shrouded mind, rain on the roof, rhythmic, insistent, terse.

"So. We have business. In your kitchen locker you will find an envelope containing your day's wages and a second envelope with your severance pay. My sister would be appalled at the notion of severance pay for a maid, but she need not know, being dead. I can't live my life to please her bigotry. I hope you find it generous."

She paused, staring at the floor, then drew a fierce inhale. "You may be aware that employers have no obligation to offer reasons for dismissals. In the long run it avoids unnecessary pain, at least for the employer. So that is what I have to say and I wish you the very best. I do. I believe you'll make a very good life for yourself and your loved ones, whoever they may be. I've been very appreciative of your service and will certainly be pleased to give you a reference should you need it. Now I have spent enough time on this matter and have other things to attend to. You are welcome to stay until morning if immediate departure would be inconvenient."

The girl's immobility held Sophia there. Neither spoke. Finally, with lowered gaze, Grace took a breath, restraining her voice like a muzzled dog. "My mother is going to ask me why."

"Say the old woman is a lunatic. That's not so hard to credit, is it?"

"Why? Why, Miss Weatherlee?"

Their eyes met. Sophia's lips flattened, drew taut. "Because you witnessed me, Grace. You stood in the shade and heard me speak. Not your fault, not at all, you followed my directives and stood there and absorbed my confessions. As if you saw me stripped naked. That is not to be done. I am not to be seen. There are no mirrors here."

Grace turned away, went to the cabinet, began to remove clothes from the top drawer. A muffled cry from the doorway stopped her.

The old woman, through a slur of tears, spoke in clipped articulation. "Whatever your politics, it is historical fact that a country is in grave danger when its upper classes are discontent." The door shut.

I slipped my fingers behind my black glasses, pressing my lids to squeeze out the sight. The room diffused into shatters, dissolving into black. I groped for a wall. Tiny whines rose in my throat.

The scene had never happened, of course. The lady was only shadow, illusion, India ink, or my own quirks aged and ripened: the vile old lady within me.

On the cusp of change, with your past life looming like a slag heap of soiled undies, there comes a sorting out. For me the job had been a snug distraction from life. Always the tour timed out the same. It offered health benefits, sick leave, paid vacation, a pension plan and a half hour for coffee between excursions. The staff was friendly, and most of our patrons were truly entertained by my tales of this tart old eccentric. Harmless fiction has its place in a world of lethal fact.

So there was no earthly reason for my urge—often considered though never fulfilled—to come in some dark moonless night, feel my way to the master bedroom, and shit on the rug.

Sixteen

Dee Ratowitz sat in the deep upholstered armchair, heavy dark brown against the light teal blue of the living room walls that glowed in the noonday sun. She rarely sat in Chuck's chair, but right now she needed to be embraced, swallowed up, contained. She felt safer in its arms. Her pulse was racing. The pills made her feel alive and she hated that.

Third Saturday of September. Chuck had to work and her mother took Joey to the zoo. By now Mom knew that Dee wouldn't let her take him to church to clog his brain with Jesus, but the zoo was fine. Dee was thankful—or as thankful as possible—that her mother loved her cute little grandson more than she'd ever loved her daughter.

Dee had never lost all the weight she'd gained during pregnancy, and when Joey started school she put on another ten pounds. Chuck said he liked it and playfully pinched that bulge of fat at the waist of her jeans, so the next week she'd started the diet pills. Two pills twice a day, then more. She lost some of the weight but kept taking the pills. For energy, she told herself, though she could hardly stand still for five seconds. Right now she was stuffing her face with candied popcorn, salt and sweet. She still had the bulge of fat.

Now Joey was into second grade and she had way too much time on her hands. She quit the bookkeeping job when the dealer made a fumbling pass at her, and for a while she looked for a job that fit Joey's schedule. She had an appointment for an interview at a fabric store, but she sat in the car outside the little shop unable to move. Oh yeh, panic attack, that's a side effect, she thought, and resolved to stop the pills. The resolve lasted nearly two days.

Chuck was always working late or hunched over the kitchen table studying plans or slouched stone-faced in his armchair watching some sit-com. One night he came home late and as she was warming up supper he asked if she was still taking pills. "You act kinda nervous," he said. She was grateful he'd noticed, but she hid the pills. Often she was on the verge of screaming. A couple of times, by herself in mid-afternoon, she did.

Dee finished the sicky-sweet popcorn. Nausea struck her. She went to the bathroom, vomited, then dutifully brushed her teeth. Eleven-forty. She couldn't face an endless afternoon alone in the house. In the paper she'd seen a listing for an outdoor art fair: something different anyway. She checked the listing, changed into bluejeans and a long pullover she'd picked up on sale, mohair or part mohair with a yellow-brown camouflage print and little flecks of yellowish red. She'd never worn it but it had an artsy feel, so why not? She liked the way it hugged her hips.

She took the bus downtown—forget the damned car—and walked to the park, feeling free for the first time in weeks. She hadn't even brought her afternoon pills. All kinds of art there: paintings, statues, weird shapes she couldn't figure out, a few nice pictures of dogs or trees or the ocean. Mostly she observed the artists sitting by their stuff, and she wondered how they coped with people just walking past. Checking prices, she smiled to think somebody would pay five hundred bucks for a picture of the ocean. Maybe to remind yourself it was there. She and Chuck hadn't been to the ocean—ten miles away—for, what, three years?

There was a stage for entertainment. A folksinger came on, a guy with a funny two-pronged chin beard, sideburns and a big scuffed leather hat. Maybe her age, maybe older, but he had the jaunty glee of a kid. He leaned in to the mike, murmured, "And now, friends, here he is, the man who needs no introduction," and hit the first chord. He didn't have much of a voice, but his guitar sang. Dee stood listening for about fifteen minutes and he smiled at her a couple of times. He finished, got scattered applause, and she walked away. Then she walked back.

He was packing up his guitar and had some CDs on a little stand. On an impulse she bought one. At some point he had said his name, Randy, Ranny, something, but she hadn't caught it and didn't want to ask. He commented on the weather and she heard herself make some kind of joke about his two-pronged chin beard—then reached out and touched it. She watched herself from a distance, as if acting in a movie—smiling, tilting her face, flashing her eyes. Then he was looking at her, and she knew what was happening. "You doing anything right now?" She shrugged, shivered. "Want to come to my place?"

He said it so simply. No one had ever been so direct. She hadn't been wanting that, or had she? She couldn't say yes or no. Finally she gave a little nod and a tense smile that said *Why not?*

She wouldn't actually do it. She would give him a friendly wave, turn and walk straight away, congratulating herself on being a coward. Instead, she followed him to his car, a blue Chevy that had seen better days, and got in. He lifted a grocery sack from the passenger floor into the cluttered back seat. "It's a jumble," he said.

He drove to a working-class neighborhood not far distant, chatting about funny experiences with audiences, but he must have known she wasn't listening. She was watching Dee Ratowitz in her new badly-cast role as free-wheeling adulterous wife. She felt the tremble growing in her spine. She saw herself driving straight through all the stop signs. Crazy.

They went up the back stairs of a square brick apartment building. His room was clean, posters and wall hangings, a mattress on the floor with a Mexican bedspread—kind of a friendly hippie feel to it all. She knew he could tell she was nervous and he was very sweet. They embraced and he led her over to the bed. They lay down and he held her head in his hands like a gift he'd just been given. "I noticed you . . ." He spoke of singing for her, even though he guessed there was scant possibility, watching her walk off, come back. He said he loved her smile and the little frown she had when something struck her funny. His fingers massaged the back of her neck and down her spine. She stopped fighting it and the tenseness ebbed. Then she forgot who she was and followed her instinct.

A surge of pure lust carried her through the outset, but when he came into her a switch turned off. She was frozen, numb. He was there pumping away and it was all a mechanical stunt, no more feeling than at a doctor's exam. Such a relief. If she was indifferent she wasn't really doing it at all. The sounds coming up from her gut weren't bestial growls of pleasure but only the grunts of being thumped on, whacked like a rug—some distant female whining *Yes!* She could let him do it, clean up, hug him goodbye, say how much she enjoyed his music, go home to make dinner, having not been fucked at all.

Then she felt herself coming. The gathering clutch, the wall giving way, the balance before the fall. She fought against it, but then she was hit by the shock, the tremors, wave after wave, accepting the flood to the well and the long long slow dissolving.

She was Dee again, with a stranger beside her stroking her hair, a bearded little boy with a smile as if he'd found a turtle or a shiny lost quarter. She was Dee, but a Dee she had only just met by accident. She had to leave now, say the right things if she could manage the words. After a while they got up, she went to the bathroom, they held each other a long minute at the doorway and he drove her home. She asked him to stop at the bus stop a couple of blocks away from the house, gave him a peck and quick hug, got out of the car. He said something she didn't catch. She leaned down to hear.

"Thank you," he said.

He had been good with her. She sensed that he accepted that this was a one-time thing, that she wanted nothing more or couldn't afford it. She told herself that it was one of those beautiful sweet happenings, as when she was little and found a shell with its magical whorls of purple and white. She had put it on her shelf, where its brilliance faded though she held a fragment of the memory.

Then the guilt rolled in: dank winter fog off the sea. It engulfed her so thickly she thought her legs wouldn't get her the two blocks home. She wanted to stumble, to rasp her knees on the concrete just to let pain erase her. Nobody was home yet. She got in the shower and scrubbed and scrubbed, scouring away an imagined smell. She folded the sweater into a box of giveaways for Goodwill. It was all an accident, she told herself, an impulse, one of those crazy things people do.

Her mom brought Joey back promptly at five o'clock and Chuck arrived soon after. She fixed dinner and the evening passed—all back to normal. She was anxious what might happen if Chuck touched her when they went to bed. He did. At first she was numb, could hardly feel him, but then she was on fire. It grabbed her harder than she'd ever known, and she had to clamp her teeth so as not to scream. Afterward, Chuck whispered that she was like an earthquake under him. She lay awake for hours reaping the aftershocks.

In the next days and weeks the guilt kicked back hard. It would come in a rush, fill her, leave her void. She recognized that she was getting addicted to the diet pills. They would jangle her nerves and she'd drink a beer to flatten out, but that added up to jumpy depression. She told herself that of course she would never try the cheating thing again, and she knew she was lying.

My cheeks were wet. I had never had tears since I lost my sight, wept only dust. Now there was dew. I stood there the way I stood at the edge of the playground wiping off grit. The way I feared Shirley would be mad if I tried to kiss her or mad if I didn't try. The way I told Brian that it wasn't working out. The way I stared at my mother stuffed into her coffin.

It was terrifying to be as deep inside a woman as I was with Dee. From boyhood I was drawn to girls but dreaded their proximity. Men bore no threat of closeness, no entry without a password. Women were wetlands, quicksand, milk, blood. Seeing my denuded sister spread-eagled, I could only weep with a heart beyond joy or grief.

For three decades on the tour I had faced no greater challenge than cantankerous geezers, sprained ankles, panic attacks and a schizophrenic episode. Now there were ghosts looming in flagrant nakedness. I cast my ears about to locate my flock. (*Cast my ears about*, clever, I could work that into my spiel—but no more spiels.) I ached for my tourists to distract me, but they seemed to be lost in the bughouse or dangling from the horns of the Minotaur. Perhaps I had never had tourists: I had wandered the streets babbling for thirty years.

I heard wheezes and panting. A pale conflux of patient faces came into focus. "Well then," I said, "let us now cast our ears about—" I did hear a chuckle, perhaps from the chicken man. I couldn't think of a single thing to say, so I offered some facts about the Spanish-American War. By now I could trust that nobody listened.

I wagged my finger and our nomadic gaggle forged on.

Seventeen

The Ballroom again. Sophia sat under the same Shakespeare window in the corner where Marty and Chuck had faced off across the Porter-Cable saw. Now her chair was a heavy oak rocker with spiral leg posts, a wide golden seat cushion, and vine carvings along the back. She was winding a ball of dark red yarn from a tangled mass in her lap. She would pull at the snarl, then work the ball through the tangle to gain a few more inches. Her face was bloodless.

As before, Chuck stood across the room. In contrast with his heavy work shoes he wore a navy blue flannel suit, a white shirt and a blue-gray necktie. He fingered the jacket buttons.

"No. Always leave the last button unbuttoned." She tugged at her yarn. "For reasons unknown," she added. She removed her reading glasses and looked up from her tangle. "So let me see. Well, not so bad. This is English tailoring, better in the shoulders, they tell me. Of course I prefer three-piece suits on a man, but those are hardly appropriate for your sort of work. You're not an attorney, after all. I've chosen only the one tie and you'll want several, but keep them subdued. Neckties must be housebroken."

She regarded him closely. "Up straight." He shifted his weight, stood straight for inspection. "Arms out." He raised his arms. "Yes, the jacket should come to the first knuckle on your thumb. We can have it adjusted. I was going by guesswork but I have an instinct. Your build is similar to that of William. You'll need something lighter in summer, but flannel has durability, and it does get chilly in these quarters. You'll want to steam it every three or four wears, or hanging it in the shower stall will do as well. And we'll find you an overcoat. You can't wear your old jacket with that. It would look wretched."

She put on her reading glasses and continued disentanglement of the yarn. "Shoes, we'll do something for shoes that are more suitable. But overall it fits?"

"Fits fine."

"I have always had an eye for fit."

"Well, ma'am, I'm wondering, do you want to tell me what—"

"Did you see the sun this morning?"

"Yes. Yes I did."

"That side of the house is lovely in the morning. Were you there overnight?"

"Yeh, the elevator shaft, there was some questions on that, I had to make sure—"

"And how is your little boy?"

"Well, he's not so little now. He's in school. That's good for my wife, gives her a lot more time." She busied herself with the yarn, pulled a strand free and began to wind.

"I'm sorry," she murmured.

"Ma'am, I— The suit's great, fits fine, but what I wondered is . . . what am I doing in a suit?"

"I said I'm sorry!" She spoke under her breath, face clenched, then managed a tight grin. "Not you. My cat, when I was very small. I talk to my cat, her name was Tigger. Is that a sign of dementia, to talk to the ghost of your cat? Better than talking to walls." She worked at a thick knot in the yarn. "Well yes, the suit. The suit is yours. This is your proper attire. I expect to see you in proper attire."

This was her way. Once he'd told Dee that the old lady was like a dump truck without a backup signal: she'd come at you backwards without your knowing it, then dump her load. Dee had laughed at that. Those days she still laughed a lot.

"Well, it's obvious, isn't it? This project is too large for a single foreman. You're already working overtime. And so I have decided there will be a foreman for each shift. Lloyd will be a foreman, he has proven reliable, and you will select two other foremen, perhaps the previous man if he is still here, and you will supervise. Your salary will be commensurate, and you may arrange more flexible hours, which should help in regard to your family. Your new title is Construction Supervisor, and supervisors wear suits."

The previous man. Yes, the previous man was still there. He was drunk most of the time, but Chuck couldn't bring himself to fire him. Earlier that day Marty had staggered in late to the new wing where they had just begun to plaster. He sat dumbly regarding the job before him, launched into it with clumsy fury, then walked away.

And two days ago Chuck was eating lunch at a table set up for the crew under a canopy by the gasworks. The other men were back at work, but Marty appeared and stood unsteadily at the far end of the table. "Hey, Chuckie!" he called out with a smile, waving hello.

"Marty."

"Hey, Chuckie, here's an idea. Let's build a real house. Get some lumber, hammer, nails. No, forget the nails. Maybe Scotch tape? Let's do it." The further the man got into the bag the less he slurred and the more he spoke like a college prof with a screw loose.

"What's going on, Marty?"

"Or a preacher's pulpit. Big fat preacher. Or a birdhouse. Maybe just walls. Walls, yeh, we're great at walls. Walls of Jericho, toot toot, come tumbling down."

"Marty, you're drunk. Listen, take off. Take some time off."

"With a gazebo. *Bring me a julep, butler.* Hire me a butler named Butler."

"Marty, I mean it. Let me give you the day off. I won't dock you. You'll be better Monday. Take off till Monday. Hear me? We don't need this."

Marty slumped down heavily on the bench beside him. Their glances ricocheted. Chuck took a sip of coffee, waiting it out. A minute of dead air, then with a broad inhale the drunken man rose from the table swaying, pulled out a wadded handkerchief and blew his nose. He grinned at Chuck and shrugged.

"But what you could do, I'm saying," Marty spoke with the old lady's crisp articulation, "is build a real house. And live there. House to live in, how about that? What a fuckin' weird idea. Friends, family, kids in every room." Marty's face softened and his eyes took on a funny gleam. "*Hey! How's it goin'! How you doin' there? Come on in! Hey man, I can't stand that music, can you turn it down? But I love you, man, we're neighbors, okay? Wanna get a pizza?* Crazy house, but we're all alive. Fifty rooms, hundred rooms, a thousand, all fulla people, alive and flying high!"

He turned and stumbled down the path. Chuck caught only a few last words. "We could build that . . . hey, yeh . . . and not be total fools."

"Mister Chuck?" Sophia's voice cut through the silence. She hadn't called him that in a while.

"Ma'am?" Chuck jerked himself out of Marty's presence. Yes, he was here and wearing a suit.

"Is that agreeable?" She was squinting at him.

He brushed at his lapels. "Well sure, ma'am. Only thing is . . ." The slant of the sun on her reading glasses hid her fishhook glare. "Thing is, with foreman I do get a chance to get my hands on stuff, do some work, actual work sometimes, and I enjoy that, especially that inlay work, I learned a lot from Tomaso, the new Mexican guy. I'd miss that. I mean, I'm a carpenter, is what I . . ."

She stared at him, through him, past him. Ragsie had stared that way, lying on her side, cold fish orbs, and he'd started to pet her until his mother cried out, "Don't touch her! She's dead!"

"But sure, yeh, it'd be great to have some time off, or more flexible, I mean, although Dee and I, we've kind of adapted, but— And the truck's great, it gives us a lot of flexibility— But I really feel, I don't know, funny wearing a— But it's great, fits fine. Actually I've got some shoes, black shoes, kinda dress-up, they'd work for shoes. With a suit."

"Now we must discuss the window."

"Ma'am?"

"The question of the window, it needs to be finalized today."

"Well, the window, if that's what you're—"

"Today, thank you."

"Whatever you say, Miss Weatherlee, I just need to—"

"I'm aware of your feelings. But now you have no excuse since I'm not asking you to do it, other people can do it, Lloyd can supervise. You just have to see that it's done."

Chuck felt the suit jacket tighten across his shoulders and the trousers ride up in the crotch. Just his imagination. "Miss Weatherlee, I'm only saying— Whatever you want, sure, but my job is to make certain the work is the best craftsmanship that— I mean that wall would cut off the sun in there, and that's a Tiffany window, you spent a lot of money on that, and that woodwork, that's cherrywood, and it'd cut all that off. And that window is so beautiful."

Marty had installed the window a couple of years ago when he was on the wagon a while, and when the job was done, the last dab of filler in the woodwork, they had both stood staring at that radiant miracle ablaze with sun and heard themselves laughing like buddies.

"But what I was thinking, those stairs, we could take those the other way and then you wouldn't have to cover the window, and we'd have the sunshine in there—"

"The stairs are there for a reason."

"Miss Weatherlee, they go up to a ceiling and stop. They don't go anywhere."

"I have nowhere to go."

"That's not what I mean, I—"

"This is hardly a question of life or death!"

There was nothing more to be said.

"Mister Chuck, you are under stress. Perhaps your home life, but that's not my business. I'm sure you have considered quitting. I can't suppose what would keep you here. To deal with the daily rants of a woman whom they say is directed by spirits of the murdered dead, this requires forbearance to say the least." Her fingers clawed the tangle of yarn and froze there.

"So you will stay or go. You will wear your new suit or no. The wall will appear there in any case. The walls have a will of their own, and even if I should proclaim, *No, there will be no more walls*, there will be walls. You know I rely on you, Chuck, but we are all so expendable."

I saw the two figures facing each other like porcelain statuettes on a knickknack shelf. I felt a tightening in my lungs, but a scream might incite my tourists to flee, and then they'd forget to tip.

I could envision Chuck coming home that night in a business suit. His wife would be standing in the kitchen holding a jar of applesauce. She would take one look and drop the jar. He would tell her he got promoted and his hours would be more flexible. The minute he said it he'd know it was a lie. So would she.

She had three suits to try on and this was what fit, he'd tell her. *Well that's wonderful, honey,* she'd say, then clean up the applesauce.

Sophia spoke. "Mister Chuck, how is it you have never learned to tie a necktie? Come here." She beckoned, he crossed the lustrous floor, leaned over and she retied it. "Much better." She playfully pinched the tip of the tie and smiled.

Eighteen

We stood there like flies in amber, zombies at the mall, used cars under red balloons. No more than fifteen minutes left to the tour, but it seemed to stretch out like late afternoons in seventh grade. I waggled my finger more forcefully.

Once in my youth I dreamed that I was a ferocious beast, perhaps a tiger. Very vivid. On waking I tried to hold onto that dream, but tigers don't waggle their fingers.

Perhaps not a tiger. Perhaps a cranky poodle.

Now we looked into a kitchen. Not the yellow kitchen: the walls were a pleasing warm gray, and the table had been replaced with an off-white drop-leaf and four matching cane chairs. Dee Ratowitz sat at the table drinking tea and reading a magazine on home decor.

Six months had passed. Dee had managed to slack off the pills and actually lose a few pounds despite a beer in the afternoon and another with Chuck before dinner. Joey had Cub Scouts and was tooting his trumpet in the grade-school band, so Dee was satisfied, she told Chuck, just to be home with a lot of leisure time. She had never repeated her artsy adventure, though she told herself that she was grateful for it: she needed the shock to shape up.

Another move: they had bought a new house. Chuck still said he intended to build but not any time soon, and real estate values were going sky-high. They found a two-story, four-bedroom Victorian on a half acre in an older section of Santa Cruz close to a shopping center, plenty of room for a garden and maybe a dog at last. The neighbors were doctors and lawyers, no riffraff. Too big for them now but a good investment, and they were still thinking about another child. So they said.

The months flew by. Dee tried to feel sorry for Chuck. His responsibilities had multiplied. Now he was running up the Peninsula and across the Bay meeting subcontractors, ordering supplies, checking invoices. He talked about going out to the worksite whenever he could, watching the work, even taking a screw gun from some guy who was sinking the heads too deep and showing him how to do it—just to get his hands on tools again. He joked to Dee that being in a job that went on forever, no rush, no deadline, meant there was never any time. She tried to laugh.

And he would still joke about Mrs. Weatherlee. Every morning he walked through hallways that got longer by the week, he said, finding her each time in a different room. She might be reading a book, playing solitaire, sipping tea, knitting, without really noticing what she did, and then she'd say something crazy. "I see her there I think I'm working for a ghost." Dee kept silent on the subject.

Today was their anniversary. They always celebrated the date they first made love, not the legal thing. This time there was more at stake. They had had dry spells before, but the rains always came. They found a babysitter who could be there till all hours. Chuck would get off at six and they would drive up to San Jose for dinner at a fancy restaurant. Dee put on her old blue dress, still Chuck's favorite, pleased that she could get into it again. She spent a long time with her hair, then sat reading about drapes and Venetian blinds.

The sitter came a little before six. When Chuck wasn't home at 6:30 Dee tried to call but got no answer. He had an office on the grounds but was almost never there to answer the phone. The girl sat around for a while, then Dee paid her and let her go. She put Joey down at 8:30. He whined for Daddy to tell him a story, and it was all she could do not to slap him. Then she sat at the kitchen table and waited. She had had only one beer, yearned for a bourbon but felt too heavy to lurch out of her chair. He walked in at a quarter till ten.

"Hi."

"Don't even say it."

"Dee, c'mon, I'm sorry, but we're at a stage where we've got supports going in, and the night foreman had to be late, some kinda family problem, I don't know, so I couldn't leave the crew just standing around—"

"We were going out."

"I know we were but—"

"Babysitter's come and gone. I didn't put dinner on cause we were going out for dinner."

"Okay, I'm sorry—"

"Why didn't you call?"

"Last time you said don't call, you said what's the difference?" He knew in his gut this was different, their anniversary, but couldn't she see that he was sorry about it too?

The clouds were gathering. She rose without a word, opened the fridge to see what she might fix for dinner. No point in making a scene. Here was this beautiful man stuck between his duties and his sneaky bitch of a wife. She asked if he wanted a beer. He didn't answer. She reached two bottles from the back of the fridge and set them on the table with a church key. He pried off the caps and sat down.

"What's that shirt?" Dee asked as she put pork chops in the skillet. Pork chops were quick, and some leftover yams.

"What?" He sensed what was coming.

"You wore your blue shirt this morning."

"It got dirty. I got a couple shirts there. I got a room there. For when I need it."

"You got a room?"

"I told you that." Had he told her that? He must have told her that. Why should he have to tell her that?

"You got a room."

"Well, so what?"

She was steering toward a fight, she knew it. "Well, I don't remember I signed a contract for single motherhood. Chuck, goddammit, I see you I think, *Hey, he's good-looking, maybe we could get together, my husband's away a lot.*"

"What, you think I got something on the side, is that the deal?" It was moving too fast for him.

"I wish you did, Chuck. I wish you did. If you were cheating at least I'd know what I was up against—" Stupid, stupid, stupid thing to say. She tried to slam on the brakes but the brakes wouldn't hold.

"How am I finding time to cheat on you when I'm working fourteen hours a day?" Far distant he heard the old lady exhale: *Mister Chuck?*

The pork chops began to sizzle. "Well how about you work eight hours, then take a couple hours to go fuck some cutie, and I'll still have four hours of you that I don't have now." She turned away. He stood up, grabbed the back of a chair and banged it on the floor. "Go ahead. Make noise. Wake up Joey. He asked for Daddy."

"Goddammit, Dee, I'm just trying to keep the job! I'm working my ass off! I don't know where the hell the money's going—"

"Kids cost money."

"Kids cost money," he echoed, clutching a scrap of reason, "and that's why I'm trying to make money, but it's going out so damn fast. You show me a necklace you bought, it's cute, you oughta have a necklace, but we're owing a couple thousand bucks on credit cards—" He hated talking to her back.

"So it's my fault?"

"I didn't say that. I said you're asking why I gotta work and I'm saying I gotta work to pay the bills—" He heard himself sounding hysterical. He pushed his voice downward to the pitch of a reasonable guy. "Dee, I don't want to fight. If I had a choice I would spend every damn minute with you and Joey. But it's not like I can go someplace and get a job that pays this well. She's paying three times what I'd make—"

"He cried the last time you put him to bed. Eight years old and he cries."

He had. Chuck had tried to make it a joke and Joey cried more. "That was once." Once, and it burned his soul.

A tide of weariness engulfed her. She didn't have the energy for a fight. She turned off the burner and the sizzle died: silly to burn the pork chops. She straggled to the table and sat down. Chuck sat down opposite. They sipped from their bottles. Just sit here, shut up, no need to make it worse. But the words had to come.

"So Joey's eight years old. When's he going to have a little sister? Did we talk about that?" She tried to keep her voice neutral, not angry, just a practical conversation. But the edge cut.

"We said that if—"

"Did we talk about that?"

"I don't think the timing's good."

"I'm talking about having a baby."

"I'm talking about reality."

She resisted the urge to slam down the bottle and let go the scream she'd been holding back: it would be sure to wake Joey. He'd been having nightmares, so best let the scream stay coiled. "Well then," not knowing what the words would be, "you just go ahead and keep that job and see how long you keep me." That wasn't what she meant. Not at all. Never.

"Dee—" *Slam down the bottle, upend the table. No. Control.* "Dee, hey. We stay with the plan. Stay with this fucking job a while, save up, and then I start my own company. Isn't that what we planned? Very specific plan? Dee?" She focused on the table. Tears came. She wiped them in rage then let them run down. "I mean, we both made the plan, didn't we? So we gotta roll with the punches. But, I mean, the experience, I was in way over my head, but now— I'm telling you the chance for craftsmanship, working with hardwoods, mahogany, teak, Japanese cherrywood, fantastic. Now she's got an idea for this dome, I didn't think it was possible but I found something in a book like in 1832, and what they did was . . ." Was she listening? "You listening to me?" She gave a stiff-necked nod.

"As soon as it's more stable. I mean, this wing we're working on, when that's finished— I talked to her Monday for some time off and I'm working on it, but I can't push it cause Lloyd can do most of what I'm doing and then maybe all of a sudden Lloyd's in charge. Same thing happened to me." Her eyes were dry. "And now you've got the car all the time, isn't that a help?" She nodded. Things were back on track. "Hey, did you get Joey the toy pickup? Red Ranger pickup truck? Maybe he's too old for that, but—"

"And a football."

Where are you! He heard Sophia's distant cry.

"I love you," Chuck said.

Dee looked up at him. "Love you too," she murmured, then rose to turn on the burner under the pork chops. The phone rang.

Chuck went into the front room, answered the extension. "Yeh?" Mrs. Weatherlee, of course. There were noises, she said. "Noises?" Noises in the walls of the Daisy Room. "Well, it's probably the plumbing, Miss Weatherlee. Couldn't that wait for morning?" No, it could not.

"*No, it could not!*" Dee called from the kitchen.

"No ma'am. I'll be right there, ma'am."

"*No ma'am! Yes ma'am!*" from the kitchen.

"Yes ma'am. Soon as I can." He hung up. "Dee—" He came into the kitchen. Dee was leaning face against the fridge sobbing, her fists pressed to the door. "Okay, I know— I know you put up with a lot, but listen, I'm getting it from both directions. I'll be as fast as I can and then—"

He droned on. She heard words, meaningless words swarming like gnats from the garbage. She heard his pain, she wanted to hurt him and she hated herself for wanting it.

"*Yes ma'am!*" she cried.

"I'll be an hour, maybe less."

"*Yes ma'am!*"

"She's my boss, goddammit! What you want me to say, *No, bitch, I'll be there tomorrow?*"

"*Yes ma'am!*"

"Stop it, for chrissake."

"*Yes ma'am!*"

Chuck grabbed his jacket from the back of the chair, started for the door and turned back. "You didn't complain about buying the living room set and new dresses and a car that runs. You didn't complain about the fucking Christmas presents—"

She turned to face him. She could see herself: red-faced, mascara running down, blubbering like the little fat girl on the playground when the boys pulled down her underpants. Humiliation burned her eyes. "*Yes ma'am!*"

He started out through the back door. "Oh hell—"

"I spent years watching my dad walk out the door and I'm not gonna watch you! You walk out that door, I'll go out and get laid by the first guy I meet!"

"He's welcome to it!"

Then she was rushing at him, stumbling into a chair, hitting his shoulder with her fists, trying to make him feel what she felt, and he came around with his forearm hard against the side of her face.

She sprawled on the kitchen floor. A moment of blankness, then she saw that the tile floor was dirty. She needed to mop it. She touched her face. There was blood.

"Oh honey—" Chuck was babbling to her. "Oh God, honey— I just reacted—" He must have hit her. "I just reacted. I wasn't trying to hit you, I would never do that. I would never do that! I just automatically put my hands up and—" He made a funny wheezing sound.

He must have hit me, she thought. She started to get up. Pull up the legs, get the knees together, roll up. Nosebleed, not bad, get some kitchen paper. Hands were on her arm to help her up, Chuck's hands, he was helping her up. He was saying something she couldn't make sense of.

"Thing is, we gotta save some money, then I'll have my own business and then I'm the boss and I just make phone calls. All these guys working their asses off and we're on a Florida vacation."

She was sitting in the chair. She touched a bruise in her thigh. Right, she'd stumbled into the chair.

"Is that gonna— Yeh that's gonna be kind of a bruise there . . ."

His fingers were touching her face. No, the bruise was in her thigh. She'd bruised her thigh.

"Sorry, my hand just came up automatically and you were coming forward and I kinda lost balance . . ."

Her mind was clearing. There was a paper napkin on the table. She held it to her nose to stop the flow of his words. She swallowed nausea. She saw him standing there sorry, sorry, sorry, trying to make it all better while desperate to get out the door to kiss the old lady's ass.

"Look, I'm going, I'll be back pretty quick, I think, and okay, let's talk about a baby, maybe that'd work out— So I'll be back and we'll talk about a little sister for Joey, okay? And if I get tied up out there I'll give a call. I know I shoulda called, but I think it's just the plumbing, maybe windows banging, you know how many windows we got there . . ." He was zipping his jacket, fumbling for the car keys. "Okay?"

Okay? All okay? She touched the ache in her thigh, murmuring, "I want you here. Just think about that when you're out there tonight. Just think."

His voice was distant to her. "Dee, I can't do any more than what I'm capable. I'm doing the best I can. That's all I can do." Then he was gone.

She sat there, dumb. The bruise on her face began to throb, and she wept, but more a tired leaking at the lids than anything with feeling. After a while she got up, went into the bedroom and changed out of her blue dress. It had a rip at the waist, must have caught on something. No matter, it was pretty much worn out.

Chuck returned after midnight. She had finished mopping the kitchen floor. She put the mop aside, met him at the door, embraced him, mumbled that it was her fault, that she realized he couldn't help it, that he was doing his best. He said again that he should have called her. She said she wasn't blaming him though she knew she was. It would all be fine, she told herself, if she could be a better liar.

They sat at the table and talked—stuff they might buy, Joey's little friends at school, a TV show that was supposed to be good. He was about to bring up the notion of a baby, said instead, "Hey, the floor's clean." She thanked him for noticing it. His neck and shoulders were still as tense as rock. He'd been in over his head from the day he was born.

What happened over the next four years— I knew it in a flash. I fathomed it from my fight with Dwayne and his falling apart. What happened might have happened anyway, but the fight gave Dee an excuse. Not only had he hit her but he'd let her take the blame on herself. The more she could punish him the more she could flog herself for punishing him. Guilt was the drug that she needed more and more.

Nineteen

I once knew an actor, Joseph, tall, bony face, cigarette breath, who told me about the Actor's Nightmare. You're on stage, the audience is watching, but you can't remember your lines or what character you're playing or even what play you're in. "Not much different," he giggled, "than being born." An odd duck, Joseph.

Now I felt I had landed in the Tour Guide's Nightmare. I'm standing there in my uniform and my haircut. I'm the responsible adult, duty-bound to inform, entertain and lead my charges back to their exit through the gift shop. But I lurched through the maze, lost and befuddled and blind, at the end of my stock of jokes. I still had nineteen minutes to go.

My stoppered eyes made out what I'd cruised past for thirty years: the ghosts, the yearning, the torn blue dress. The spirits summoned us into their presence with blatant disregard of the floor plan. My throng huddled about me like mutants with leaden feet, brains of sludge, lidless corneas. I smelt something dead. Must be seepage.

Creeping up to the top of the hour, my little band clung like bird lice. I was five years old when my mother told me that birds had lice. *Don't touch the canary, it might have lice!* After that I could never watch birds.

❖

An outbuilding had been converted to an office. Chuck leaned over his desk consulting blueprints, making notes on a clipboard. He was older. His dark blue suit, lighter weight than before, was slightly rumpled, but he wore it comfortably with the knot of his necktie loosened, his collar unbuttoned. A brisk rap at the door. He tightened the knot, sat at the desk. "Yes?"

The door opened. Marty. "It's me." He stepped in, stubbed his toe on the sill, steadied himself against the jamb, gave a small wave to Chuck and grinned.

"Right. Right. Marty." Chuck swiveled in his chair still focused on the blueprints. "Marty, well, I guess you know what it's about."

Marty closed the door and shuffled to the desk. "Lemme guess." He waxed thoughtful for a moment. "Nope, no clue."

"Well, you know I've cut you a lot of slack."

"Don't they say seventy times seven? Somebody said that. Maybe the Pope. He's kind of an asshole but nobody's all bad." Marty was drunk but acted a little drunker than he was.

Chuck picked up an envelope and held it out. "So here's your severance check. It's pretty generous, I think." Marty was unresponsive. "Well, it's there if you want to pick it up." He put the envelope on the edge of the desk and swiveled to open a file drawer.

Marty picked it up, pretended to peek through the envelope. "Well, maybe you ought to explain to me," he said, "cause I figured you'd be satisfied. I mean, this work is something only a drunken slob would do, so I tried to live up to the job requirements."

Chuck swiveled to face him. "Marty, dammit, you know as well as I do. You've had three formal reprimands for lateness or drunkenness or drinking on the job, and that's not counting all the times I've just looked the other way or all the times I've ignored your sarcastic cracks that maybe you thought I couldn't hear but I think you knew it." He stared at the blueprints. It was more than he had intended to say. "I've tried to deal with what I owe you from way back and what's under the bridge, but you've just . . . Anyway, that's it."

Marty waved at him, grinning. "Better loosen that necktie, it cuts off blood to the brain." More water under the bridge. Mercifully,

Marty spoke at last. "Well, yep, fine, okay, thanks. Very generous. Pleased to contribute to the vision, the master plan." His voice changed. No sarcasm, just one guy to another guy, workmen on the job. "How's the family?"

Chuck hesitated, replied in a voice to match. "They're fine. Joey's in high school next year."

"Time flies like a wounded duck. My dad used to say that. His only joke."

"How about yours?"

"Oh, my wife got a better offer. She also got the house." Marty teetered on the verge of a dismal chronology of his marriage but veered away. He made a vacant gesture and to Chuck's relief shambled to the door.

"Sorry."

"Hey, not every day you can make somebody happy just by getting out." They avoided each other's eyes but the silence held them in its fist. "Well, okay. Gone but not forgotten." He opened the door, waved goodbye and disappeared.

Chuck looked at the blueprints without seeing them. They would come into view soon enough. Yes, dammit, the man was gone but not forgotten.

After making some phone calls he decided to walk up to the current work site to see if Lloyd had any questions. Sometimes he needed to be there just to imagine the feel of the tools in his hands. It was never easy. Watching another guy squaring that doorframe was like seeing somebody kissing your wife.

No reason to lock the office, but Mrs. Weatherlee liked locked doors, so he locked the door. He'd heard that one of the grounds crew had no other job than to lock the dozens of doors at night and unlock them in the morning. He walked with his eyes on the walkway before him, rarely seeing the house from a distance. Maybe it was only the slant of the light, but its sluggish bulk seemed to breathe.

Rooms were breeding like rabbits. At last count they stood at two hundred forty. Work was underway on a northwest extension intended to rise three stories, twenty-two rooms—unless she changed her mind. During the day no more than a half dozen rooms would ever be used, as far as he could tell, apart from the servants' quarters.

It had been a steep learning curve—steeper every year—but he'd managed it. Whole realms of construction were still Greek to him, but the old woman at least understood when she needed an expert. Dynamic loads, settlement loads, thermal stresses—it would take a guy with an engineering degree to work it all out, or else it'd take a very smart lady with lots of time on her hands and a bug up her butt.

Some days he walked into any one of twenty doors and had a feeling he was in her dream. She was back in another century and the world was like a story she'd read or some old movie on late-night TV. Maybe it was just all that money she wallowed in. She'd rambled on about a doll house she'd had as a kid, her own little world that she could stick people into, pretend what year it was, make up your whole life story and tell it to yourself. That's what dollars could do.

With her it was never smooth sailing. From the first interview he still felt the marble in his mouth. She had some itch that could never get scratched. The wall that would close off the Tiffany window: he'd suggested three or four alternatives, but they built the wall. One day make it beautiful, next day mess it up. Still, there was so much he could be proud of having a hand in as long as he didn't ask himself Marty's question: what was it there for, this enormous bulge on the landscape? When his dad built a bridge it was for people to cross.

You study the blueprints, you talk to your foremen, you make your calls, and some odd moment you catch a glimpse of the vast Victorian glacier inching over the acres where orchards used to be. Maybe now you could do that book report: the white whale, the crazy captain, the sailors who followed his lunatic quest. He yells, *I see it! Follow me!* and never a doubt, they follow. Maybe it wasn't even Ahab's idea. Maybe the crew ganged up and said, *You be our crazy boss, we need a nut case to follow*, and if he'd said, *Forget the damned whale, let's go home!* they might have torn him apart.

Sometimes Chuck did think about cutting loose. He could be building houses for people to live in, something besides this empty elegant crypt. But Dee liked spending the money and never came right out to say, *Chuck, quit the job, we'll live on love.* She was more distant sometimes but they never had another big scene. She couldn't know his ache in wanting to read a bedtime story to the little boy, then realizing he's not that little any more and he doesn't want that stupid story. Or knowing you're in over your head, that you're not qualified, and every day you're faking it no matter how good you are. And goddammit, you know you're the best there is.

He told himself, hey, but this was providing jobs, not only to the crews and servants but to a whole chain of suppliers. It was keeping skills alive that were dying out with prefabs. Her vision was crazy, sure, but the Pyramids were crazier and people still gaped at the Pyramids. Even *Moby-Dick*, you might hate it but still you're amazed that he could write all those words when you couldn't even write a one-page book report. And *crazy* wasn't so bad if you made good money at it.

Of course he realized where the money came from. Killing people. Rifles, machine guns, bombs to blow his brother to bits. Was that the price of their big new TV? But the good thing about being a boss was that you didn't have time to think. You're working in your head, not just hammering nails while your mind runs wild. Joey asked, "Daddy, where do they get the money?" But her people didn't start the wars, they just responded to the need. There would always be the need.

My mother, before she had to start working full-time, was always watching soap operas—folks with great hairdos having a lousy day. That must have been the source of my current fantasies, my stunted cultural heritage.

A little after eleven a.m.—a quarter till five, my time—Chuck was talking to Lloyd about the floor studs. A mile away, in the kitchen behind my eyes, Dee took a sip of bourbon from her coffee cup, glanced at the new cabinetwork and picked up the phone, though I tried to blot it out.

"Hi. Wanna come over? Joey's at school till three. Okay. I'm here."

Chuck's talk with Lloyd, who had an unerring instinct for swerving any talk toward football, took longer than he'd intended. There was a subcontract to finalize so he had to get back to his office. He cut across the gardens. Perfect weather with a tang of autumn chill. The gardener had planted large splotches of brilliant hues, a whole range of hot yellows, oranges, and reds against a low silver foliage. Across the garden he observed Mr. Kurosawa standing like a stone statue, staring in his direction. He gave a brief wave and walked on. At the fork, he turned to see if the gardener was still frozen there. No, no one, only Weatherlee House and the glare of the noonday sun from ten thousand eyes.

What happened then— It wasn't ghosts. It was only that strange shift of Time when he saw the old lady from a distance. He was back in the horse-and-buggy days, long before he was even born. He was jumped outside the calendar, the way he'd wake up bewildered before dawn not knowing who he was or where, waiting for it all to seep back into his consciousness. Was everyone like that and did they just not talk about it? Was he the only one?

An open two-seat carriage drawn by a pair of sagging horses pulled up to the front entrance of the mansion—an entrance none ever entered. Sophia Weatherlee appeared in the doorway. She was dressed in the same black mourning, the same long dress, a traveling shawl on her shoulders and a wide-brimmed hat with a veil. The coachman hopped down from his seat and helped her aboard. It was like that English movie Dee was watching before he asked her to change the channel.

Sophia took her place beside Isabella Pardee, who wore green, a light straw hat with a yellow flower. Sophia offered her hand, Izzy took it, the carriage drove off. The two women sat rigidly, determined to exist no matter what century.

Chuck was haunted by Izzy Pardee. The old lady would eat lunch with her niece when she came to visit and one day Chuck was invited. He knew by now that an invitation was a command. The niece was dark-haired, her face always smiling even without the trace of a smile. Like a pool that's deep and still, and you can't tell what's under the water. She asked a few polite questions about his wife and son, and he answered without even hearing himself.

"Mister Chuck Ratowitz is almost like family here," said Mrs. Weatherlee, "so you and he should be better acquainted." She liked any excuse to say *Ratowitz*. He caught Isabella's quizzical look at her aunt. They ate a kind of salad with fish in it, and Sophia rambled on about politics and fish and evolution and some artist he'd never heard of and kept asking him his opinion.

"Hey, better ask me about baseball or, I dunno, how to deal with dry rot," he said, trying to keep it playful. The niece smiled.

They finished with lime sherbet, *sor-bay* the old lady called it. Funny taste. Then she said, "Izzy, show Mr. Chuck the view from the west balcony, which was the product of his labor. One can see orchards from there." The young woman gave her a strange squint, then got up and motioned him to follow.

Yes, the distant apple orchards were beautiful. She stood near and he felt the silence between them. Out of nervousness he started talking—the challenge, the fine materials, what craftsmanship had meant to him from the earliest he could remember. "It's like the flowers out there," he said. "That old gardener there, I watch him with his clippers, I think how does he do all that? But then you just . . . do what you do." He stopped. He was talking like a poet or something.

She looked up at him. Sun and shadow reflected in her eyes, her lips formed a soft smile. He was stunned, as if she were standing before him naked. In that moment his whole life might turn. He had only to reach out, say some words or just move closer. A beautiful woman had opened herself to him. The door was ajar, and beyond it another world. Dee was beautiful, though she'd put on weight, but something was missing that he felt in Izzy Pardee. A future . . .

It passed. He said he'd better get back to work and thanks for the view. She rang for the maid to show him out.

When the two of them met now and then, he managed a friendly nod. Call it being faithful, call it being chicken, but he could never hurt Dee the way he'd hurt the girl in high school. Soon after, Isabella Pardee moved again, farther up the peninsula.

He kept seeing that moment. Maybe he'd imagined it. Maybe the glow in her face was just sun flashing out from behind a cloud, and only his keen urge to break free made him suppose a welcoming passion in this stranger. Movie stars always sensed when the girl was hot for them, but those guys already knew the story. He was thankful he hadn't risked it. He wished he had.

With Chuck's vision I watched the carriage moving away and the mausoleum it left behind. Perhaps that Boston spiritualist was correct, though non-existent: Sophia Weatherlee would achieve immortality by hammers, commissioning an exact replica of herself—her mazeways, her rubble, her hundreds of sterile wombs, a vast edifice with a tiny hermit crab scuttling in its spirals—to mystify future generations. She would live.

In my experience with monuments what attracts you is the insanity. Why do all that? A creation without function, expanding upward, outward, taking, taking, sucking the marrow out of lives and giving back—what? One's cancer becomes the object of devotion but not the object of delight.

In my dreams this house expands to blanket acres, many square miles and millions of rooms, some for the servants, carpenters and groundskeepers given to the tumor's daily sustenance, but most of them vacant though lit by candle, gaslight, or LED. At night the planes flying coast to coast in blackness sight down at the flaring pinpoints. Melanoma.

No matter. Chuck Ratowitz was rid of two worries, the drunken ex-foreman and the unsettling niece. He turned back to his office and his responsibilities.

Twenty

As I watched Chuck Ratowitz pore over the blueprints I recalled my mother's niece telling me about the lines of my hands. My life line and heart line and some other line predicted what would happen to me, which I wasn't sure I wanted to know. Perhaps the blueprints were like the lines of a hand, though how could he know the significations?

I was always loathe to hold hands, afraid that Kathy's or Reggie's lines would tangle into mine the way my mom said that bubble gum would glue your guts together. If my ghostly waifs Chuck and Dee held hands more tightly through these years, might they have kept entangled? Could he read her long afternoons like the lines in the blueprint?

Chuck hated to see his hands. The calluses were soft.

Dee saw herself on the freeway in solid fog going hell for leather. It was four, five years since her crazy art-fair fling, and here she was carting Joey off to eighth grade. She'd gone through shopping sprees, daytime talk shows, romance novels, all the ditzy-homemaker stuff. She stopped the diet pills cold and put on ten pounds—good excuse to start up the pills again. She resembled one of the whiny soap-opera gals that her mother used to watch, stewing in their own sour juice. *Thank God I'm not doing what that stupid cow is doing*, she would tell herself, but now she was the stupid cow.

She didn't jump right back into it. It took a long time before she went out hunting for whatever she knew she couldn't find. Chuck was driving the truck to work, leaving her the car so she wouldn't be stranded. Joey had band practice after school on Wednesdays, so early one Wednesday afternoon she went out to a bar.

Nothing happened. A couple of geezers were shooting pool and a stone-faced couple down at the end of the bar sat stupified. A young black guy came in, perched two stools away and started chatting up the horse-faced redhead tending the tap. She came home, cried a while, ate half a pint of butterscotch ice cream. She hated butterscotch but Joey liked it.

Two weeks later, at a tavern in Capitola, she got picked up by a salesman, got driven to his apartment, got screwed. They hardly even spoke, which was fine with her. Next week another. It wasn't that hard: guys in bars in the afternoon were needy and she was wearing a target on her butt. There was no feeling to it, no thrill like the first time, no tenderness. Beforehand she felt scared, afterwards sour and dirty. That's what she needed to feel.

Then, shaking so hard she could barely stand up, she brought a man back to the house. Luckily she didn't have to stand up long. They did it on Chuck's side of the bed. That brought back the heat, but after he left it took her two shots of bourbon to stop the shaking. Then she went to pick up Joey.

And then Ralph. An accountant, clean-shaven, married. A couple of times a week he'd come to the house—she was used to it now—and she'd lie there being handled, waiting for Chuck to walk in and her life be blown to shreds. *Suicide by dick*, she told herself, and once she came close to laughing, but the loneliest thing in the world was laughing alone. It lasted about a month and then she broke it off. Ralph was nice about it.

By that time she was drinking quite a bit. Between the booze and the pills she was on a wild swing, the way her babysitter Midge pushed little Dee higher and higher until she squealed. One day Chuck mentioned the level in the bottle. She'd used it for cooking, she said, then got a bottle she could hide.

She wasn't always out hunting. Sometimes she just wandered, went to the park, to a coffee shop, to the mall. Over that span of time there were six or seven guys, but she lost track of the months and maybe the number of guys. It was all a blur—though not a blur in the long long minutes of doing it, when they were doing her, when it was being done. Then it was all sharp edges.

Dee Ratowitz was jarred off the playground swing by a trip to the laundromat. Some people go to church to get saved, she went to the laundromat. No need: they had a washer and dryer at home, but she had to escape. She knew she was trying to self-destruct, and some part of her—maybe the silly kid in the yearbook photo—didn't want to. She had a teenage son who needed her, a husband doing his best, even a goddamned unloving mom who loved her. She had to escape her swamp of frazzled inebriation, so she went out to do the laundry.

She had envisioned sitting in the machines' silent rumble, paging some glamor magazine. But there was a guy by the dryers awkwardly folding clothes. Tall, on the heavy side, wearing an Army jacket. Mostly bald, with a big bony nose.

Her laundry sack she set on top of a washer at the far end of the room. She felt out of place. It hadn't been that long since she went to the laundromat weekly but now it was alien territory. She'd forgotten she needed coins. Digging in her purse, she noticed the man holding up a blue pinstripe shirt as if he didn't recognize it. Her purse's contents spilled onto the top of the washer.

The man looked around. She coughed out a laugh. "That's the second time today. Boyoboy." She fumbled to pick up the contents and scraped for change in the bottom of the bag, then gave a sigh and turned to the man. "I'm sorry, I'm dumb, I forgot change. Do you have any?" He gestured toward the change machine by the door. "Oh sure. Yeh." She went to it. "Out of order. Wow. This is my day."

"Well, lessee . . ." He dug in his pockets.

"You were looking at your shirt kinda funny."

"I was trying to think when I ever wore it." He took a coin purse from his jacket, came toward her. She noticed a limp. They exchanged bills for coins.

"Hey thanks. I figured I'd have to take a paper cup and stand on the street." She laughed. "Course I'd have to borrow the cup." She went back to her machine, slotted the coins, started the load. For a long minute she watched the tall bald helpful man folding his laundry, then heard herself speak. "You don't do that real well." Why did she have to speak?

He smiled. "Well, they get wrinkled, but I put'em on they get dirty so the wrinkles don't matter. Less work the better."

"Let me do it." He gave her a quizzical look. "I mean you did me a favor and I just have a thing about wrinkles." He shrugged, laid the pin-striped shirt on the pile as she came past the row of idle washers. She picked up the shirt, rubbed a stain. "Did you pre-soak this?"

"Pre-soak?"

"Pre-soak. You need to put some detergent on the stains."

He stepped back, leaned against a washer. "My wife used to do that, I guess."

She started folding. "She's not doing it now?"

His smile flashed, then vanished. "She kept doing my laundry right up to the time we split. Retained her affection for my overalls."

"Oh hey, you got buttons off there," Dee said. No response. "Tell you something funny if you wanna know," grinning at this man with the big crooked nose. He was scanning the floor but she sensed he felt the grin.

"Why not?"

"I got a washer and dryer at home."

He nodded. "Congratulations."

"But this gets me out of the house. I used to have a job, but then I thought great, I don't have to work, just sit home, be a wife and mommy. That wears pretty thin." She kept folding more aggressively. "I'd go out and buy stuff, any piece of crap, run up these credit card bills and then spend the rest of the day standing at the fridge getting fat." She began sorting socks. "But then I found other distractions."

She saw where she was taking this. She had picked up the moves like a pro. She didn't know she could do it cold sober in a laundromat. Right now she wasn't a muddled Dee or a hopped-up sister to Dee. She was Dee, right there, deliberate, pumping higher and higher on the swing.

"My husband wears a suit and tie. He looks so funny in that."

"White collar, that's the ticket."

"No, Chuck isn't really white collar, not by a long shot."

"Chuck?"

"Chuck. Yeh, Chuck."

"I knew a Chuck. Where I used to work. Nice guy."

Dee leaned against the counter. He was still scanning the floor. She stared blankly at the line of dryers. If you acted indifferent, their eyes would be drawn toward you. She pictured him ogling her.

"No, I had all these expectations," she said. "We were high school sweethearts. And then I was a waitress. I used to do a thing where I closed my eyes and the door would open, I'd look up and see if it was him." She smiled, shrugged. "He'd come in, he wore these boots, and the boots made me feel really small and slender and pretty, just because of his wearing boots. And he'd pick me up, whirl me round, I felt really light. Thought, wow, I would love to feel this light for the rest of my life."

"Well, this was a different Chuck."

She imagined his ugly hands. "Well, this Chuck, my Chuck, is this— What, no, now he's what, Construction Supervisor. In a suit. He works for this nutty lady and he builds a big house that nobody lives in." A sudden impulse: Dee wanted to flee out the door but her laundry held her there, and her demons.

"And his son doesn't hardly remember what he looks like. And his wife is running around behind his back and making herself ridiculous. And doing the laundry a lot but hey, we got clean laundry." No, stop babbling, they don't want to hump a crazy woman, too risky. She was counting the line of dryers over and over.

"No, for a while I was really nuts. Compulsive stuff. Got started on diet pills, then take the pills and run around. Who am I, just three layers of fat with some guy laying on top of it? But I told myself I gotta hold onto Chuck, I gotta keep Chuck, I can't lose Chuck, I'll die." She caught her breath, held it, trying to suffocate the words that clogged her throat.

He was looking away. That was better. They could go somewhere and fuck without ever seeing each other. If she opened her eyes while he was doing his thing she'd see only the baldness. That must be the attraction. She couldn't stand bald guys.

"No, this was a different Chuck. This guy's happily married. Happy wife, happy life."

"You're a poet."

"I must be. I'm out of a job."

Their words were low, brief, pulling the walls in around them. She was on a familiar track: the tremor and the sinking.

"Quit your job?"

"Fired. My old lady bitched about me working all hours but she liked the money, so I just kinda wore out my welcome." He picked up a sock with the heel out. "Like the bottom of my pocket. How long I'm even gonna have a room."

"What's your room like?"

"Come on over and see."

"You'd be surprised if I took you up on that."

"I don't mind surprises."

"Except I have to pick up Joey. My son. From school."

Why say that? There was time. There was plenty of time yet. That was the stock excuse that got her off some smelly bed and out the door. All at once she was the little girl dragging her feet against the swing.

"Well then I could give you a call," he said.

"How about I call you? You got a number?" Back away now. Keep the door open. Even more of a rush when she made that call.

"I got a number. Got my number, got your number, got everybody's number. None of 'em add up."

"You got a sense of humor. Course this is kinda funny, in a laundromat. But it's a place where people go."

"And pre-soak. Pencil?"

Dee laughed, dug in her purse, found a marker. He tore off a corner of newspaper from the counter, sports section, wrote a number. He handed the marker back, stared at the scrap in his hand.

She put her hand on his arm. "I'm Dee." Their eyes met. Slowly a swell of soundless laughter rose in Marty. "What?"

His voice turned on edge. "Pretty romantic. Two losers making it together." She looked at him. "Sorry, I didn't mean that. I meant two free spirits. They meet in a laundromat, she needs change or she needs a change. And he's got just what she wants. He's got some quarters." Her mouth stiffened. "And his wife's a bitch and her husband's a sonofabitch so they got a lot to bitch about. They complain a lot and that's so sexy they can hardly wait. Cause they'll be able to fake it pretty good."

"What's going on with you?" She felt she was shouting but could barely hear her words.

"I'm insulting you, right? I'm just a happy guy acting like an asshole. Marty the Asshole, glad to meetcha."

"I'm doing my laundry!"

Abruptly she turned back toward her washer, banged her hip against a cart. She opened the lid and began pulling the wet clothes out of the machine, stuffing them into the bag. She knew who he was and he knew her. The guy from work, Marty, the man Chuck talked about. She stood as if stark naked.

"No, you're okay, Dee." His voice froze her. "Not two losers. Just one loser, me, and you still working on it." She started for the door. He was saying something, and it wasn't until she was in the car, door locked, that his words penetrated. *Yeh, I knew a Chuck. Happy guy. Big plans.*

She couldn't recall if she sat there crying or just drove home. The man would tell Chuck, Chuck would leave her and Joey would know. For a week she couldn't sleep. Tomorrow would be the day. First time that she truly believed in Hell. One night Chuck came in, no fake smile, barely nodded to her, nothing. She was going to say it before he said it: *Okay, I know he told you. Right, that's me, that's who I am.* As she drew in a breath he went into a rant on the plumbers missing a deadline.

Nothing happened. Maybe the guy hadn't known her or maybe he thought Chuck deserved the slut he got. Whatever, the mirror's reflection showed every wrinkle and blackhead.

No big dramatic change, the way some movie star gave up booze and made her comeback. She didn't flop into the arms of the church, discover a miracle vitamin or start to write her bestseller. She did cut out the pills. That made her so fuzzy for a while that after lunch she would just flick on the TV and sit there hearing the cackle. And she still drank in the afternoon, until one day she went to pick up Joey, ran a stop sign and realized she was driving drunk.

In her mirror she was still the fat ugly cow, useless except to a beautiful son who was already twisting free of his clinging mom. Chuck was making good money now, apologetic—sincerely, she thought—that he was absent so much. He tried to make it up with a motorboat, charge accounts, a home entertainment center and a jolly smile when he came through the door. But something desperate lay underneath. She never lost her respect for him or the longing, but he seemed to be fading like another face from high school. Their plan of building a house was long gone. They bought a new residence—ranch-style, four-bedroom, vaulted ceiling, picture window, perfect lawn. It was bigger, much nicer, much better investment. Unbearable.

Chuck Ratowitz, I could tell, had no notion of this. Parts of us go eyeless long before the eyes snap shut. Nor did he ever suspect that he and his wife and his son—Joey at band practice after school on Wednesdays—were only ghosts conjured up by a gray-headed uniformed runt. None of us do.

Ghosts are scary, movies tell us, but I wonder about the horror they feel themselves, trapped in the soft sticky webs of their palm lines. Did my poor dad Barney Smollet in his slow Arizona demise—wheezing into a pillow, hearing the gasp of his heart—feel trapped in his dying forever? Ghosts have so little privacy. We walk in on their dishwashing, childbirth, copulation, squabbles—all the tiny humili-ations. I hadn't courted these sights but I must have willed them. Perhaps I was seeking kinship with my own fugitive selves. *Hello, are you me? Glad to know you, I'm me too.*

I reached out to touch a doorframe, a tourist, anything real. I felt the foundations shaking. I staggered down a black corridor, light at the end, and it hit me like a fist: this must be death. I wasn't ready. Who'd feed my cat? And, goddammit, I had a good pension plan!

Twenty-one

False alarm. I couldn't escape that easily. It was only a panic attack, and in this world if you don't live in a state of abject terror you're nuts. As a child I was scared of the dark, and yet when darkness became my abode I would only rarely be seized with a vertigo that plunged me down to the slithering inky tongues of the crocodiles.

I slapped my hand to the wall and steadied myself. My gawkers stood huddled in a doorway as if posed for a snapshot. Each was etched in my mind, but now the faces cross-pollinated. I saw the floppy hat on the black guy, his nose bandage on Sammy, the pompadour on the dad, the Mexican lady's teddy bear in the clutch of the college prof, and each one with the killer's eyes.

Is this the Midnight Tour? We wanted the Midnight Tour.

I was hearing a chant, a stutter, that asked for the Midnight Tour at ten till five in the afternoon. Indeed the Midnight Tour was popular: all were given candles to hold, ominous music played, actors flashed through shafts and banged on pipes. In fact these tourists were seeing much more—real spirits, teacups, laundry—but they wanted designer ghosts.

Is it real ghosts? Do people die?

Of course people die. String out any story far enough, people die. Perhaps that's what I told them, but for the first time in my dutiful career I didn't really care. I had lost all orientation. Three decades' trudge over the same route had engraved it deep in my sinews. I was the old horse who drew the carriage through the historic district, trained to the cobblestone ruts, blinders on, shit-bag under my tail. But now the streets were a jumble. I groped my way, heard my bedraggled goon squad following like whipped dogs panting to please. I had never come through these passages. Some walls were finished. On others the plaster had cracked away, exposing lath strips. Still others were only bare studs. My blindness was dim except for ancient slivers of sun through ceiling cracks. I wanted to scream but Management frowned on screaming.

"We are now in the subconscious realms of Weatherlee House. Watch out for Freudian symbols," I joked. The only one who laughed was the skinny man with the eyes.

Then I heard a stumble and muffled curse. Down the passageway the ex-foreman Marty Wenger limped toward us, cap pulled low, army jacket unzipped, shirts layered beneath, carrying a heavy duffel on his shoulder. Nearly upon us, drunk or very tired, he veered into a room to the right. I made my way to the entry. The room was bare, its drywall screwed clumsily to the studs, a sheet cracked down the middle, another loose at the top warping out like a flagrant tongue. No, they didn't use drywall then, but by late afternoon history had lost all credibility. We were simply wading through Time, its sewage up to our chins.

My grunts edged forward behind me. Marty mumbled, as a lost boy might. "Musta built this . . . retirement home . . . love nest . . . Now figure where to crap." He tossed his duffel to the floor, pulled out a sleeping bag, spread it on the boards. I strained to erase him from my sight. His woe was revolting.

I began jabbering whatever came into my wits. "Thirteen bathrooms. She scarcely needed that many toilets, but you don't want to toddle for twenty minutes when nature calls." My words came in a steady spurt. "There was a study done: the number of times we defecate over a lifetime is divisible by thirteen." I couldn't stop. "Public facilities are restricted, of course. Only taxpayers may evacuate. The dispossessed must keep a tight grip." My bowels were seized by an urgent strain to excrete all prattle, all madness, all nonsense once and for all. *Sightless people are invisible!* I shouted in my head.

The tipsy ghost stumbled to the far end of the room. "Good as anywhere . . ." He swayed, wedged himself into a narrow unfinished airshaft, unbuttoned his pants and squatted.

"Hey!"

"Dios nos ayude!"

"Hey, buddy!"

"Beschämend! Vollkommen unannehmbar!"

"We really don't need to see this."

"Sammy, don't look!"

"Mo-om!"

The air crackled with rage. Were they scandalized or envious of his privilege? He caught sight of us. "Hey, it's okay! I'm going! I was checking— I had a thermos here, aluminum thermos—" He stumbled to his feet, pants at his ankles, stark sober.

And at that moment Planet Earth began to shiver. I watched it happen through the narrow vision of Chuck Ratowitz.

Late afternoon, he was at the shed that served as the office of Project Manager. He'd been promoted again and the office was slated for upgrade. He had just finished a pleasant phone call with his Uncle Frank's widow when he felt a tremor. He ran out into the open. The next thirty or forty seconds stretched out forever. The mammoth edifice shuddered and swayed. He was frozen to the spot. The monolith drew a deep breath of indecision, and then it came down.

A third-floor balcony split off, crumbling like a cracker. A jerk at the south wing, like a chiropractor adjusting the neck, and the elegant little sixth-story gazebo launched a slow-motion dive. Weatherlee House shook like a massive wet dog. The fifth floor pancaked, then the fourth. The rest held.

It ended as brusquely as it began, then a terrible wait. His crews and the household staff were scattered outside staring. Chuck saw people turning to him. He was the guy in charge. How would he know when it was safe to go in, when nothing more would collapse? Danger of fire? Was it his fault? Some weight-bearing wall? Miscalculation of torque? In his months of supervision he had brought in county inspectors, corrected code violations, enforced the standards, done all he could. The last thing anyone could expect in earthquake country was an earthquake.

Then he realized: she was in there. He could hear screams. He could see her tiny figure buried under rubble or clawing the curtains with broken fingers. He would crash through the door to find her face down bleeding into the carpet. He set himself into motion, organized crews to work their way into blocked passageways. Then he remembered Joey and Dee. He called. They were fine.

The crews worked all night and into the next day. The fire department came and went. Other union men showed up to volunteer, so they had as much manpower as it was safe to use. Every time they moved a fallen joist Chuck went cold with fear that a clutch of rooms would come rumbling down, but nothing happened.

And Sophia Weatherlee wasn't there. Mid-morning he got a call: she and her visiting niece had been on her houseboat in Burlingame. She had bad dreams the night before and a tremor in her hands, but otherwise only a nasty slosh of the boat. "Our moorings held," she said. Chuck reported that none were seriously injured: two maids suffered abrasions but that was it. Later it occurred to him that there had been at least thirty others indoors—maids, cooks, the old guy who tended the furnaces, repairmen fixing an elevator—but his only concern was for Sophia Weatherlee.

The crews went to work clearing rubble. There had been well over three hundred rooms: now that all of the fifth and sixth floors were gone, a hundred and sixty remained. It was testament to the quality of the workmanship that the damage wasn't worse. That was Mrs. Weatherlee's opinion, and Chuck nodded in agreement to her empty words.

She ordered the upper stories cleared, new roofing for the remainder. There were oddities resulting from the repairs: doors opening to absent chambers, a little yellow room opening out into empty space, stairways to ceilings.

"Could we do a balcony there?" Chuck asked of the door to nothingness.

The old woman's stare was the way his mother had stared when her little boy asked for an elephant. "Things taken away are taken away for a reason," she said. Henceforth the building would expand outward, not upward. The orchards would give way to more cells of the organism. Weatherlee House would metastasize.

"We're fine," said Dee when he called forty minutes after the quake. The first shock had hit right after Joey got home from band practice. They ran out to the front lawn, felt it shake for fifteen, twenty seconds, then the heavy shock that seemed to last forever, but the structure held. They waited a while, went back in. She tried to call Chuck, but the phone was out. He finally called. All they lost, she told him, were some dishes she hadn't put away and the pink glass cat, a gift from her mom. "Its tail snapped off," she said. "Good riddance."

"Lotta work went into that rubble." He tried to sound chipper but couldn't suppress the cry in his voice. She told him how sorry she was for his pain. He thanked her.

Years later she looked back in wonder at those few seconds. It took an earthquake, she confided to a friend, to wake her up. After her crazy season of self-destruction she had settled into numb routine—being mom to a son who was hither and yon like the wind, wife to a man she used to know. *The fog comes on little cat feet*—some poem from high school ran in her mind—but the fog was closing around her like a big beefy fist. Now something had reached up out of Mother Earth and shaken her like a frantic mom snatching her kid out of traffic. Something had snapped besides the glass cat's tail.

The Beast of the Apocalypse heaved, bellowed and stilled. My goslings' faces were blank. The quake cut off all questions. "So welcome to California." I gave a reassuring chuckle and waited for someone to ask how we might be feeling the 1906 earthquake more than a hundred years later. Or was it the 1989 Loma Prieta or one of the countless rock-waggles that shook up the yuppies on special occasions? I chose to let them wonder. I had to accept the flimflams of Time.

I stumbled ahead with my lecture. "Mrs. Weatherlee was trapped in her bedroom, hysterical. The workmen, trying to reach her through the rubble, heard her playing her grand piano to appease the savage spirits. She played a Chopin polonaise over and over again." I heard myself telling lies I'd never told before. "The front thirty rooms were boarded up. She feared to repair the damage she presumed was punishment for her guilt." Why was I spouting this crap? "Oddly, there was no damage to the six kitchens of Weatherlee House. Why six kitchens? All the staff to feed, plus the hungry ghosts."

Get me outta here! This is nuts!

Somewhere below, a heavy pounding and a voice. Where the ex-foreman had squatted over the air shaft the flooring had collapsed. The bony-nosed man was trapped at the base of my brain.

Call the crews! Get me outta here! He pounded. *I'll die in here, you fuckheads! I'll stink! You'll smell me in every room!* Yes, he stank. *Call the cops, dammit!*

Call the cops to rescue a spook? My troupe turned to me like a musical chorus who'd lost their lyrics. The Austrian, the Mexican lady, the corn-fed Iowans, the lady prof, the black nose, the psychopath—my multicultural clump. Only teenage Samantha was impassive. She dug in her fanny pack, found a lipstick, removed the cap, then held it absently as she fingered a scar on her lip.

A smile squirmed across my face. A prophetic glimpse: future generations by the thousands, millions, would make pilgrimage to a cathedral haunted by a defecating ghost.

Twenty-two

We had walked miles from the sealed-off wing. Burrows branched like arteries meandering out from the beast's dead heart. A blank wall twenty yards ahead would dog-leg toward another blank wall twenty yards ahead. I led, they followed—an odyssey within a hamster wheel. In my bones it was precisely 4:53 p.m. but each minute took years. My ghosts were aging fast.

The corridor bent, doubled back, made a squiggle of jogs, then opened to a hall that stretched like the endless trudge between airport terminals. When had this vast new suburb come into being? Had Weatherlee House consumed orchards, colonized neighbors, licked whole valleys with its thick coated tongue? Or might we be in those underground shadowlands where they store the great bombs for Last Judgment? I could hear the deep whine of missiles rising.

I saw a dim figure, an ambient smudge whom I seemed to be following. Of course my eyesight was nothing more than a metaphor, winking out at the top of the hour.

It was Chuck, a silhouette in a well-tailored suit. His gait was lumbering, tense, as if pretending calm while pursued by a bear. At intervals he passed through sharp light and I could see his rigid face. A lamp shone at the end of the passage. He paused, entered the room. I came forward with my breathless flock of goslings.

We found ourselves in a dining room with an oval table of heavy walnut and four upholstered dining chairs, a dark dappled yellow. The walls were a gentle off-white with several paintings of sea and surf reflecting the glow of a ceiling fixture. The room decor appeared unnatural to Weatherlee House. The couple had balked at living there, but Weatherlee House had ingested their neighborhood.

I stood in the doorway but my acolytes filtered past me into the room. They spaced themselves along a sideboard over which hung the print of some fruit by Cezanne that I recognized from college. Or perhaps it was there because I recognized it. The little black man Ike walked briskly to the far corner, sat in an armchair and picked at the Band-Aid on his nose. I wasn't about to interfere.

Dee sat at one end of the table, a coffee cup before her. She nodded to Chuck. He set a leather briefcase at the opposite end, unlatched it, took out a manila folder and sat, adjusting his necktie. He always had trouble with knots.

"How's it going?" he asked.

"Fine. Coffee?"

"Sure. Yeh. No, I guess— No, thanks."

Chuck fingered the folder. "So I got the idea we might work this out."

"Fine."

"You need something to write with?"

"I'm okay. You take notes."

"Where's Joey?"

"He's at the play. Didn't he tell you? He's in the senior class play."

"Yeh, I'm trying to get there to see it. Maybe tomorrow. It's still going tomorrow, isn't it?" No reply. "Funny, I wouldn't have figured he'd be interested in plays."

"He's interested in Sally Jarvis and she's interested in plays."

"Oh. Yeh." Chuck forced a laugh. "Yeh, he's at that age. Wow." He took a small notebook and pen from his breast pocket. "So I thought we might work this out." No, he'd already said that. "You sure that's what you want?" No reply, but it wasn't really a question, just a reflex. "So okay, the idea is we work this out before the lawyers get it tangled up any worse, okay?"

"Okay by me."

The Austrian edged up to the table and sat in a chair, staring intently at Dee. The skeletonic Dr. Quint came forward to sit across from the Austrian. She was writing in a small blue diary. I noticed Dee glance toward her. All was clouded but Dee was in keen focus.

Chuck turned the pages of his notebook, clicked his pen several times, pursed his lips. His eyes glazed over, then closed.

He had seen the change coming. At supper one night after the earthquake she said, "I guess I got pretty shaken up." That's all she said, just left it up in the air. He supposed she was starting to feel empty-nest now that Joey was finishing high school. With Chuck's encouragement she had been taking classes at the college, and in January she started back to school full-time. It seemed to do her a lot of good, as if she'd thrown open the window and gasped fresh air. In a way he was jealous—it wasn't long ago that she'd looked at him that way—but he thought that it'd be good for the marriage and for a while it was. The marriage was the main thing after all.

Wrong. Three years from the start, right after they'd finished redecorating their new house, she graduated with a B.A. He took her out to dinner to celebrate, and as soon as she'd finished her salad she asked for a divorce.

"How come?"

"You're already married," she said. It took him a while to figure that one out.

He moved to rooms on the grounds. It was a relief in a way, since he was constantly on call. Dee stayed in the house with Joey, though she talked about moving to San Jose to care for her mother who was bedfast with arthritis and what all. Chuck was surprised that after all the bad blood between the two there was a kind of a truce.

It had taken some time to get around to serious talk. Finally, when the lawyers kept dragging their heels and piling up fees, they decided to sit down and work out a settlement. For the first time in three months they were together in a room whose decor they had marveled at. Now it was alien to them both.

"Feels strange," he said. "I guess we'd only been here, what, ten months, twelve? Beautiful, though. It should bring a pretty good price, I mean, real estate's going sky high. Although it'd definitely do better if we held it a while, rent it, say, but I guess we better settle it." He waited for her to respond or at least to sip her coffee. She sat without expression. "So, savings. Any thoughts?"

"Is there any?"

"Some. Not a lot. The house kinda shot most of it. Even split?"

"Whatever. Except for Joey's bonds. That's his."

"Right. Car: you should take that, you need it." He was about to mention the new company vehicle he had just acquired but references to the job were better left unsaid. "So, the house—" Back to the house. "Assuming we still want to sell it we should do pretty good, according to the agent, he says even already it's appreciated, although there's gonna be capital gains to pay, but we just split the equity, I guess, unless we want to hang onto it, rent it for a while, just to see if—"

"Sell it."

"Right."

Chuck made a note. Dee took the first sip of her coffee. Ready again with the notes, he asked, "What about all the various stuff? Household stuff?"

"I don't want much. Some kitchen things. I'll come next Saturday, take what I need, everything else can go. I'd like to start fresh."

Start fresh. Chuck tasted the sourness rising. He heard her ask something about his mom. Had he told his mom? Why was she asking about his mom when she knew his mom didn't give a shit about him, that she was in Arizona with some new guy, starting fresh. He shook his head.

"I like your mom," she said.

"That's news to me." Sharper than he meant it. There was a scene like this in a movie he'd seen. They'd sat down to work out the settlement and came to see in a flash how much they were still in love. Dee must have seen it too. Or maybe he'd seen it on late night TV. Long time since they'd gone to a movie.

Several tourists edged closer. Were they moved or amused? Felt a kinship with these lonely souls? Or saw only the torment of clowns rehearsing their pratfalls?

I half expected Chuck to rise, fling the papers, scream an obscenity, flee down the corridor pounding the prison walls as he ran, cracking the bones of his fists. But he just sat there watching her sip her coffee. After a moment he picked up the thread of what he'd practiced saying. She could stay on the group health insurance for six months. He'd send her the papers. Alimony, fine, if it wasn't more than they were spending now, whatever she considered was reasonable. "And if we could maybe call it something besides alimony," he mumbled, attempting cheeriness. Child support and Joey's college, sure—he wanted to be a good father.

"So what do you want for visitation rights?"

"Well, I'll do my best."

Her lips formed a faint smile. Had he said something wrong? He was trying to be agreeable. She started to sip her coffee, then set the cup down abruptly. He forced a laugh.

"Hey, this is pretty complicated. Could we just talk a little?"

"Talk about what?"

"Well, how are things going? I'm kinda worried about you, not that—" Dead end. Try to back out. "Not worried, but I just— I kinda wonder, you know, how it's going or if . . ."

She took a quick sip, set the cup down, pushed it away. For the first time her eyes opened directly to him. "Well, the only pills I'm taking now are vitamins, and I haven't cheated on you for quite a while, so I think I'm doing okay."

He heard the words, but it was like listening to Mexicans talk—he guessed they meant something but didn't know what. Why was she saying that? Did she think he'd done the same? Did she think he deserved it? Did she just have a mean streak he'd never seen before?

Dee spoke. "How about your power boat? The storage bills are coming here."

"Power boat. Well, it's not mine, it's ours. I named it after you."

"Whatever."

"Dee, Christalmighty, I'm just saying— Can you just look at me and—"

"Shut up!" bellowed one of my band. The others turned in surprise. Bud Padgett, the smiling Iowa insurance man, the hat lady's husband, wasn't smiling now. His face was squeezed tight, pink with rage. Abashed, he stammered, "Just . . . kinda . . . I mean . . . keep it down?" There must have been a story there, to be told on tours of their three-bedroom Craftsman home in Cedar Rapids, Iowa, if anyone signed up for the tour.

Neither ghost gave a sign of having heard.

Dee gave a slight flick of her hand that might have meant *Sorry* or it might not. She had resolved not to get emotional or say anything hurtful, to take her coffee in even sips with a deep breath in between. Now she despised herself for what she'd said. She knew Chuck loved her as best he could, that in his inarticulate way he was crying out, that she was as cold and mean as her mother always told her she was. He had helped her draw back from the abyss. "You've got free time, we've got the money, why not go back to school?"

She'd enrolled for two courses, Intro to Art and Intro to Lit. Strange being this chunky housewife among all the trim tanned kids. She managed to burn off a few pounds and congratulated herself that she'd suffered as much as all the crazy geniuses they studied. At least she knew more about life than her kiddie classmates and she didn't have their worries about the future. She had no future.

At first she coddled that cozy old rush of guilt. Here she was reading books while Chuck was slaving away, blaming him for what he was making possible for her. But she tried to cook a good dinner whenever he was home, stop complaining when he wasn't, and be loving when he needed that. But there came a dawning: there was a world out there. Every book was a secret and she was the snoopy little girl again. Sometimes what she glimpsed cut too close to the bone. Penelope waits twenty years for Odysseus, then he shows up—and takes off again. That hurt so much she had to laugh. And the day she started to see those dull supermarket faces through Rembrandt's eyes . . .

Second semester she got into poetry with a different prof. He was a young guy, funny and smart. She found her mind wandering off the structure of sestinas and onto his curly red hair. One day after class she stopped to check an assignment and he asked if she'd like a cup of coffee. They walked down to the college snack bar and she wondered where this was going.

It went to having coffee frequently after class, nothing more. A spark, no question, but neither took the risk of blowing it into flame. If he had made a move she wasn't sure what would have happened. He was married and in a funny way that gave her more license. But she had never known there was so much pleasure in talking. Closeness had always meant sex, simple as that, but this was a closeness she hadn't known. Chatting about Yeats, for godsake! *The silver apples of the moon, the golden apples of the sun.*

Next year he was gone to a better job in Milwaukee. But that was her first *friendship* with a man, and it made more difference in her life than all the grinding on mattresses. If she could only tell that to Chuck—but she never could.

She had accumulated college credits willy-nilly but then she enrolled full-time. Chuck appeared to be relieved that he wasn't coming home to a slow-boiling crock of resentment, and they felt a spurt of renewal. It didn't last long. Something in him was . . . inert? defunct? What word would Yeats have come up with? After five semesters taking nearly a double course load she graduated with a B.A. in Comp Lit. And she asked Chuck Ratowitz for a divorce.

The night before graduation they made love, the first time in three weeks. It was good. She lay sleepless all night, hearing her mother's old graven words: *cold . . . unloving . . . liar . . . sneak.* Stay with him till he pays your way through college then dump him? By dawn she'd accepted that she'd have to put off telling him, at least till Joey was out of high school. By then maybe something would change, maybe. But next evening at the restaurant she finished her salad and the words came out.

He hadn't seemed surprised. He made some half-hearted quibbles, suggested maybe a counselor, asked what he could do to change.

"Chuck— What I see— How do I—" *Find the words, you've got a B.A. for chrissake.* "Okay. Say you've got a hobby and you're absorbed in it. But you get involved in other things, and you really miss your hobby. You think you'll get back to it some day, but you never do. You never do. I'm your hobby. You want to get back to it and you never will."

He had sat staring at his plate with the bits of gristle he'd trimmed from the steak. Several times he started to speak, then finally managed it. "What's that, one of your metaphors, like in English class?"

No more negotiations for the present. Chuck rose from the table, said something inaudible, put the folder in his briefcase, turned and left the room.

Start fresh. What would be my fresh start at the five-o'clock bell, at the end of the tour, on the first day of the rest of my slow decline? My spirits might be revealing something to me besides my own blindness. If I could ask them what I really wanted to know, if I knew, it would be like seeing babies born. But I could only see the sad farce they played before me—the slapstick thwacks, pies in the face, squeals of pain, the same old routines, same old, same old.

"Questions?" I asked my flock. When they spoke at last, they spoke in whispers as they might to a child awakened from a dream. And I heard her speak, though her lips didn't move.

What happened? Didn't you love him? Why do you need the car?

"Well, we split. I thought it'd kill me but it didn't. I found a job."

Do you have a job? How did it make you feel? What are they asking for the house?

"Saddest moment of my life when he didn't care about visitation rights. Giving up being a father. But he'll be okay on child support, he'll be good on that."

What do you dream about? Do you go to church? How do you cope with divorce?

"Well, I decided on library work, went back for a master's in Information Science, what they call it now. Sounds better than just lending books. Joey's off to college."

How old is your son? What's he majoring in? What time do you have? Que hora es? Wie spät ist's?

Dee looked directly at me. That instant my vision was as keen as a razor at the wrist. I believe she saw me. I believe she was speaking to me.

"The first thing we ever got, we got a waffle iron. We never made a waffle."

Twenty-three

Dee and I were alone. My entourage was still there, but their faces were faded into the dappled upholstery or Cezanne's basket of fruit. In that minute she must have needed to tell someone—even a blind stranger with a terrified smile—that she was in fact pregnant with a future. She saw into my black ovals and she spoke.

So I didn't see Chuck again till we were in court for the formalities. We said what we had to say and that was it. He did manage to get to Joey's graduation and we said hello. He asked me how things were going, I said okay. His graduation present to Joey was a new red Honda Civic. Mine was a Timex watch.

Joey applied for the Naval ROTC scholarship. I said that was nuts, that his dad could afford the tuition. It meant four years in the Navy after college, then four years in the Reserve. "The Navy isn't Boy Scouts, they fight wars," I told him. "I'll be an officer," he said.

After all my nagging about his grades I kept hoping his grade point would be too low to qualify. But he just scraped by, and off he went to Cal State Fresno to study engineering and how to get himself killed. "Why Fresno?" I asked. "Some of my friends are going there." I said nothing. I didn't want to sound like my mom.

And Mom, she went downhill faster than I'd expected. I'd hoped this might be our chance to get closer, make it up, but between my studies and her pain meds that didn't work out. When she died I had more free time, took a heavy course load, finished my master's in less than two years. Damn tuckered out, as my grandpa would say.

I'd had it with ceremonies, so I got my diploma in the mail. Joey was funny about it. He came home for the weekend, said he'd cook us up a big dinner to celebrate. For him it was a challenge to fry an egg, so I wondered what he would do. Here he came with two big TV dinners, popped them in the nuke and that was our celebration. We laughed together about it and I remembered how I used to laugh with Chuck. He had Chuck's laugh.

He wore his uniform and it suited him. He looked a lot like Chuck: curly hair, good shoulders, same little curve to the lips. I was glad he'd started to get along with his dad. His ears were like my mom's.

I was lonely. Library jobs were hard to come by unless I moved to Montana. I told myself I wanted to stay closer to Joey, but I think I was still a little bit married to Chuck. I put Mom's house up for sale, found a small apartment in Sunnyvale and a job as a dental receptionist. "I could use the LC catalog numbers to shelve the patients' teeth," I joked to my boss. He didn't get it.

No time for men, not that I wanted that, so then of course I met a guy. Me and arts fairs: this time it was one of the artists. Tall, skinny, bony face and crazy mad funny eyes. He did these landscapes in big blocks of color, dark clouds, sun blazing through, and somewhere there were always a couple of skeletons dancing or snoozing or making love. No woman would want something like that in her living room, but she surely might want Zachary. I was free and I did. Long story, but it didn't take long.

Then I wanted something else. I told myself no, that's nuts: I had my freedom, a guy who was fun to be with, no strings. But it hit me like the swatter swats the fly. My common sense didn't want it, but the core of me wanted another child.

I was forty-two and didn't have time to go shopping. I had a boyfriend who'd been married twice and stated firmly that he didn't want to risk strike three. But it wasn't a husband I wanted. Zach came to dinner one night and I made lamb shanks. Chuck had been a sucker for lamb shanks. After dinner I took the risk.

"Zach, I'd really love it if you gave me a little present."

"Like what?"

"How about a baby?"

Before he could dive for the door I managed to lay it out. I didn't want a husband or a responsible daddy—Zach barely had change to feed the parking meter. I would pay for a lawyer to draft the agreement and he could see his offspring as much as he wanted or as little. "I know it's nuts," I said, "but something tells me it's right." I pretended some deep feminine intuition, but there was no little chickadee twittering in my ear. It was just my ovaries' last wild yowl.

He sat a long time staring at his cup with those mad funny eyes. "Okay," he said and got up to make more coffee.

Zach was the right choice. There wasn't a conventional bone in his head. We worked out all the contingencies with the lawyer, signed our names a dozen times and waited to go "bareback," as he called it, until I'd sold Mom's house and had the savings to quit working a year or so. The day it went into escrow we banged our brains out.

Nine months later, Millie. Camilla, actually, after my grandma. Zach was there at the birth, and Zach's other girlfriend Patty—he'd told me that at the outset—and their friend Deena, a midwife. Zach looked at the baby the way he looked at one of his paintings: he liked it but he wasn't sure where it came from or what it meant.

About my sixth month I had called Joey to tell him what was happening. "Oh," he said, and then, "How'd you do that?"

"The good old-fashioned way."

I think he was a little bit shocked, but I figured it's okay to shock your kid, he'll survive it. A few weeks after the birth he came home and saw his baby sister. Millie peered up at him and they were in love. That was a time I thought again of Chuck.

I quit my dentist job and lived on savings for a year, just a mommy, nipple-on-request, reading my way through Neruda and Mary Oliver and Stephen King—once I learned the word *eclectic* I was shameless in my choices. Zach was helpful without hovering. But then he and Patty had the chance to move to a farm in Oregon, and we all hugged a sad goodbye. I told myself, hey, you know better than to feel abandoned. Sure, I knew better but my tear ducts didn't.

The road runs smooth across the years, it hits a bump and then runs smooth again. It's three years later, I turn around and my son's finished college, headed into the Navy. Millie is three, rips around like Joey did at that age. And I've scored a library job in Mountain View so I'm learning to juggle well enough to join the circus.

One day a little round Mexican guy comes into the library, puts a book on the counter and tells me, smiling, that it's idiotic, offensive, shouldn't be on the shelf. I think he must be some kind of religious nut but I check the title: *Basic Motorcycle Repair*. I'll pass the word along, I tell him. "Adios," says he.

Two days later I run into him at the coffee stand where I stop before work, and we chat. He does motorcycle repair, he says, and invites me to his shop. "Sorry, no time." He invites me to dinner. "Sorry." He invites himself to dinner at my place. "Sorry, gotta run." I'd have been annoyed if he hadn't been so jolly about it.

Jump forward two months and we're lovers. I would have never imagined I'd feel attracted to someone dissecting a carburetor, but that's what finally hooked me: watching an artist. Like watching Zach painting or Chuck planing a shelf. He'd come roaring up on his Harley in a cloud of boyish glee. He'd stir up a batch of *gazpacho*. He'd run his hand across my face, mumbling something in Spanish, and I liked not knowing what he said. Millie loved his clowning and played with his little brush mustache.

Then Zach showed up. Turned out they hated farming and every drizzly square inch of Oregon. I had told Diego the whole tangled story of Zach and Millie and Patty, not sure how he'd react, but he had just looked, well, thoughtful. Now they were coming to dinner. I was on pins and needles. I had never lost my feelings for Zach but I accepted that I couldn't have it all. I was afraid of some glance striking a spark and leaving cinders and ash. But Diego made *chiles rellenos* and everybody was happy.

They left and Diego read my mind. "You want him, that's fine." I panicked: he meant he was walking out. Not so. He embraced me, patted my butt. "Whatever makes you happy, Dee." I had heard those words before. This time I accepted them.

It took some getting used to. Zach was dubious and Patty could hardly believe that a mustachioed Mexican wouldn't wield a jealous machete. But these were peculiar people. So was I, and I had to accept the fact. I could be with Diego or Zach unless they had other things to do, and sometimes Patty and I would leave the guys and go to the ocean with Millie. The Three Weird Sisters we called ourselves. And thanks to the wonders of the Web, weaving past and present, I got an email. It was my chummy poetry prof with whom years back I'd drunk flirtatious coffee. Sweet to be a memory. I bookmarked his website.

I was forty-nine, Millie was seven and Joey was twenty-eight when he was killed. I swore to myself he'd be safe once he finished his active duty, but they called up the Reserves. He'd been there two weeks. The coffin was closed for the funeral. There wasn't enough left of him to look at.

She stopped speaking. No wonder: none of that had happened yet. I was only reading the furrows in her face.

Tben it struck me. In this world unfolding to me, in me, of me, I had never directly seen a child. These ghosts spoke of children, bore them, named them, read stories, but no child's face appeared directly before me. No future beckoned them, except by hearsay. There were mothers, mothers bereft, mothers nagging or loving or drunk—all in a childless world.

Like the rest of us, the ghosts had to trek across the calendar day by day trying not to step on the cracks. Dee Ratowitz would rise from the table, take her coffee cup to the kitchen and feel her way through the years.

Twenty-four

I removed my glasses, wiped my cheeks, rubbed the bridge of my nose where the frames bit in. I suspected the ghosts had filched my eyes and the old lady was rolling them in her dish of marbles, ripe to be sucked. I put my glasses on and lo, night was night and my tiny sparkling fish swam in black water. All of us—myself, my seekers, my ghosts, the black widow at the core of it all—were counting off each cricket chirp till the top of the hour.

"Don't we feel a pulse?" The old lady's words crept out like timid mice. "We know so little what makes our so-called heart beat so implacably. Some spark at the core? These heartbeats go on . . ." She held another wad of tangled red yarn. "Well, so be it," she snapped, letting her clot of yarn fall into her lap.

I clutched my sanity like a rock-climber groping for a finger-hold, held in a timeless dangle. I heard my tourists shamble in but could see only the black-clad figure against Shakespeare's frenzy of sunlight. Then I noticed the tube. From the back of her wrist proceeded a thin plastic tube that ran up to a Y-connect, two ducts ascending to bags of fluid suspended from a stainless steel stand. One bag of liquid was clear, the other had a greenish tint. Delicately she touched the tape securing the tube into the back of her wrist, as if to calm it. She was getting on in years—from old to ancient to legendary.

The Project Manager stood at a distance, his blue suit vivid in the sun.

"So you're late." She spoke distractedly.

"Yes ma'am, I am. Medication all right?"

"I feel this thing in my hand." She brushed it as if brushing away a fly, then regarded the bags that dripped into her. "Nutrients, do you suppose? Poison? Dishwater?"

Chuck Ratowitz smiled, nodded, letting a silence settle between them. Answering too readily, he had come to know, gave the impression that he hadn't really absorbed her words. She would immediately forget whatever she said, but she wanted it remembered by someone in her employ.

"Well, it's what keeps us going," he said. "Nurse says you're stable. I guess the doctor just wants to make sure. Not take any chances." She raised two fingers of her intubated hand and made a tiny gesture: *Cut it short*. He halted: another silence. "So now, the paper-hangers are coming in today, coming to work in here as I mentioned? And so I expected maybe you'd want to go out to the Sun Room?"

"For the pink?"

"Pink wallpaper, yes ma'am."

She stared at him. The sun caught her glasses and for an instant her lenses were glaring blank holes in her face. She glanced up again to the IV bags. "Yes, pink. As a girl I was surrounded by pink, of course. They need to make sure you know you're a little girl, though I was quite aware of the fact. I was muffled in pink, suffused, marinated in pink. I hated pink." She touched the tape that held the tube in her wrist. "Though now I find it comforting. Uplifting, somewhat. Although my brother once made a joke about Negroes never being in the *pink* of health. He thought it was funny. A sweet man, really, but stupid."

Again her eyeless stare. "Did you know it's my birthday, Chuck?"

"Yes ma'am, I do." From behind his back his hidden hand brought forth a small cake, vanilla frosting with seven pink candles in a circle. "Happy birthday."

She peered at it a moment. "That's cute." She ran her free hand over her face.

He set the cake on a side table, took a book of matches from his pocket. Putting down a thick folder, he lit the candles, stuck the burnt match in the matchbook, put it in his pocket. "Da-da-dahh-dahh-dahh . . ." He mumbled a few notes of the song, then picked up his folder and let the tiny candles burn. She stared at the IV bags.

"So here's the report on last week, ma'am. Photos of the South Quarter, with plans for the extension, based on your plans." He handed her the folder. She placed it gingerly on her lap and opened it. She glanced through the photographs, unfolded a blueprint and studied it.

"These are my plans?"

"These are based on your plans. These are faithful to the spirit of your plans."

"What does that mean? *Faithful*? Are these my plans?"

Chuck started to answer, hesitated, spoke. "Well, as I explained, Miss Weatherlee, these days we have to conform to code, and so your consultants, your licensed architects, do have to make adjustments to bring everything into conformity. Being that now the project is so extensive that we're dealing with a lot more than just residential construction. There's whole systems that require a level of engineering and that's why we have to—"

"Are these my plans?"

"—Why we have to do things a bit different than we did before. But we went through all that, that's why we brought Perkins-Westerfield into the project—"

"Are these my plans?"

"Yes. These are your plans."

The sun had changed and her pupils hardened to pinholes. The eyes of a bird, Chuck thought. Even the songbirds who sang in the morning peeked through eyes like tiny black stars. She scanned the blueprint vaguely and ran the fingers of her intubated hand across the lines of a section. A candle winked out.

"There are other people here."

"As I said, the paper-hangers are coming. I can ask the girls to bring you out to the Sun Room. We need to clear this out completely so nothing gets messed up."

"Damaged."

"Right."

"I am already damaged. Not fatally as yet." She picked up the tangle of yarn, began to pull at it. He took the folder, folded the blueprint. "Very well then, please call Miss Grace."

"I think it's Hallie, ma'am. Grace is long gone, as I recall."

"Dead?"

"Not that I know. Just gone. People go."

"They do. I have in mind a maid named Grace. The name strikes a chord. She had a mother." She let go the yarn, touched the tape on her hand, straightened the plastic IV, spoke in a half-whisper. "The maids were speaking of derelicts."

"There have been derelicts."

"How many?"

"A lot."

"Why?"

"It happens. That's just the way it happens."

"What are we doing?"

"More security."

"What about the people?"

"We deal with'em."

"How?"

"Different ways."

"Well, it's not adequate. There are odors. An odor, you can smell it. I'm not imagining things. Voices, there's a voice. The foreman."

"Foreman?"

"The man who brought you in. He had a limp. He lost a leg in some stupid war. We joked about it."

"Marty? That's Marty Wenger. That's taken care of. He had to be fired. He had a drinking problem."

"Don't they have treatment plans for that?"

"Yes, they do have."

"I make donations for things like that." She busied herself with the yarn. "It's all in a tangle!"

He was used to these spasms. He had learned to stand still, to wait through the minutes her ditties required. Now he was waiting to drive up to San Mateo for a meeting at noon. It would take him through Sunnyvale, where Dee lived now. Last time through he had turned the radio loud to blot out the thoughts. Another pink candle expired. He turned to go.

The sun had dimmed. Sophia looked up. She was in a soft afterglow. "There are people in this room," she said in a quavering voice. "Who else is in this room?"

"Well, paper-hangers pretty soon. Would you like to go to the Sun Room?"

"Who are these people?"

"Dennis, Arturo, Reggie, they've worked here before, they do a good job, I can vouch for'em."

"Put your hand on the back of my neck." Her face was twisted like the wad of yarn in her lap. A smile frosted over the terror beneath it. Chuck took a ceremonial pause, stepped forward and placed his hand as directed. "You're not afraid of me now."

A burst of hushed voices. *We kinda got lost. Is the cake to eat? My sister had diabetes.*

Sophia tensed against the hush. She sensed the watchers. "Are these people dead?" she said faintly.

"No, nobody's dead."

"Did I kill them?"

"No, Miss Weatherlee, that was the box hedges. There was a frost. They're replanted. Mr. Kurosawa took care of it." He stepped back.

"Leave your hand!" He placed his hand again on the back of her neck. "That's enough." He removed his hand. She touched the plastic tube, gently picked up the lump of yarn and began to stroke it softly as if petting a cat. After a moment, "And how is your little family?"

Oh fuck, not that. His little family. A wave of rage, then an ebb, the ocean sucking back its tide. Years passed in a hot jag of pain, a slash of memory.

Stagnant water. He had expected that when the divorce was final he could search for companionship. Stupid to think that he still should be faithful, but there was something in him that made him that way. Several times he drove all the way to San Francisco and paid for sex. Then the long drive home.

Isabella Pardee had been living in one of her aunt's houses, but she would come to visit the old lady. Once, Chuck met her in the garden and they said hello. Other times he saw her from a distance. Then he heard she was moving back East and hoped she might stop to say goodbye but she didn't. He dated a few women but he never could think of much to talk about.

Things happen for a reason, his uncle always said, and he tried hard to figure the reason that he was alone. At least he didn't have to feel guilty juggling a home life with his obligations. He ought to do something for enjoyment, but he had never cared for TV and followed sports only because that's what men talked about if they didn't talk politics and on the job you couldn't do that. He only wished he had something besides the work.

Three years after the divorce he heard from Joey that Dee was having a baby. Who with? Just a guy. He had kept photographs of Dee, and after the phone call with Joey he went to his files and tossed them into the trash. Later he wished he had burned them. It would have been more final. He still tried to sort out what he could have said—to get the anger out, to apologize, or at least so she'd understand. If he'd had a dog he could talk to the dog. Sometimes he woke up mornings thinking what he'd name it.

He encountered Dee again at Joey's college graduation and they nodded. She had a little girl with her, maybe three years old. He tried not to watch her from a distance but he couldn't help it. Joey had done well in college, was going into Naval Air, wanted to be a pilot. Several times Chuck dreamed about his brother Stan, but Stan was more impulsive than Joey. Joey would be okay. He'd have to be okay. He was the one bright spot.

Chuck slowly lost track of time. He was aware of the seasons as they affected construction plans, but otherwise things went day by day, week by week. He would sit at his desk signing purchase orders and glance up at the calendar to see what year it was. He found himself wondering what age Dee's daughter would be. When would he stop hearing his ex-wife's name?

"Mister Chuck?" The old lady had asked about his family.

"They're okay, I guess. My wife, ex-wife, I haven't seen her. She lives a kinda funny life. And my son, he's in the Navy. Naval Air. He's training to be a pilot. Doing fine."

"There will always be wars."

"And rumors of wars, don't they say?"

"Not only rumors."

She scrutinized her tangled skein. *How does this happen?* She found an end and began with meticulous patience to work through its loops and kinks and gnarls.

"So anyway, happy birthday. I'll call the maid. I better get back—"

"Why are we purchasing acreage?"

"Well, that is something we can talk about. I'll have some updates on that. By the way, I've ordered some Italian marble for the—"

"Why are we buying land?" She picked at a knot. "I don't need more land. It only takes six feet to bury me."

"Well, it's not completed yet, and I've got a meeting up in San Mateo so—"

"I don't want land. We have no need to expand beyond our boundaries. We displaced the people to the southwest, that was necessary, I made my donations, but there are limits. I will not displace more people. We should remind ourselves they're human after all, whatever their deficiencies." Her fingers tugged at the knot spasmodically, then froze.

"We've made provisions."

"What?"

"Lotta things."

Their features sharpened, etched by slashes of light. A sour odor was seeping in. Chuck's voice was muffled, distant.

"So we've reached the perimeter to the north. So what we're doing, we're acquiring, here, the west half of the northwest quarter and the southwest quarter of Section 33 south of the center of Darwin Road in Township 12 North—”

“Darwin Road. You lived there. You lived in that neighborhood.”

“Matter of fact I did.”

Her fingers clawed the knotted yarn and their voices rose.

“I want it to stop. We shall continue building on the land that we have.”

“It’s taken care of. Miss Weatherlee, this is important to the town. We’re providing jobs.”

“Jobs doing what?”

“Building.”

“Building what?”

“Building the future. Miss Weatherlee, we’ve donated for a civic center, there’s gonna be a gym, swimming pool, new wing on the library. All the things there wouldn’t be if it wasn’t for this investment. You’re aware of that. You know that. You’re the one telling me.”

“People are being evicted. I absolutely refuse. I want it to stop.”

“Nobody’s going to be homeless. Nobody’s gonna starve.”

“There are derelicts.”

“I’m not talking about derelicts. I’m talking about people who’d have homes if they did but they don’t.”

A sigh. Sophia flung the tormented wad of yarn to the floor. Chuck stooped and picked it up. He laid his folder beside the cake on the stand and placed the tangle upon it. She closed her eyes, let her head rest on the back of the chair, flattened her lips as if tasting the acrid fluid that trickled into her vein.

“Chuck?” Her voice was straw. “Do you still remember how to frame a roof?”

He glanced away to the window. “Yes ma’am, I could frame a roof better than anyone working here. But I don’t do that now.”

“You look good in your suit. New suit?”

“I’ve got a couple. Same color. I like navy. My son’s in the Navy in fact.” He smiled. Like his suits, his smiles all looked alike, he knew, but none of them real. That would be another joke if he could find the words to tell it.

The seven candles had expired. She touched the tube that wormed its way into the back of her wrist. "I need to increase the level."

"I'll ask the nurse. So if you'll check over the plans at your convenience. No hurry, we're pretty much under way. They're very faithful to your intentions."

A shiver. The first twitch of an earthquake? Squirrels on the roof? Sophia shivered in panic. She was phobic on squirrels. The watchers pressed into the doorway were stirring.

"Stop them! Stop them, Chuck! Get away! Go out! You're gone! You're dead!" She covered her face with her hands.

"Miss Weatherlee, there's nobody here. They're waiting, the paper-hangers, and it's up to you but I think you'll enjoy the pink." Chuck was in full charge now, he in his navy suit. She was wide-eyed but silent. "Hey now, how about that cake? Seven candles for good luck. You taught me that." He took out his lighter, lit the candles again. "Hey now, Miss Weatherlee, how about a smile? Little smile, come on. It's your birthday."

She looked up at him pleadingly, and then with great effort a smile crept over her face and consumed it. A hideous smile.

"Okay, so the paper-hangers are ready whenever you are. Just call Hallie. I gotta run. See you later." He turned and disappeared.

Sophia's face was pale, the glare blotting out her sight. Her lips were tight shut but her thin bat voice hovered.

"The suit makes such a difference."

Twenty-five

I must have been five or six when Daddy first took me to the barber shop. The barber put a booster seat in the great revolving chair and lifted me up. Now I was a big boy, with the nightmares that came with it. Joy or terror, I wasn't sure. I sat there as he clipped and clipped while an old guy was telling dirty jokes. I didn't understand them but the other men's laughter was dirty. Then the barber undid the bib and brushed me off. I wriggled from bits of hair down my neck and Daddy paid and we left. I was still little Raymond, now facing a lifetime of haircuts.

Now I was little Raymond on my last stroll through Time. I suppose I expected some kind of epiphany, though as we crept ever upward to the five-o'clock witching hour it came clear that I'd fall short of any truly meaningful apoplexy. From Sunday School I recalled that St. Paul fell off his horse and beheld the light, but my daydreams would never rate a Biblical write-up. No revelation, no thunderbolt, no helmeted club-wielding angels crashing the door, no money shot to ring the box-office gong. On my deathbed I would be waiting for an epiphany as Gertie awaited her pinch of mackerel.

No wonder that other lives were flashing before me: there was so little flash to my own. I would do my job till the clock got ticked off and I cracked my very last joke. I would wave my flock off to the gift shop's bowels, mumble goodbye to Corlene the box-office girl with the bright orange lips, and walk forth into oblivion. I would go back to my rooms, give Gertie a generous head-scratch and sigh the first sigh of the rest of my life.

But the extraction was not to be so neat. In my twenties my dentist went after my lower left wisdom tooth. It wouldn't budge. He pulled and dug, pulled and dug, his palm dislodging my jaw, but the roots held firm. "It's coming!"—and then he crushed it. Chunk by chunk he plucked it out inelegantly. In these last minutes my ghosts were plucked out one by one.

We fumble for a semblance of finality but we never quite manage. The lovers finally get laid, then call a couples counselor. The soldier wins the war, loses his job. Zombies suck out our brains, but who needs brains? Once the gods moved mountains, promised rainbow or plague. The good guys slew the Amalekites—man, woman and little crapping baby—and that was the happy ending. These ghosts held me in their hunger, their thirst, their ache, but how to satisfy them? Their stories lay dormant in the walls and my tour guide's patter was the wallpaper sealing them in. Strip it and the ghosts emerged—the carpenters, the maids, the ancient gardener clip-clipping their lives away. They spoke with urgency, horror, hope, though I could hear only the backwash of hearts with damaged valves.

By now at first glance I could narrate their lives.

We were in a waiting room. Reception desk, faceless receptionist, a row of padded chairs and decorative potted plants, a ponytail palm and an elkhorn cactus. A three-foot cactus was not the most appealing foliage for a waiting room.

Dee Ratowitz stood looking at a nodule on the crown of the cactus. A funeral darkened her face. She had stood with ten-year-old Millie, whose pain anesthetized her to her own, at the lost boy's funeral. The little girl had rarely seen Joey except when he came home to visit, but he was her beautiful big brother. Millie knew that soldiers got killed but not if it's your brother who flies a plane and teases you about your braces, then gives you a bear hug. When word came Dee had tried to mumble some words of comfort, but Millie screamed, "Stop it, Mom!" She sounded years older then.

Diego, Zach and Patty had been there, wise enough not to slather balm on a wound that went twenty-eight years to its depth.

Chuck was there. He walked over before the service, asked, "How's it going?" and Dee tried to smile. She introduced her friends. He shook hands stiffly, nodded to Millie, then stood waiting for his ex-wife to speak, but she didn't. She felt so sorry for him then and so enraged. She sensed her silence was killing him and she just let it kill him. He walked away.

A week later Dee got a call from his secretary asking if she could meet him at his office. She came on a Saturday when it wasn't so busy, though she still heard the hammers. She hadn't seen the place in years. He had offered many times to give her a tour but she'd declined. Now it was like a city, stretching on and on. She got lost three times before she saw the low building marked ADMINISTRATION.

The receptionist buzzed Chuck a second time and after a minute he appeared. They gave the usual nods. He ushered her into his office. It was small, plain, with a window facing out to the rear of another building. He gestured her toward a chair but she remained standing by the desk.

"So. Well. Hi. Thanks for coming."

"No problem." She glanced at a blueprint spread across his desk. Cryptic hieroglyphs but better than looking in his face.

"Can I get you some coffee?"

"Thanks, I'm a little pressed for time. Stuff piles up on weekends but they said it was important, so—"

"So how are you?"

"Better, I guess."

"You changed your hair."

No reply. She sensed his loneliness and feared being near it. He was trying to lead up to something and she didn't want to follow him there. Her finger traced an outline on the blueprint, a little square with numbers on it. Another cell in the slammer?

"Well, I just wanted to say . . ." He sat in his desk chair, gestured again. "Have a seat?" She remained standing, fingering the edge of the blueprint. "So, yeh . . ." Their first car was like that. Starting in wet weather, it would sputter out a few chugs, then sit dead. She wondered if he remembered.

"So, yeh, when I heard about Joey. Your friend called, what's her name, Patty called, and course she explained that you were pretty hard hit, so . . ." He paused. Pretty hard hit.

"Accident on the carrier, she said. Fatal, she said. Didn't say he was killed, just *The accident was fatal.* Funny way to say it." He was silent for a time. "You know, he'd write me, I guess he probably called you on the phone but he'd write to me. Kind of more formal, but they were great letters, not just email but actually written out, so that was kind of special. Stuff about the carrier and all the— And then a couple times he'd talk about the launches off the catapult, going zero to a hundred sixty-five in two seconds, amazing, twenty-four tons of aircraft? He was thrilled, just . . . thrilled." Chuck breathed it in.

"And your friend said the airplane broke— That's the way she put it. I guess she meant the towbar, and just pitched off the end of the deck. *The airplane broke.* Funny way to say it." He came to a halt, then added, "And it all went dark."

The phone buzzed. "Scuse me," he said. "Yes?" She looked at him then. She could hear the frantic squawk through the receiver, the way her grandma used to shout into the phone to carry over the distance. "Which green?" he said. "No, I'm asking which green is wrong? New bathroom, which one?" He forced a small laugh. "No, okay, I'll bring a new sample. Not so strong. I'll tell Willard: no *digestive* green." He glanced at Dee. She focused on the blueprint.

Odd, she thought, listening in to the other woman in his life. Same as their years together. It would be easier for Chuck, easier for them both, if she just turned and walked out the door and let him devote his life to painting bathrooms green. But her finger went on tracing the blueprint.

"Miss Weatherlee, sorry, I've got an appointment right now—" Dee saw his apologetic grin. "What? Seepage, yeh, no, we don't have any problem with seepage. No, the weather report is clear skies. All stations, no rain, they said. Out the window? Yeh, okay, I will." He sat with his hand over the receiver, staring at Dee. "Yeh, I'm checking out the window. Clear skies." He was looking at the floor. "Okay, no problem."

He hung up, grinned at Dee with a you-know-how-it-is gesture. She checked her wristwatch.

"Is that your mom's watch?"

She touched it. "Yep, funny. Last thing I ever supposed, wanting to look every day at something of hers. Mom, damn you, Mom. But then, well, the one thing she gave me, she gave birth. She gave me the gift of Time." Dee smiled wryly at the watch. "And what I do with it, well . . ."

"That's kind of a change."

"That's kind of a change, yep."

"So you're doing okay?" She raised her eyes to him. "I mean except last week. Right, stupid question."

She walked away from the desk to the single window. Blue sky. "I was glad the Navy took care of stuff," she said. "They do a great job with funerals. They must have admirals just in charge of funerals. It was pretty hard on Millie."

"She's what, eight, nine?"

"Ten."

"Wow. Time flies."

"She really loved Joey. He was like a dad." No, like a big brother, not like a dad, Why did she say *dad*? Just to hurt him?

"Anything I can do?"

"Like what?"

The phone buzzed. "Scuse me." He picked it up, rose from the desk and turned away. "Yes?"

She watched him. Clearly he had something to say to her. He must be lonely. If he'd just come out and say it all in one flush she might be moved to say, *Yes, Chuck, we're old enough now, the past is the past, let's keep hold of the good, let's be friends.* That frightened her but she realized she wanted it.

"What? Yeh, I've got a meeting. What's— Squirrels? No problem, no, they'll go away." He tried to edge a word in. "Well there's no way to keep'em out of the bird feeder, I know it's for birds but—" Dee could feel his frustration. "Okay. Okay. Hold on." He punched a button on the phone, glanced at Dee. "Bob? Chuck. Go out back, out south toward the supply shed, there's a squirrel problem, shoo away the squirrels, okay?" He punched the button. "Okay, it's fine."

Dee heard the telephonic squawk take the tone of a whining dog. Chuck made little grunts of assent. Dee tried to stop listening. He hung up, sat down at the desk. "It never stops," he grinned. "*Is the door lock working? Which one, we have lots of doors? The one I'm thinking about*, she says. And I say it's been fixed and she asks which door and I say the one you're thinking about." For an instant Dee saw the boy she had known. Then he clouded. "If you're rich your flunkies are supposed to know what you're thinking. Ten minutes ago she said she smelled onions in the atrium. I dunno . . ."

"What don't you know?"

He made a feeble gesture. "You told me once how to deal with squirrels on a bird feeder. I recall we had a bird feeder."

"Joey built it. It was all rickety. You were gonna help him but you didn't."

He looked up at her. "Is that what you came here to say?"

"No. I figured since you called me, or your secretary did, that you wanted to talk. But it doesn't seem like a whole lot's changed. I opened a door back there, coming in, it was a brick wall. Just like old times."

He slouched into his chair. She noticed that his suit jacket didn't quite fit. Baggy in the chest or a slump in the shoulders that she'd never seen before. She heard him mumble something that sounded like *waterbugs*.

"Waterbugs?"

"Nothing." Aware of her gaze, he straightened. "Old times, okay, I guess. Just start to lose track. I mean go day to day, week to week, just kinda float. I ever told you, there was a little pond down from Uncle Frank's in Fresno. I'd go down there, watch the waterbugs, water striders they called 'em. Skimming the surface back and forth. I loved that. Really loved those little guys never stirring the water. Why that comes to mind . . ."

She had never heard him talk that way. Another time she would have welcomed it. Not now. "Chuck, it's good to see you, but I've got a whole week's groceries to—"

"Dee, I saw you there and I realized—" The phone buzzed. "Hold on, okay? Hold on? Please? Please!" He picked it up. "Yes?"

She tightened her grip on her shoulder bag and drew in the breath that would take her out the door. He reached out an empty hand. A squawk and crackle cut the air. He knew Dee could hear the voice.

"Chuck, this is intolerable. Your man ducked out to the bird feeders without a jacket. It's cold, he's going to get sick and I'm sure he has loved ones."

"Miss Weatherlee, I'm in the middle of a—"

"And there's a draft, I can feel it."

"Ask the maid to close the window."

"Someone has opened something that should be closed. Please find out what's opened and close it. Don't you do it, have your people do it." He tried to speak but his lips wouldn't move. "You sound upset," she said.

"No problem."

"What is it now?"

What was it? "My son," he said without thinking.

"Is he in trouble again?"

"He wasn't ever in trouble, Miss Weatherlee." Dee was hearing this.

"No, that was the other man. Marty. I called you Marty. Your son is in the Navy. Fine young man, I'm sure."

"He was killed."

Silence on the line, then a sound like paper crumpling. "Yes, you told me, I remember. Is there a war now? I lose track of these wars. My father spoke on the subject. Father-in-law, I think of him as my father. He was against it. All wars." A pause, then a cry. "If there could only be *finality!*"

"Yes ma'am." He was staring directly into Dee's eyes, holding her with his pain.

"I'm terribly— Sorry, I'm sorry, Chuck, I'm very sorry, I'll get off the phone, but your man is out there freezing! There is suffering enough! I won't have it!" The call broke off.

Chuck shrugged. Dee stood, impassive.

"She asks me, *Is there a war?*" He gave a dry laugh. "Course, military honors, all that, they make you think there's something meaningful. Flag, ceremony, all the sharp-looking guys. He always looked sharp in his uniform. This little kid I read bedtime stories to."

"If that's what you asked me here—"

"I just thought we ought to—"

"Talk, talk, okay, we talked, I'm sorry but I've got to—"

"Okay! Go! Go!"

It was like this the first time they were naked with one another. The desire to see, the fear of seeing, the startle, suspended between embrace and flight. She didn't want to see him stripped but she couldn't look away.

"I guess it was stupid," he said. "I wanted to— Wanted to say something at the funeral, but— Words don't come easy. Never did. I guess at a certain point people run out of words and then they just repeat themselves or— And you were with your friends, I guess, whatever—"

"Friends, yes."

"I'm glad." He shrugged. "I don't know if I'm glad. I'd like to be glad— I just thought we should talk. We'd gone through so much together— I guess they say, well, that's life . . ."

She managed to glance away and a silence settled in. She turned to the window. A flowering vine partly covered the panes. She saw a whir in the air. "You've got hummingbirds," she said.

"Oh yeh, yeh. They like the jasmine. That's winter jasmine, according to the gardener. Funny old guy. Old Jap. Uncle Frank, he always respected the Japs. I miss him."

Their quarrels had always taken this pattern. Mindless back-and-forth, spiky blurts, then a hiatus like driftwood caught in an eddy. Next day they'd try to be all smiles, but each year trying less. She clenched her jaw against weeping as the hummingbird took its pleasure. She would pull free from this eddy—in a minute.

"Dee, dammit, I'm sitting here signing purchase orders—" He made a wave of his hand as if waving the words away. "But I think all the years I've got left to go, and what's the point? Once the old lady asked me what's my purpose in life. Chrissake . . ."

She felt the slow cramping behind the eyes, in the throat, that would bring on the tears.

"When you and Joey left, at least that was one thing off my neck. I didn't have to apologize any more for doing my job, for trying to— But out there the other day, seeing you, seeing your little girl, and your . . . boyfriends, whatever, I just— Joey. I never knew him."

"I knew him. He was kinda wild for a while but he straightened out. He was all right. He's dead, you know." She winced at the needle stab of her words, no reason to—

He rose to the bait. "You got a cute little girl. Does her father pay child support?"

"Never did."

"I always did. More than my share."

"That's true."

"I fulfilled my responsibilities."

"Yes you did."

"Doesn't that count for something?"

"It ought to."

"I worked. I provided. I did productive work—"

"Hammering."

His voice pulled in, nearly inaudible. "I stayed sober. I was faithful. I never played around."

Dee glared at him, a bitter flux in her throat. She was the cause of his pain and she hated him for it. "Well I did. Maybe you missed something." Their eyes met again and she saw the little boy crying inside. Then he stared at the blueprint.

She sat in the chair he had offered. It reminded her of the start of labor, when she imagined the baby would be dead but the cramps would go on. "The first times I cheated on you, I flogged myself with it, but I thought, hey, it's his fault, so it's not cheating, it's just lying. And I messed myself up every way I could, diet pills, drink drink drink, stuffing my face with Twinkies, can you believe it? Living my life like a really sappy movie that I kept sitting through again and again. I wouldn't live that time over, never, for godsake, never. But I will say that I learned a few things."

He slumped into his office chair, picked up a knickknack on the corner of his desk, fingered it. Dee recognized the toy compass they'd given to Joey for Cub Scouts. She struggled for words.

"I'm sorry I'm being mean to you, Chuck. I had in mind, I guess, maybe we could be friends. Seemed like maybe that's what you wanted. Why hold grudges? You'd say funny things, make me laugh. And my friends, yeh, they do things just as crazy as this . . . loony bin, whatever it is. One guy, he paints these pictures, I don't understand'em, nobody buys'em. The other's a mechanic, he talks the way you used to talk, how you'd love it when you did the job perfect and it worked. I guess I'm still drawn to crazy guys . . ."

The years lay between them, flickers dying.

"Chuck, I'm sorry, I try to pull back from hurting you. You can't help it. You just walked in the door and put on the suit. You look really awful in that suit."

She met his dull gaze and managed to hold back her tears. His voice was flat. "Okay, you made your point."

The phone buzzed again. He sat frozen. It buzzed, buzzed, buzzed. Dee rose, strode to the desk and picked it up.

"Hello?"

A gasp, then the voice of a startled ancient anemic girl, "Who is this, please?"

"Is this Mrs. Weatherlee?" Dee asked.

A thin whine. "I don't think so." Click.

Dee felt the current pulling her free from the eddy. "I have to go."

He rose. "Could we keep in touch?"

"I doubt it."

"If I could say what I want to say—"

Dee was at the door. "If you could say what you want to say, you'd have said it."

"If there's anything I can do—"

"You'd have done it."

They stood across the room from one another. They grasped that it was the end, but neither could make the first move. At last she turned, opened the door, walked out. He stared at the door left ajar. He would never see her again except in dreams. His hand ran across the blueprints, smoothing the folds.

Twenty-six

I stood watching this man with the curly receding hair and a baffled heart. He smoothed his blueprints, the ex-wife watched a humming-bird, the son lay dead between them. Her words echoed my break-up with Laird when I was twenty-two, twenty-three. I spat out my crude honesty and saw his soul die in his eyes. Then the world spat it back at me: a life of petrified groping relieved only by the nuzzle of my fluffy pitiless cat. I wished better for Dee.

The clock's hand in my psyche moved upward. We were in the final two minutes of the tour, but as things were going it might take weeks. I had floundered my way room to room, ghost to ghost, ignorant of what impelled me. Perhaps like my tourists I surmised I was stumbling toward revelation, that out of this grim chrysalis I would squeeze forth and stretch luminous wings. I would emerge with a new spirit or at least a new hat. I would open the perfect gift, though I had no clue what it might be. Or I would stand there like the one remaining cuspid in a foul blackish mouth.

I might have spun the simple tale of a lorn little lady who built a big house, but no question the official story was better: guilt, slaughter, specters, the number thirteen, all funneled into this preposterous hulk. In my mind the construction went on. The house was no longer a hundred sixty rooms or three hundred twenty-seven: it was thousands. Stud walls rose and extensions spread over hills and valleys, devoured farms and villages, covered the landscape with death-row cells. Ghosts sped room to room on freeways, surfed on chemtrails. Armies advanced, unstoppable glaciers of steel scraping out all life in their path. Thankfully I was blind.

I had spoken these reflections to Gertie some night after three jiggers of Scotch. "Stories beget," I said, slurring it into *shtories*. "They engender the peristalsis that we call war, with its acrid diarrhea. What's a war but a story told with vim and vigor? No tank starts its belly-growl without a story to fuel it." Gertie hopped off my lap and hid under the sofa.

Again I was losing track. One moment I was with the man and his blueprints, then straining the patience of my aging cat. Now I envisioned Dee. She was in a bathroom, a bedroom, a kitchen, I couldn't say. She stirred mixed feelings in me. No wonder: she was my emanation. She existed only in the fantasies of Raymond Smollet, who existed in lumps and shards. She flowed out of me the way as a child I had nosebleeds, which came whenever my nose had nothing better to do. Dee was my blood.

She turned halfway to me. Nothing was visible except the slur of her tears. *Tell me*, I said.

I thought it was funny almost. His secretary called for the appointment like he was some high school kid scared to phone for a date. If he'd just leveled I might have said, *Sure, Chuck, we're old enough, let's be friends.*

It didn't go that way. I wonder what he did when I left. Maybe stood there with his blueprints, planning the time it'd take to cover the face of the world with his sticks and stones.

That was nine years ago. It passes in a minute. Millie's just off to college, same age as me when I went with Chuck. And I'm sixty-one. How did that happen?

I still see Diego, Zach less often, and a circle of friends, all sorts. That's the gift of aging, I guess. I went into my sixties flying high, big party, dancing, more hugs than I ever knew there were hugs in the world. Then two weeks later the diagnosis.

What did I do to deserve it? Lots of things, in fact, but just being human was enough. They told me, "Hey, no big deal, we caught it in time, it doesn't mean that you'll lose a breast, that's mostly a thing of the past." But I lost a breast.

I wondered, should I call Chuck? I decided no. Even though I'd hung on to the name Ratowitz.

Diego and Zach were there when I came awake. One on another, they put their hands very softly where the breast had been. That gesture told me what had happened and that I was loved, way beyond what I ever deserved. Patty came in later and we chatted about books, recipes, women's rights, so on, but like the play of Patty's needles as she sat knitting it knitted a fabric. Chuck told me once that the old lady knitted. I wonder what she made and if anybody wore it.

And Millie brought me a photo on a postcard. This woman, I don't know who she was or if she's alive, but she'd lost a breast. And where the scar was she had a tattoo, this blazing feathered dragon flying out of her chest. Colors, flames, and her arms reaching up to the desert sky. So I think I'll do that. I'll get a tattoo. For spring.

Dee disappeared. She went out like a candle. That's all of her I ever saw.

Twenty-seven

Last stop, last minute, last gasp of the tour. Normally, our little group would return to the entrance patio, where I would invite them to stroll the grounds, buy crap at the gift shop and enjoy the rest of their so-called lives—stationing myself at a narrow passage, available for tips. Tips were officially discouraged, which meant only that I needn't report them to the IRS and could budget for quality cat food and Scotch. My tone poem would end in a whisper.

The fact is, though, that everyone has a breaking point.

The old woman lay in the Ballroom, propped with pillows on a metal hospital bed, adjustable to need. The only touch of luxury was a fluffy yellow quilt, held by one talon, drawn up to the chin. Her head appeared beheaded. Vague whispers in her features hinted at pain or nightmare or chill, but her sunken eyes were alert as squirrels, focused, then darting away.

An IV rack by the bed held a yellowish bag of fluid. Its plastic tube, as before, ran into the vein in the back of her visible hand. Another tube clipped into her nostrils led to a green steel oxygen tank. The room was bereft of frippery. The blotches of the Shakespeare window shone above her. Its words were muddled. Were we seeing death?

"Death? Whose death?" her dry lips murmured. "Someone being honest with me here?" Her glances flashed aimlessly, following the shadow of a moth, perhaps, or walking through hallways searching for the Daisy Room or Seance Room or the patented kitchen sink or those hydraulic elevators to take her aloft to a floor collapsed, picking her way through memories of blueprints.

"Marty?" she said. Suddenly a hideous odor. Her hand brushed her nose, recoiled from the tube. "What stinks?"

Me! It wasn't a voice, exactly, more like vibrations in the odor.

"When will I die?" Her words were squeezed out of lungs the size of small fists.

Now!

"Marty?"

Out!

"Have we finished the doors? Are there doors? Of course there are." Her voice was manic, flat, a hiss. "President, who was that President who came to visit here, or the newspapers said he did even though he didn't? And I refused to see him? How could I see him if he wasn't here?"

Now!

"We need to discuss— No, this hieroglyph, its legs, ascenders, descenders, serifs. William loved typography. He had a letterpress. All those terms, the stem, the bar, the bowl, leg, shoulder. Take care of that! Marty!"

Now!

"Now!" She brushed at the tubes in her nostrils.

"Easy, Miss Weatherlee. The tubes, you need to let'em be. The tubes are there for a reason." Chuck's voice, the face a blur. "Rosella stepped out for a minute. Your nurse Rosella. She said watch out with the tubes."

Sophia's lids flickered, dazzled by sunlight. The pupils sharpened then scurried away—now dodging traffic, now meandering endless rooms, fingers palpating the walls, pressing prints into lush velvet papers. She might have been a bird carried by wind, seeking a place to perch.

She came to focus on Chuck Ratowitz. Her face wrinkled up in puzzlement. He was older, or his suit, still blue, always blue. His tie a sour red.

"Who?" She glanced away, as if to ask someone else.

"Me. Chuck."

Her hand rose a few inches and fell. "Chuck, yes. That smell?"

"Might be the fumigation."

"Stifling."

"Infestation maybe. Stuff in the insulation."

"Who?"

"Me. Chuck. I'm here."

She peered at him. "No clipboard," she said. "Your clipboard. You always have the clipboard."

"Oh yeh. No. No need." He felt naked without it, but there was no real need. It had been several weeks since his usual morning report and long past the time when she said anything that mattered. He had several meetings, one in Santa Cruz, the other in Palo Alto, but a small pocket notebook sufficed. Clearly she was coming to the last days, though she refused to go to the hospital. He looked for any signs: slurred speech, imbalance, sagging in the face? Her vital signs remained stable. She talked about a smell. Maybe the dying were able to catch a scent.

I'm here!

Sophia startled. An eyelid fluttered.

"Chuck?"

"Right."

"These tubes . . ." She brushed at the air.

"Well, we've gotta have the tubes. Doctor's orders. You're feeling better maybe? More energy?"

"I smell it . . ."

"Well, that's what I said, the fumigation. I could open a window but it's kinda chilly out."

"Closet . . ."

"What?"

"Tigger . . ."

"No, Miss Weatherlee, you gotta relax. You were just dreaming. Rosella stepped out for just a minute, she can give you something. Maybe you want to sleep a little more when she comes back? She'll be right back—"

"Tigger . . ."

"No problem with Tigger, Miss Weatherlee. That was a story you told me long time ago. That was a long time ago."

"Didn't give her pills . . . she died . . . stuck her with a fork . . . Others! Millions!"

These episodes upset Chuck. She had fallen into spans of delusion and the doctors warned of a stroke. There had always been rumors about her fantasies but now there were actual signs. The maids told him that until she became bedridden two weeks ago she would wander through the passages at night, rolling her IV stand ahead of her, talking to the walls. She would spasmodically cry out as if fingers were touching her. Her thinking had always been rational—bizarre, yes, but not like popcorn. *Rational?* Maybe not the right word.

"You feel any numbness, Miss Weatherlee? Anywhere? Vision okay? Headache?" She stared at the ceiling.

"Help me here." She fingered the pillow. He held it as she pulled herself more upright, then sank back again. The intubated hand rubbed the back of the other as if to rub life into it. "The odor, I woke, it was there."

"Well that's natural. You smelled it in your sleep."

"Obviously!" In her voice the same cutting edge but dull as a butter knife.

"Well, or it might be the water treatment plant. Food service, cooking oil, dead rats. Lotta smells out there."

"You smell it?"

"No ma'am."

Her eyes tightened to shut out the smell.

Chuck had been thirty-eight years on the job, and at some point he had been given power of attorney. Her lawyer had died and Chuck was the only one she trusted now. He would have expected she'd rely more on her niece Isabel, who was now back East. They seemed to be close, but maybe the old woman didn't trust closeness. Maybe she could only trust her puppet. He had lived his life in service to her obsession. What better qualification?

"So, quick report, just so you know. Things are on track. Sun deck in the south quadrant—"

"People here . . ."

It was fruitless to tell her there were over a hundred people working on the premises and more every day. She was never satisfied with his answer. She would whine that people were sneaking through the house, spying on her, lifting her tea cup, letting in sunshine. He would nod and then she'd lose track. He thought the left side of her face was drooping.

"So, right, I have a number of things to do now, Miss Weatherlee, and Rosella should be back in a minute. Maybe you want to tell her to increase the drip, cause are you kind of uncomfortable, you think? Any pain? Numbness, maybe? Just make sure you tell her if you feel any—"

She pulled herself up in the bed like a ghost popping out of its coffin. He saw what was coming. She'd said it a dozen times before.

"It's time to stop."

"Well . . ." He'd heard it before. She always got over it.

A fist tightened. A cramp. A tension in the walls, the way a uterus contracts whether giving birth or expelling its burden. Her voice rose, full lungs, sharp lips.

"It's time to stop. It's time. I have said this before. We are done. We have our rooms. Our rooms and alcoves and archways and flooring, they are done. We can stop."

More and more often, out of the blue, she would babble that the work should stop—"Not one more hammer on one more nail!" she would howl—but he never took her seriously. Immediately she would spin out new inspirations, fumbling at the tangle of yarn in her mind. Once she had scrawled marks on watercolor paper as building plans. Now they had a whole office of architects for that. Chuck would sign off on a three-year plan and give her a briefing on what her intentions were. She might ramble on about a porch or portico they'd already built five years ago, but she didn't interfere. As long as he said, "Fine, we'll see to that," she was tractable. His job this past year was to keep her contentedly out of the picture.

"We shall end our endeavors."

"Miss Weatherlee, I have to be in Palo Alto—"

"Now!"

"Lemme call Rosella—"

"Minor elements, I'm sure, so you will develop a plan for phasing out and select a maintenance staff—"

Same old stuff. "I understand your concern, Miss Weatherlee, but we're taking care of—"

"It's finished. It's done. We have hammered our hammering and we are done."

Chuck knew this moment would come—the moment he heard that she meant it. He had dreamed it in sleepless dreams. The standard protocol was to nod, nod, *Okay, fine, no problem*, glance at his watch, make a note in his notebook, then go on with the day, the week, the years. But now her eyes dug into him and he had to say it.

"No."

This wasn't high school. This wasn't his oral book report where he'd stood frozen like a stick. This was life, and he was in charge. He was Project Manager. He had told her no.

"No, the thing is, Miss Weatherlee, our current phase is over the next three years, and there's a ten-year projection— Listen, I have to go, I've got appointments. We'll talk and I'll go over what's already planned, what you've approved, but right now—"

The stench hit him and he heard the howl.

I'm here.

Was it Marty? Joey? Some victim of fallen beams? Himself trapped by drywall? "Miss Weatherlee, I have to go. There's no problem. I have to go."

"Your neighborhood, your family, your son, the dead boys, where are they? The stench is pervasive. Stop it."

He tried to look away, like looking away from nakedness. When his senile grandma was staying with Mom he'd walked in on her standing naked. He had tried to look away but was trapped in the dazzle.

"We have housed our dead. They are accommodated."

Sophia's glasses had always made her pupils like pinholes, but now they were round black stains in her face. Her lips were paper-thin. "I cannot be responsible for housing the full population. One hour at Chancellorsville would fill the East Wing. And they come to the door, they say, *We're here from Gettysburg, from Verdun, Okinawa, from Dresden, from*— Oh, where they came into that village and they lined them all up— *We're from there.* I can't house them all. They wander about and have babies. In my rooms they have babies. They have names."

She had derided the journalistic fantasies that portrayed her as insane with guilt, haunted by the dead from a thousand battlefields, beating off zombies with hammers, but now she believed them.

"No."

He had a right to say no. He put his hands on the rail of her bed. "There's nothing gonna stop. Miss Weatherlee, I'll have to call the nurse if you don't relax. You'll have your headaches." She flailed her hand weakly. "There are straps on the bed, Miss Weatherlee. She'll have to strap you down."

Out!

"Your perky wife."

"What?"

"Your perky wife," she said, "and your perky little baby boy, they have names."

It hit him blind side. She began to claw feebly at her tubes. He held her wrists and looked around for the nurse. "Rosella!" He tried to lower his voice, to sound calm, but the words burst out. "Miss Weatherlee, we are not stopping and you are going to be fine. You will be fine. Everything here is fine. It's got a life of its own. Your orders were that the hammers never stop and they are never going to stop."

"They have names!"

Her strength gave out. She sank back into the pillows. He released her wrists and backed away, bracing himself against the wall. The nurse, a thick blue-garbed woman in her fifties, appeared at the bedside, felt Sophia's pulse, making small bird sounds to soothe her. "Rosella's here, honey, Rosella's here."

At the hefty nurse's touch the old woman closed her eyes. Chuck pressed his back hard to the wall. Her words spasmed up from her throat. "My sister was fat. Revolting. Whereas I built walls." Her face was a mask of terror. "What? Tubes? Chuck?"

His glare locked onto hers: something like an intercourse, the deep hate special to lovers. Only an instant, no more than the whine of a rocket's streak to the sky before its bloom. "You hear me?" he murmured. "Hear me?"

Sophia spooned out her words as if to a cranky child. "How to respect a grown man who sucks a marble!"

I loathed him then: a caricature of myself, his life dribbling through his fingers, blaming others for his cowardice. Yet I grasped his rage at the gross injustice. Was he not owed a bonus that would never be paid? Was fidelity worthless? Craftsmanship? Guilt?

His image hovered in sunlit air like a soap bubble floating an instant before blinking out. No more the kid coming out of shop class, no more carpenter, foreman, Project Manager, only a tense graying stranger crying to survive. He was backed against filigree woodwork, pale as death.

Everyone has a breaking point.

Chuck plunged forward off the wall. He grasped the steel rail of the bed, spitting his words. "You're okay! You're feeling fine! You've got a lotta years! Dozens of people depend on you, hundreds, thousands! Listen!"

She grabbed his suit by the sleeves. The window flared: *Wide unclasp the tables of their thoughts.* She was one mad stare.

"Don't start that with me, Miss Weatherlee. Cut it out. Didn't we start here together? Haven't I been good to you? I did it for you. You owe me."

He shook the steel rail. The nurse Rosella stepped back terrified. Mouth half open, she raised her finger to her lips. Chuck's voice rose to a shout.

"Stop that! Stop it! There's nothing to cry about! You got what you wanted! Everything you said! You're happy!"

Sophia's face drew into the ferocious hiss of a maddened cat. Rosella shushed fiercely.

Chuck was red-faced, sobbing. Somehow his hair had been mussed and a strand stood up like a tuft of weed, ridiculous, horrific. He was in that groove where the hero charges the machine gun nest, where the fullback hits the line, where hubby stabs wife with a butcher knife thirty-nine times.

"I built this house. You wanted this house and I built it. That's what the job is. I do the job."

Out!

"You can't make it stop. I've got power of attorney and I can do anything I damn please. It's a major enterprise. We're talking the economy. It's bigger than people. People don't mean shit."

He choked, caught a breath. My tourists scattered like pigeons.

"You don't have enough corpses to fill the fucking rooms, we'll order'em. I knew it a long time and I kept right on because the money's good and I had a family to support who are gone and dead, but I have a suit and tie and I look good in a suit and tie, and stop staring at me. Stop it! Stop it!"

Sophia's owl shrieks rose above his roaring. Shuddering, she ripped the tubes from her nose and her hand. Rosella cried out, reaching out, backing away. Chuck shook the rail in frantic resolve to bring on the final quake. He grabbed the hammer in his tool belt to batter her skull to a pulp—but he hadn't worn a tool belt for thirty years.

A power saw ripped through the clamor. Then silence over the face of the deep and a tiny snip in the garden. The ancient gardener clipped a blossom. We were at the top of the hour.

Twenty-eight

These final moments before my retirement were memorable, though I had no desire for the sight as part of my pension plan. Memory is as fickle as a cat. My playmate Rollie and I wrote our names in the snow, and then Rollie peed on mine. I could never recollect if I hit him or if I peed on his or if we both dissolved in the melt. Memories are stains that resist the pre-soak.

Over the next days that final tableau would rise in me like corpses to the face of the sea, floating sunward then sinking back to the primal ooze. The old lady's head lay cocked to the left, her sockets white. Her lips were drawn back in grotesque pretend like a boy bent on scaring his baby sister. The pressure of blood had found the crack in the artery, a crumbled partition, an unbolted door. It must have been a massive stroke. Aha, I thought: *the stroke of five!*

To be sure, she was only fantasy, so the gong that freed me from my thirty-year stretch would be the end of her span. From mist she came, to mist she went, leaving only seepage. Chuck too was frozen there, clasping the rail. And my tourists were etched in Sophia's bifocals, drifting back from their diaspora. A belly, a hat, a lip, hair and nose, teddy bear and merciless eyes.

They were all ghosts, of course, ectoplasm from my cranial waste bin. Dee perhaps was the woman my mother might have been if she weren't who she was. Chuck mayhap was my first love Billy or a hundred men I passed every day making their voiceless pleas to a senile god. The old lady was perhaps my fourth grade teacher Mrs. Schumaris, who would have fired all her students if only she'd been able to. The word *perhaps* is glued to my face.

But I was clueless as to how my flock found their way out. They might have become floating dandruff, or perhaps the Ghost House absorbed them like flies in the stickiness of Venus. I may have called Security and had them deported. Sadly, in any case, no tips.

I had fretted that I might have to wade through a gauntlet of well-wishers or even a surprise retirement kick-him-out with a dribble of cheap champagne, Mr. Bottoms offering me a wormy handshake and a blaring smile. Or the new box office girl, who sounded fat but sweet, might cradle my face in her hands, give me a butterfly kiss and whisper, "Have a nice day, Mr. Smollet." No such luck.

I took the bus home and fed Gertie. I had thought of calling a taxi to a restaurant where I sometimes ate Sunday brunch, but I couldn't stand the image of a little man sitting in solitary frolic, poking his fork in dead cow. I had thought of presenting myself a thirty-year service plaque. I had thought of eviscerating Gertie on the front steps of Weatherlee House. In the end I just warmed up a supper of pasta with chorizo. Later I listened to an audiobook on the War of 1812—as pointless as my life had been—until I nodded off.

I woke early next morning in my armchair with Gertie curled on my belly. She did that whenever I'd drunk too much, I suppose because then I didn't turn over. The first thing I felt was my nameplate. I ran my fingers in its grooves. That wasted fool Raymond Smollet was still in his wrinkled uniform and had countless minutes to fill before he confronted death's dreaded white light. Once in a hellish gym class I wore a tee-shirt stiff with rancid sweat, and now I was fated, it seemed, to wear parts of my uniform until they were threadbare. I uncrinkled myself, set on water for coffee and filled the bowl for that frizzy intestine called Gertie.

My life had reached equipoise. Secure in my small pension, supplemented by savings and Social Security, I had no serious worries.

The Blind Center had a speakers' series and hosted social outings. They offered volunteers to assist with paperwork and reading. I could learn ceramics, Spanish, yoga. There were tours you could take. They celebrated birthdays the last Thursday of every month. I could buy a talking watch. It all sounds rather dismal as I list it but it promised peace. My frequent mac-and-cheese was no great gourmet treat, but at least I allowed myself to taste it and it satisfied.

It was only Dee I missed. True, I wanted all voices to cease and desist along with the reflux from thirty years of chewing my cud, but I yearned for her words to be the last of all, leaving a little echo of dawn in my mind along with her quirky smile. I envisioned a sister holding me, giggling *Raymond, Raymond . . .*

It didn't work out that way. The last sight I had was that of the unfinished man.

Dozing myself awake on Saturday morning I had left something incomplete. Turn in my beeper and restroom key? Already done. Pick up my lifetime pass for the standard tour? That could wait till Hell froze. I ate my oatmeal, drank coffee, sprinkled a handful of litter over Gertie's purpose in life, picked up the umbrella I kept by the door—I could hear a gentle sprinkle—and wafted my back-to-bed dreaming way to the bus stop.

Still an hour before the first tour assembled. From habit I made my way past the ticket booth and nobody noticed. The rain pattered gently. At an outbuilding smelling freshly of paint I peered into the window. I dreamed him bent over a desk.

Chuck Ratowitz had assumed he was high in the chain of command, with a major say in the future of Weatherlee House. The old lady fooled him. She had turned off the spigot. The lawyers shielded him from all worries till a visit from the executor to bring him up to date. By order of the new owner, an entertainment conglomerate, construction would stop. Chuck was given a month's notice and a severance package. The executor explained the provisions, but what he was really saying was *You don't mean shit.*

"Don't I have some say in the matter?" Chuck said. Not really, he was told.

He straightened, viewed the rain through his office window. Rain made it all appear different. I imagined him as a kid watching drops run down the pane, seeing the world through dribbles. The house was smaller than he'd seen it in years, the orchards were gone and the road was no longer the lane bordered by jasmine but a parking lot full of cars. He saw a billboard—*WEATHERLEE GHOST HOUSE*—and tried to call to mind constructing that, or if it had gone up without his noticing, like when the neighbors built a tree house for their kids. But he couldn't complain. He had savings, a house, investments, a condo in San Jose, two cars, a motorboat and a closet full of suits. He touched the blueprints on the desk—what would never be built.

I didn't want to see him. I was finished with the smell and the sweat and the sobs of spooks. I had never managed to control my dreams, but I had to get rid of this starving ghost. I was partner to his achievements or his crimes, such as they were, a carpenter on his crew. His hammer blows, my wisecracks, they may have had no vast effect on the world, and surely we did no great harm beyond the daily wastage wrought by the human race itself. We could only hope for a verdict of *Innocent by reason of insanity*, though in the green eyes of Gertie I beheld no mercy. And I could only fantasize that her eyes were green.

He fingered the blueprint. "Mahogany for the atrium," he mumbled, or something like that. I opened the door discreetly lest I wake either of us. He looked up. "You have an appointment?" He surely realized that I was blind—the glasses were unmistakable—but many people are confused as they see me focus directly at them: I don't act blind. I knew then why I was there.

"I would guess that it's time." I said it, not knowing precisely what time it was or for what.

"Sorry?"

"You can take it from here."

He appeared to understand: that hesitation before sucking the marble, but no question that he'd suck it. He took off his suit jacket and handed it to me. I unbuttoned my jacket, not certain it would fit him, and we exchanged. Surprisingly it was a perfect fit. All the clothing, right down to the shoes and the hat, a perfect fit. The nameplate might change over time, though it hardly mattered.

I had been the bearer of a story. Like a parasite from the jungle, a story infests your gut, your heart, your retinas. It's yours for life. You spit it out, vomit, excrete it five times a day to those mortals who queue up their mouths like birdies for worms. You come home and scream it at your cat, but it just roots deeper. A novelty song when I was a kid told of a guy finding a thing—never said what it was, just went *boop boop boop*—and never ever being able to ditch it. And then one day the rare sucker appeared.

"Just tell the basic story," I told him. "They know what they want to hear so they'll hear it the way they want it. Toss in a little personal stuff to give it tang."

I adjusted the half-windsor of the necktie formerly known as Chuck's, and for me a brighter future beckoned. I could try new recipes. I could listen to music and hear it. I could find a way to get to the ocean. I could sit in coffee shops and listen to silly sweet lives. I could speak my soul aloud to Gertie and take note of what I said. I could let Time take its course, easing me into my gentle night.

"Personal stuff?"

"Make it humorous. They like it if you sound kind of nutty." I handed him my black glasses. He fumbled, got them on. Now we were brothers, beclouded.

Right. Okay. Well, personal stuff. I got a job here, good pay. Then I was foreman, pretty much round the clock. We had a son, my son was—

But how it happened, this guy Marty, my mother's friend's cousin—

So the architecture, Queen Anne Victorian, they call it, but Mrs. Weatherlee— I built that, by the way, hammered the nails. But then I got promoted, foreman, so I didn't have so much opportunity—

Man, you could get lost in here. You need a map, almost.

Okay, so that's the corridor to the south quadrant, we built that, but that was a stairway, very low steps for her arthritis, thirteen steps there. Clyde made a joke about that, kid named Clyde, he was a joker—

This is the Ballroom. Like they say, *Have a ball.*

And then a number of years. I put on a suit and that was the end of the marriage. But we expanded. Huge impact, jobs, development. This all used to be orchards. And the boy died, he was killed. Joey, they called him a hero even though what he did was run his plane off the end of the boat.

Which way's north? There was a door there, you go through there you're in thirty rooms. Is that south? Where's the sun? There. There you can see the stained-glass window, that's Shakespeare, don't ask me what it means, but that's where she— Isn't that weird? By the sun that must be east, but who should know better than me? Cause I built all this, I mean I supervised it, being the Project Manager. I had the responsibility. That's one thing I can say. I took responsibility.

So it's the story of— What I liked about the book was— Hey no, c'mon, I get this dream I'm back in high school and I have to do this stupid book report—

But you wonder. Like with Stonehenge, did they know they were going to put up all those stones? Or the Pyramids, the wall in China, skyscrapers even, did they ever think, hey, that's enough, that's all we need, that's it? Did they ever want to stop?

Okay, now we got our bearings, we're okay, we're cool. Funny, those colonnades, that was west, that wasn't— Maybe through there if it's— I always got— We kinda need a map, I guess, cause you get kinda lost, cause— Some kinda map or they oughta put up directions or—

I think we're lost.

Shadows flickered through the naked studs. Chuck was distant now. He had passed into the house through a jag of walls, groping deeper into the whimsical grotesquerie, trailed by a gaggle of noses and hats. Soon he would see Sophia Weatherlee in her rocking chair—with her marbles, her knitting, her tea cup, her keys, her Shakespeare, her scribbles—and lose himself in her tortuous maze.

*B*lind Walls had its genesis many years ago when we took the guided tour of San Jose's Winchester "Mystery" House. Its legend was irresistible. A wealthy recluse, haunted by the guilt of her inherited armaments fortune, was told by a spiritualist that she would live only so long as the sound of hammers rang in her ears. And so, goes the story, she employed squads of workmen—crews working 24/7 for 38 years—to create a labyrinthine mansion with mysterious architectural anomalies. The legend, fueled by journalistic speculation, turned the edifice into a tourist attraction five years after her death. And in 1996, it served as the basis of our play *Hammers*, produced at Philadelphia's Old City Stage Works and the Baltimore Theatre Project.

The legendary heiress was crucial, of course, though her name was changed to acknowledge that our Sophia—or anyone's—was fictional. But we recalled that the tour guide had spoken of a carpenter who had been on the crew for the entire 38 years of the project. Who would spend his entire working life in the service of another's obsession? Well, millions do. Thus the story of Chuck and Dee emerged, a composite of so many people we've known and been.

The play was deeply indebted to actors in our Philadelphia developmental lab and grad students at Towson University, where we explored characters and scenes improvisationally. We were grateful for their contributions of verbiage or scenic ideas, but the true value was in the questions that arose: those are what always spur us to press beyond the obvious.

At the time, the blind Tour Guide was a memorable but minor role. We knew, at the outset, that the action would be on two levels—the interplay of the imagined characters and the tourist narrative of the story as we had encountered it. In many of our dramas and subsequent fictions, we've explored not only the story but the telling of the story—its motive, its occasion, its anomalies. Every story has an untold story within it, and that story changes with the teller. Our Raymond Smollet was indebted to the weird magnetism of the actor who embodied him, but eventually he demanded his own voice in the narrative.

None of the characters have changed radically from those in our drama of twenty years ago, but none are quite the same. And it's evolved a more radical seismic shuffle in its relation to reality. Raymond is blind, yet sighted, yet blind. It's the 1880s, then the present day. We're in a scene in Weatherlee House, then in another part of Raymond's head. And we can't plead genre convention because we're not providing the full wad of condiments for Horror, Science Fiction, or Fantasy.

Perhaps it's our living now in earthquake country; perhaps the political landscape; perhaps a perverse instinct to live a life between pigeonholes. But we prefer to think of it simply as the way that life is experienced. Years ago, one of us spoke with a friend in the late stages of AIDS, still ambulatory but gaunt and distracted. "Weird thing is," he said, "two minutes from now I won't remember we had this conversation." The friend is long gone, but the words remain shimmering.

In the process of work on the novel, we encountered M.J. Ignoffo's biography *Sarah Winchester, Captive of the Labyrinth*, which casts doubt on key elements of the "legend." Her arguments are compelling, and we've incorporated them not only in the Tour Guide's futile burst of truth but in Sophia/Sarah's own ambivalent persona.

Why tell a story that varies radically from the one that initially attracted us? Why tell any story? For us, it's no great moral fable, and its "mystery" isn't in the anomalies but in the normalcies. We believe truth is found in the intersection of multiple perspectives. We love the flutter of butterflies when they visit us, but we're more fascinated by the earlier stage, in the cocoon, when its imaginal cells revolt, when the worm becomes an inchoate soup that inexplicably sprouts wings.

At the end of *Blind Walls*, one character dies, one finds joy, one wanders in limbo, and one goes home to his cat. Not unlike life. We ourselves profess no tragic or buoyant vision of "what life is like"— life is like everything, life is like life. In our view, the suffering in *Blind Walls* derives not from tragic inevitability nor even from characters' lack of insight—their vision at times is focused like a burning glass. But they're trapped at crossing points, perhaps like a donkey balking at a rickety bridge, perhaps like the cars squashed in the Oakland Bay Bridge's collapse. Somehow we have to risk crossing those crossing points.

—Conrad Bishop & Elizabeth Fuller

Other Books by Bishop & Fuller

REALISTS

A singular comic novel of dystopian optimism.
In the near future, insane politicos reign and dreams are taboo. A motley band of innocents, targeted as terrorists, plunge to certain death, but by a stroke of lunatic physics plop onto Smoky's ramshackle westbound tour bus, pursued by an empire gone loco. Amid ghost buffalo and disappearing cities, improbable lovers split and rejoin, children find magic, and a ragtag bunch of loners and seekers bond into a tribe of survivors, weaving a new reality with magic as the warp, love as the woof.

GALAHAD'S FOOL

A year after the death of his co-creator and soul mate Lainie, a grizzled, acerbic puppeteer struggles to build a solo show. What Albert Fisher intends as a lightweight spoof turns sharply personal, and he labors to birth a raw myth of love and loss. His aging Galahad, no longer a glittering hero, launches a second mad quest for the Grail. To follow him, his wife secretly changes guises with their frail androgynous Fool. As the work evolves, Albert finds kinship with Galahad's despair and dogged vision, and opens to the risk of new love.

CO-CREATION: FIFTY YEARS IN THE MAKING

In the course of their fifty years of marriage, Bishop & Fuller have collaborated as performers, playwrights, and puppeteers in bringing hundreds of stories to thousands of audiences nationwide. Now they tackle their own story—a chronicle of parenting, uprootings, successes and failures, spiritual quests, dancing naked around bonfires, strict accounting practices, and perpetual improvisation.

www.DamnedFool.com